THE
MYSTERY
OF
ALBERT E. FINCH

ALSO AVAILABLE BY CALLIE HUTTON

THE MYSTERY OF ALBERT E. FINCH

A VICTORIAN BOOK CLUB MYSTERY

Callie Hutton

CROOKED LANE

NEW YORK

Copyright © 2022 by Colleen Greene

Published in the United States by Crooked Lane Books, an imprint of The Quick Brown Fox & Company LLC.

Crooked Lane Books and its logo are trademarks of The Quick Brown Fox & Company LLC.

Library of Congress Catalog-in-Publication data available upon request.

ISBN (hardcover): 978-1-64385-802-9
ISBN (ebook): 978-1-64385-803-6

Cover design by Bruce Emmett

Printed in the United States.

www.crookedlanebooks.com

Crooked Lane Books
34 West 27th St., 10th Floor
New York, NY 10001

First Edition: January 2022

10 9 8 7 6 5 4 3 2 1

To my husband: beta reader, brain-storming partner, and support system. You are truly the wind beneath my wings.

CHAPTER 1

Bath, England
22 September 1891

"I, Lady Amy Lovell, am a bride." She stared at her reflection in the looking glass and burst into gales of laughter.

"I am a bride," she repeated, leaning forward to take a closer look at herself, examining her visage, and wiping the tears of laughter from her eyes.

She, an independent woman who earned her own money—although her brother had taken all her royalty payments and invested them for her, insisting she live on the allowance provided her by the family—and here she was getting married.

To William, of all people.

That is, The Right Honorable, the Viscount Wethington. Goodness, such a long title. In a couple of hours, she would be The Right Honorable, the Viscountess Wethington. And never to forget her no-longer-hidden alter ego, E. D. Burton, renowned author of murder mystery books.

"Here is the bracelet you wished to borrow from your aunt, my lady." Sophie, her new lady's maid hurried into the room, the gold and silver bracelet clutched in her hand. Aunt Margaret had insisted that Amy adhere to the new trend to wear *something old, something new, something borrowed, something blue, and a sixpence in her shoe* for good luck at her wedding.

Amy had scoffed at the idea, but to keep her aunt, whom she loved dearly and who had raised her from ten years of age, happy, she had agreed to wear the borrowed piece of jewelry.

The bracelet was the last piece she needed to complete the silly tradition. "Thank you, Sophie." Amy held out her arm so the maid could clasp the bracelet.

Sophie was a new addition to her household. Actually, this would no longer be her household once she married. She would move into William's townhouse. Amy had gone without a lady's maid ever since her previous one had left to marry. She had shared Aunt Margaret's maid when she absolutely needed one.

Because she'd shown up at various affairs a bit disheveled, and many times wearing two different shoes, William had insisted on hiring a maid for her. She hoped he did not think her compliance on this matter meant she planned to bow to all his wishes. But then, she was quite sure he knew her better than to expect that.

"You look absolutely beautiful, my lady," Sophie said. "Your Lord Wethington will be unable to keep his eyes off you."

Amy bent and gathered up her skirts in preparation for departure. "Let's hope that is not the case, since I don't wish the man to be walking into walls all day."

They left her room and met Aunt Margaret in the corridor, coming from her bedchamber. "Oh, my dear. You look stunning." With tears in her eyes, her aunt cupped Amy's chin in her hand. "I am so pleased that you are marrying, and I can't think of another man who deserves you more than William."

Not quite sure if that was a compliment or a slight insult, Amy found tears gathering in her eyes as well, and leaned in to hug her aunt. "In case I've never said it, I love you very much, dear Aunt, and thank you so much for all the love and attention with which you've showered me over the years."

Both ladies patted their eyes. Amy had to swallow a few times to get herself under control.

"Are you ladies coming down, or do we have to come up there and fetch you?" Michael, the Earl of Davenport, Amy's brother and only sibling called from the entry hall.

"We're coming," Aunt Margaret said. "My goodness we do have time, you know."

As they reached the bottom of the staircase, Michael, and Amy's father, the Marquess of Winchester, stood gaping at her. Papa extended both hands toward his daughter, taking hers in his large, warm ones. "My beloved daughter, you are the image of your dear mother. She would be most proud of you today."

Another flood of tears arrived in her eyes, and Amy blinked furiously to rid herself of the cursed things. "Oh, Papa, I do miss her, and I truly wish she were here."

Michael cleared his throat. "Are we to keep poor William pacing in the church, nervous that his bride has changed her mind? Or should we take pity on the man, as he's losing his freedom today, and hurry ourselves to the church?"

Amy shook her head. "Michael, you always manage to say the wrong thing." With a smile and a kiss on Papa's cheek, she took his arm, and they left the house.

In the past two days, almost all her belongings had been sent to William's house. They would spend the night there and then travel the next morning to Brighton Beach, Amy's favorite place in the world, for a honeymoon. With that in mind, she turned back as she moved to climb into the carriage and gazed longingly at the townhouse she'd lived in most of her life.

The four of them piled into the carriage, and after a slight tap on the ceiling to alert the driver they were all settled, the vehicle moved forward. "My dear, I cannot tell you how happy I am to see you marrying." Papa smiled at her with a sense of satisfaction.

Of course he would. He'd spent a good part of his life trying to marry off his half-sister, Aunt Margaret, with no success, and then turned his attentions to Amy a few years ago. Why men felt the ladies of their families must be shackled to men to have full lives annoyed her. Not that she would feel shackled to William, she hurriedly assured herself.

He was different. Because of him, Amy was now known as the author E. D. Burton, instead of watching all the accolades for her books going to an unknown man. Papa had previously insisted on her using a pseudonym and keeping her identity unknown. Upon William's offer of marriage, *she* had insisted that he would not demand she remain anonymous. He agreed, then she agreed, and here they were headed to their wedding.

St. Swithin's Church stood on The Paragon in the Walcot area of Bath. Amy had been baptized there and attended church in the old building almost every Sunday. It was also William's home church, and they'd spent many a Sunday sitting side by side at the service, sharing a hymnal.

Although it was a warm early fall day, a chill ran up her body as she stepped out of the vehicle, holding Papa's hand. The church had never looked so daunting or large. Eloise Spencer, Amy's best friend—much to Papa's displeasure since he considered her a hoyden, which she was—would act as her bridesmaid. Amy had asked Aunt Margaret first, but she had declined, saying she was much too old, at one and forty, for such a position.

They climbed the steps and entered the vestibule of the church. All the familiar sights, smells, and sounds greeted her—including the irregular music coming from the organist, Mrs. Edith Newton, a lovely, partially blind woman who played every Sunday and had a propensity to miss several notes in each hymn. But Amy had not had the heart to ask for a different organist for the wedding, which would have hurt the old dear's feelings.

Aunt Margaret kissed her on the cheek, and as she took Michael's arm, they made their way down the aisle to the family bench. Eloise hugged Amy. "I am so happy for you. You and William make a perfect couple."

The doors to the church opened, and Amy had the sudden urge to glance at Papa and say, "Sorry, but this is all a mistake. You needn't concern yourself—I will see myself home."

Then she looked down the aisle and saw William standing next to Mr. Colbert, their mutual friend and now husband to William's mother, and all her anxieties vanished like a puff of smoke in the wind.

This was no stranger she was marrying. She and William had been members of the same book club for ages, dance partners at the Saturday assemblies for years, fellow church attendees and, for the last two years, partners in solving the murders of Amy's erstwhile fiancé and William's man of business.

Almost as if he had read her mind, Papa leaned in. "Have no fear, my dear; you are making the best decision of your life."

Amy took a deep breath and smiled at him. "Yes, Papa. I know."

★ ★ ★

William, Viscount Wethington ran his finger around the inside of his ascot and cleared his throat. Now that Amy had finally arrived, some of his nervousness had passed, but he knew he wouldn't completely relax until the ceremony was over.

Mr. Colbert—as William still thought of him, even though he'd been his stepfather for three months now—clapped him on the shoulder. "Your bride has arrived. You can relax now, son."

He'd known Mr. Colbert for years as the man who ran the meetings at the Mystery Book Club of Bath. Earlier in the year, William's mother, Lady Wethington had arrived from London to take up residence with her son.

Almost as soon as she'd settled in, she had decided to join them for one of their book club meetings. The still quite beautiful widow immediately had Mr. Colbert acting as though he'd been struck by lightning from the moment he laid eyes on her. William had not been happy about that, feeling a bit uncomfortable with a man lusting after his mother, but it turned out Mr. Colbert's intentions were honorable, and he and William's mother had become engaged a few days before Amy and William had announced their own betrothal.

Not wanting to take away the limelight from the younger couple's wedding plans, they'd eloped—William could still not get over his mother eloping—three months before.

Now, Mrs. Newton began playing, and Amy made her way down the aisle, holding onto Lord Winchester's arm. She looked a bit pale but he supposed wearing all white might have that effect on her coloring.

He'd always thought of his bride as a pretty woman, but today she was absolutely exquisite.

Her white satin gown was close fitted at the waist, with the fabric pulled snug over her stomach to gather in the back. She wore a white veil that trailed almost the length of her gown and was anchored to her head with a wreath of small roses.

Lord Winchester kissed his daughter on the cheek, held his hand out for William to shake, and passed Amy to him. Hands clasped together, they grinned at each other, and he knew all would be well.

The ceremony was long, and William had to keep dragging himself back from his thoughts to pay attention. His mind had wandered several times to the upcoming honeymoon and the lovely cottage he'd rented for the two weeks they would be in Brighton Beach.

Eventually, they reached the part where they would repeat their vows. At the vicar's instructions, William turned to Amy and they faced each other, holding hands. Hers were ice cold.

She stated her vows plainly and clearly. He took the ring Mr. Colbert had been holding for him and slipped the diamond-encrusted gold band onto Amy's finger:

"With this ring I thee wed; with my body I thee worship; and with all my worldly goods, I thee endow. In the name of the Father, and of the Son, and of the Holy Ghost. Amen."

'Twas done. He had a wife. And he wasn't even terrified. They continued to clasp hands as they turned back to the vicar, who had them kneel for the final blessing, which, to William's way of thinking, was much too long.

When finished, they made their way to the office, with Eloise and Mr. Colbert, where they signed the marriage book, and then joined the guests at the back of the church.

Amy's great-aunt, Lady Priscilla Granville, had graciously offered to host the wedding breakfast at her home, Derby Manor House, located at the edge of Bath. Although the ceremony itself was only attended by close family members, the celebration following would include friends and other family. William believed the last count was forty-seven guests, some of whom had traveled from out of town and had spent the night before at the Manor House.

After speaking briefly with the church attendees, he and Amy headed for his carriage. Once they settled inside and it began to roll away from the church, he leaned across the space separating them and, taking her hands in his, said, "What say you we skip the wedding breakfast and leave for Brighton Beach now?"

His new wife tsked. "Don't be silly, William. Lady Granville has gone to a great deal of trouble to host this event."

He leaned back with a sigh and gazed out the window. "I know. I wasn't really considering it."

Amy laughed and regarded him with a smile. "Oh yes. I believe you were, dear husband."

Husband. Now there was a title to which he would need to acclimate himself.

Chapter 2

A mere year ago, William would have shuddered and run as fast as he could in another direction at the thought of being addressed with that moniker.

Husband.

Glancing over at his wife, he felt a warm glow. Amy—the new Viscountess Wethington—was more than a wife. She was his best friend, fellow mystery book club member, companion, and let-us-get-into-trouble partner.

Yes. He was certain this had been a good decision and they would have a fine marriage. Maybe even children one day, to whom he would pass along his title and earthly holdings.

"It was a lovely ceremony, was it not?" Amy asked as the carriage rolled away from the church.

Too embarrassed to tell her he had spent most of the service thinking of how long it was and wondering if it would ever end, he nodded. "Yes. It was wonderful."

She laughed. "My dear husband, I believe you are a liar. You daydreamed throughout the entire service."

He shrugged and laughed with her. "Not the *entire* service. I remember quite clearly stating my vows."

"Yes, there was that."

He reached for her hand and pulled her across the space to sit alongside him. "Now I think it's time for a proper kiss. Don't you?"

"Um, yes, I believe so."

'Twas odd, as he'd kissed Amy many times in the past few months, but kissing one's *wife* was entirely different. Quite pleasant, actually. A sense of belonging, possessiveness, and protection settled on him, along with a renewed wish for the celebration to be over so they could return to his townhouse and retire to their bedchamber. He was a newly wedded man, after all.

They settled into a comfortable silence, each with their own thoughts, until the carriage drew up to Derby Manor House a mere fifteen minutes later.

"It really was quite gracious of Lady Granville to host the breakfast," William said, sliding forward as the door to the carriage was opened by a footman attired in the Granville livery. Looking back at her, he reluctantly added, "I promise I will not hurry you to leave."

"Thank you." She began to gather her skirts and veil. "As lovely as all this bridal attire is, I am unused to such bulky apparel and will be happy when I am free to remove it all and put on comfortable clothes for our trip to Brighton Beach tomorrow."

William gulped and tried his gentlemanly best not to react to her statement about removing all her clothes. They had hours to go yet.

After stepping down, he turned, took Amy's hand, and fingers intertwined, they walked up the steps to the massive wooden doors, held open by two footmen. The entranceway was already filled with waiting guests who had not attended the church service.

William and Amy immediately took their place in the front hall, alongside Amy's father and the new Mrs. Colbert and her husband. William tried not to shudder whenever he thought of that name. Yet, with the way Mr. Colbert and his mother looked at each other, William could not resent the match. His mother was happy. Happier than he ever remembered her being since his father had died.

And truth be known, he was quite relieved that she and Amy would not be competing for "lady of the household" at Wethington Townhouse.

Soon he was caught up in greeting the guests; tolerating bone-crushing handshakes; kissing dried, wrinkled cheeks; and accepting congratulations, along with bawdy winks and comments that he hoped Amy had not overheard.

After what seemed like hours, he glanced toward the front door. "The line seems to be dwindling, my dear. Soon we shall be able to join the others in the drawing room." William rotated his neck, easing the cramped muscles. "I feel quite ready for the respite."

Amy tugged on his sleeve and lowered her voice. "William, I really need to change my shoes. Aunt Margaret insisted on these dainty shoes with heels higher than I am used to. They are quite painful."

His poor wife did look as if she needed to sit down. "Well, we can't have that." William looked around and signaled to a footman. "Can you please find Lady Wethington's maid and ask her to attend us?"

After ten minutes with no maid showing up, and the last of the guests finally through the line, his parents and Franklin left to join the others enjoying drinks in the drawing room.

William leaned toward Amy. "Slip off your shoes."

She drew back and her eyes grew wide. "What?"

"Take them off. Your gown is long enough, it covers your feet. No one will know."

Amy held onto his arm as she slipped off the shoes and placed them behind a stone bust of some poet that had watched them in silence the entire time they had greeted the guests. "Have I told you today that I am happy to have married you?"

William kissed her forehead. "No. But I am prepared to hear it often."

Now shoeless, Amy took his extended arm, and as any proper bride and groom, they made their way into the drawing room, bare feet and all.

★　★　★

Amy wiggled her toes, relief swamping her after shedding the painful shoes. Leave it to William to think of something so improper. But then, instead of being outraged, as she imagined some brides would be, she thought it a fabulous idea.

"Oh, my dears. I am so very happy for you both." Miss Gertrude O'Neill, along with her sister, Miss Penelope, hurried up to them, patting their eyes with lace handkerchiefs and hugging the newlyweds.

Dressed as twins as usual, though they were not, the middle-aged Misses O'Neill were members of the Mystery Book Club of Bath as well as St. Swithin's Church. A few months past, Miss Gertrude had been a suspect in the murder of William's man of business. She had been blackmailed by the cad, but once she was removed from William and Amy's suspect list, she had confided her dark secret to Amy, which had only made Amy more sympathetic to the poor woman.

"You are such a beautiful bride, Lady Amy." Miss Penelope giggled and covered her mouth with her hand. "Oh. I am so sorry, my dear. I meant to say you are such a beautiful bride, *Lady Wethington*."

Amy felt her face flush. Even though she'd heard the appellation many times while receiving her guests, she still had a reaction when someone addressed her so. It would probably take time to get used to it. It was too bad women had to take men's names upon marriage. How wonderful it would be if they had a choice. Keep their own name, or better yet, the husband take the wife's name. Yes. That would be quite the thing. Rather freeing, in fact.

Except the name she would be keeping would be her father's name, so no matter how you worked it out, women were still using a man's name. She sighed. Maybe in one of her books she would address that problem. She grinned. Wouldn't that give her publishers something to choke on?

A footman passed by, carrying a tray. William grabbed a glass of wine for each of them and handed one to her. Amy took a sip and closed her eyes as the wonderful beverage slid down her dry throat. She immediately took another larger swallow.

"Be careful, my love." William regarded her. "You don't want to drink too fast."

Amy nodded, agreeing with his remark. 'Twould not be the thing to become muddled at her own wedding breakfast. "Perhaps you can fetch me a glass of water? I am quite parched, and you are correct. This is not a good substitute if I am to keep my wits about me."

William stepped back just as Mr. and Mrs. Colbert joined them. Her new mother-in-law took her hands. "This is such a lovely house, Amy. Your great-aunt was quite kind to do this for you."

Amy looked around, almost as if seeing the room for the first time, even though she'd visited Lady Granville many times. It was truly a beautiful space. Large enough to hold their fifty or so guests with ease, the chamber featured a patterned pale green watered silk on the top section of the walls, with cream-colored wainscoting below. Deep green and rose draperies covered all the windows, now drawn back to allow sunlight into the room.

Usually, there were several groupings of comfortable printed and striped chairs for visitors, surrounding small tables scattered about the room. Today, all the furniture had been removed to accommodate the guests.

Lastly, she wholeheartedly appreciated the deep rose Axminster carpet keeping her bare feet happy.

"Yes, it was quite generous of Lady Granville to take on the task."

"How is she related to you?" Mrs. Colbert asked.

"She is my deceased mother's aunt. Lord and Lady Granville offered to take me in to raise when Mama died, but Papa thought staying with Aunt Margaret, where I had been all my life, was a better idea. But Aunt Priscilla has been a presence in my life forever."

"And she is widowed now?"

"Yes. Fortunately for her, this property was not entailed, so she kept possession of it when Lord Granville passed on."

"It is lovely." Mrs. Colbert turned to her husband. "Is it not, my dear?"

He stared at her and said, "Yes, lovely, indeed."

Since everyone in the little circle understood he was speaking of his wife, and not the room, Mrs. Colbert blushed as if she were a debutante. Amy grinned. Who would have ever guessed these two would become a couple?

William arrived at her side and handed her a glass of water. "Lady Granville just informed the butler that we are about to move into the dining room."

No sooner had the words left his mouth than the butler made the announcement. Amy placed her partially filled wine glass down and carried the water with her. At present, she needed genuine hydration rather than spirits.

William held a chair out for her. Amy, William, Eloise, and Mr. and Mrs. Colbert made up the front table, where they were seated in such an arrangement that they faced the tables of guests.

Footmen poured champagne into glasses at each place while the guests continued to chat and visit. Amy finished her water and felt quite refreshed.

"Better?" William asked.

"Yes. Much. No sore feet and no dry throat. What could possibly surpass that?"

He inclined his head close to her ear. "A honeymoon?"

Amy was certain the flush on her face matched the one Mrs. Colbert had displayed earlier. "William, behave yourself," she murmured, darting a glance around.

Her husband merely grinned and finished the wine he'd carried with him in one gulp.

After several minutes of guests being directed and settled into their proper seats, and once the footmen had finished with their chore of pouring the champagne at each place, Mr. Colbert tapped lightly on his water glass to gain everyone's attention. "Ladies and gentlemen, I am honored to offer a toast to my stepson and his lovely new wife."

He cleared this throat and raised his champagne glass. "I have known these two wonderful young people for years through our book club." He glanced at William. "I always knew when my stepson found his true love it would be someone as wonderful as the new Lady Wethington." He looked back at the guests and raised his glass higher. "Here is to good health and happiness for the bride and groom, Lord and Lady Wethington." He looked back at Amy and William again. "And may all your *for better or worse* be much better than worse."

Laughter and cries of "Here, here," "Happiness," and "Health" resounded in the room, followed by silence as the guests drank the Piper-Heidsieck, the reputed favorite champagne of Marie Antoinette.

Conversation burst forth as the empty glasses returned to the table and the footmen began to serve the offerings from the menu Amy and her great-aunt had worked out. Eggs and bacon, kidneys, cold meats, and kippers and kedgeree. They had also agreed on a lightly spiced dish from Colonial India of rice, smoked fish, and boiled eggs.

Amy hadn't realized how very hungry she was until she took her first bite of the Indian rice dish. She closed her eyes and relished the fare as the sting of curry burst forth in her mouth. This had definitely been a good decision.

Her head snapped up at the sound of a gasp followed by a female scream coming from one of the tables.

Conversation ceased and all eyes were upon Amy's cousin-in-law Albert. He stared in shocked horror at his wife, Alice, sitting next to him, her face resting quite still in a plate of eggs and bacon.

Licking his lips, he continued to stare down at the back of her head and croaked, "I believe she is dead."

CHAPTER 3

After about five seconds of stunned silence, the room erupted into hysterical chaos.

Both Misses O'Neill, along with Lady Battenberg, and Mrs. Holland, all slumped in their chairs, hopefully the result of a swoon and not the same malady that had struck unfortunate Alice.

Alice's twin sister, Annabelle, sitting across the room, screamed "No!," clutching her throat, her eyes wild until she also collapsed in a dead faint.

William's mother lay slouched against her husband's chest, but from what William could discern was simply being comforted. A quick glance and a nod from Mr. Colbert confirmed that she was merely distraught.

William glanced down at Amy, who was quite pale but otherwise appeared well. The footmen sprang into action, quickly removing plates, probably concerned that more heads would soon take dives into their food.

Lady Granville hurried over to William. "You must do something, my lord. This needs to be taken under control."

Amy licked her lips and looked over at William. "Yes, William you must do something before the hysteria increases."

He stood and tapped on his glass.

Nothing.

He cleared his throat.

The noise increased.

He thumped on the table with his fist.

The sound was drowned out by shrieks and shouting.

Finally, in desperation, he climbed on his chair, which he hoped would not collapse under him, and shouted, "May I have your attention, please!"

No one moved or spoke, until the room resembled a ghastly diorama.

"Everyone, please calm down." He nodded at the footmen. "Please assist the distraught ladies into the drawing room, where they will be more comfortable."

Amy stood. "Albert, are you sure she is dead?"

"Yes," came his garbled reply. His face was ashen, and his hands shook as he held his wife's wrist. "There is no pulse."

Amy nodded. "Please, no one touch anything. I also think it best if we all retire to the drawing room."

In the meantime, William climbed down from the chair and waved a footman over. "Please send word to Dr. Kindle that we need him to attend us immediately." The guests who were still able to walk made their way slowly from the dining room, sneaking furtive glances at Alice. William walked to the table where Albert sat next to his unmoving wife, staring at the back of her head.

Placing his hand on Albert's shoulder, William said, "Did your wife have a medical condition?"

Albert ran his palm down his face and shook his head. "No. Wait—she did suffer from asthma, but I had no idea such a condition could be fatal."

"I've sent for a doctor. I suggest you might benefit from joining the others in the drawing room. I'm afraid there is nothing more you can do here."

Amy joined them. "Come, Albert, I will escort you to the drawing room."

"No. I don't want to go in there." He closed his eyes briefly. "Is there another room where I can spend time by myself?"

"Yes, of course," Amy said, cupping his elbow to encourage him to move. "I will take you to the library."

Once they had departed, William took Alice's cool hand and checked again for a pulse. 'Twould be good if they were certain she was dead after all the excitement, except he doubted she would remain with her face in her food had she been able to move on her own.

No pulse. He checked her neck. Nothing there either. He sighed. The woman was dead.

Amy returned and stood alongside him. "You do know we have to summon the police."

"Of course." William ran his fingers through his hair. "Had you noticed anything untoward about Alice last night?"

About a dozen guests had arrived the afternoon before and spent the night at Derby Manor. Although, as the groom, he had attended the dinner, he hadn't paid particular attention to the guests because he had been tied up with his personal affairs in preparation for the wedding and honeymoon trip.

"No." Amy paused. "Except I did witness a brief argument between her and Albert as my family and I readied ourselves to return to our home last night after the pre-wedding dinner."

William perked up. "An argument? Serious, or the usual scrapping we've seen before with these two?"

Alice and Albert Finch were not counted among the ranks of the happily married in their circle of family and friends. 'Twas rumored over the three years they'd been married that he had carried on affairs, Mrs. Madeline Davis his most recent paramour. As much as he attempted to hide it, it was well known.

"The argument didn't last long, but seemed quite bitter. At least this time they kept their voices lowered, which was a blessing."

William reached out for Amy's hand. "I'm so sorry your wedding has turned into this mess."

"'Tis your wedding too, husband. Or have you forgotten that little point?" Despite her words, she grinned at him.

William took her hand in his and kissed the back of it. "I will send for the police. Why don't we join the others in the drawing room? I believe I could use a nice-sized brandy right about now."

"I agree, my lord. Our presence may have a calming effect, and I believe I will join you in a sip or two of brandy."

★　★　★

Despite her outward coolness, Amy had been shaken to her core. Another death in which she and William were involved. Hopefully this time, they would not be on the suspect list, at least.

On their way to the drawing room to join the others, William instructed one of the footmen to send for the Bath Police and to make sure no one except for the doctor entered the dining room until they arrived.

"I believe you are turning into a mystery writer, my lord. You are doing everything I would have done in one of my books."

He offered a wry smile. "Perhaps it is due more to our real-life experiences over the past year than any desire to join you in your novelistic career."

"Sadly, that is true."

The drawing room was bursting with subdued conversations. The women who had fainted had been revived, and just about everyone held a glass of spirits or a cup of tea. Aunt Priscilla moved from one guest grouping to another, obviously attempting to soothe them. Papa, along with Michael and Aunt Margaret. approached them as soon as they crossed the threshold.

After a few hugs and murmurs of condolences, Papa asked, "What news do you have?"

William joined them, handing a cut crystal snifter of brandy to Amy. "Not much. I confirmed that Mrs. Finch has indeed left this world. Mr. Finch has requested a separate room in which to grieve. I've sent for the doctor and the police."

"The police, eh?" Papa said.

"Yes. This is an unexpected death, Papa. No doubt the coroner will arrive, and there will be an autopsy." Amy closed her eyes and sighed as the brandy slid down her throat. She opened her eyes to see Papa scowling at her.

"It seems your so-called career has turned into real life."

"Not for the first time," William murmured.

With everything in disarray, Amy decided to ignore her father's comment about her *so-called* career. Her husband approved of her work and had encouraged her to reveal her identity earlier in the year at the book fair hosted by Atkinson & Tucker, so she was quite content.

Although, she did recall with a certain amount of amusement that she'd agreed to William's proposal of marriage based on his allowing her anonymity as a mystery writer to cease. Since that conversation, she had never told him that she had been fully prepared to accept his offer of marriage with or without his consent to that condition. 'Twas best perhaps to keep some secrets from one's husband.

"As you say it is an unexpected death, I assume there was no issue with the woman's health?" Aunt Margaret asked.

William took a sip of his drink. "Albert says no."

Almost as if previously agreed, Amy and William split up and made their rounds to each cluster of guests, to assure them that everything was under control and the doctor and police had been sent for.

That last bit of news caused Annabelle to collapse again. Annabelle and Alice were twin sisters, so it was no surprise that she was taking it all quite hard. Luckily, Mr. Colbert stood nearby and caught the woman before she hit the floor.

Mrs. Colbert came up to Amy and took her hands. "This must be so distressing for you, my dear."

"I must say this was not how I saw my wedding day going, truth be known. But it is important for William and me to remain calm."

Her mother-in-law cupped Amy's cheek. "My son is most fortunate in his selection of a wife."

"Thank you, Mrs. Colbert."

"Now, my dear, we must not have that. You are my daughter now. If you are uncomfortable calling me Mother, perhaps you can use my given name, Lily."

Not having had a mother for years, and raised with having proper respect for her elders, she was not sure she would be comfortable calling Mrs. Colbert either Mother or Lily. She merely smiled and decided she would spend the rest of her life only speaking to William's mother if she could get her attention without addressing her first. She envisioned a lot of arm waving and throat clearing in her future.

Amy was on her second brandy, chatting with Eloise, when the butler arrived in the drawing room and walked directly to William. Amy hurried over to hear the message.

The butler offered a curt bow. "Dr. Kindle has arrived, my lord. I have also seen that the Bath Police have been summoned."

"Thank you." William extended his hand to Amy, and they left together, their fingers linked. She was more than thrilled that her husband did not intend to cut her out of the meeting with the doctor.

They greeted the physician at the entrance hall and directed him to the dining room.

"I am sorry to hear about this tragedy on your wedding day, my lady, my lord." The man walked directly to Alice's body and tsked. "Such a sorry affair."

He placed his medical bag on the table alongside Alice and drew out various implements. He eased Alice's head back. Looking down at her left hand and her silver and ruby wedding ring, he asked, "Is her husband present?"

"Yes. He is in another room."

"Will you summon him, please?"

The butler who had remained in the room left and returned within minutes with Albert. "Is she truly dead, Doctor?"

The doctor removed the stethoscope from his ears and placed them back into his bag. "Yes, sir. I am afraid so."

The only reaction Albert gave was a slight shudder at the doctor's words. "What do I do now?"

William drew him away from the sight of his deceased wife's face, covered in eggs, and said, "I sent for the police."

"Police!" Albert's eyes bugged. "Why the police?"

The doctor snapped his medical bag shut. "Mister—" he turned to William with raised brows.

"Finch, Dr. Kindle. Mr. Albert Finch and Mrs. Alice Finch."

"Mr. Finch, your wife appears to have been in good health, although, as I am not her doctor, I cannot say for sure. But she died unexpectedly in the middle of a wedding celebration. It must be determined if foul play was involved."

Albert's head snapped back as if he'd been punched. "Foul play? That's preposterous. She probably suffered a seizure of some sort, or possibly a heart failure."

Apparently taking sympathy on the distraught man, the doctor patted his arm. "Mr. Finch, any one of those things is possible, of course, but without an autopsy, the cause of death cannot be determined. And that, I must remind you, is police business."

"Did someone say 'police business'?"

Amy sucked in a deep breath and groaned when Detectives Edwin Marsh and Ralph Carson entered the room. Dear Mother of God, were they to be subjected to these two again? The two detectives who firmly believed she had murdered her erstwhile fiancé and, the following year, were convinced William had killed his man of business?

Their relationship with these men was anything but warm. In fact, it barely stretched far enough to be called cordial.

Detective Marsh looked over at William. "You will be interested to know I have already notified the coroner to attend us."

"Why the devil would you do that before even viewing the body?" William looked over at Amy. "I apologize for my language."

Detective Carson placed his hands on his hips and studied her and William. "Because, my lord, my lady, as amazing as I'm sure it sounds to you, I do read the society pages in the newspaper. I knew today was your wedding day, and once I received the summons to appear at this address, where I was aware the celebration was to take place, I bore no doubt that I would find a dead body here."

The stress of the day hit Amy all at once, and along with the two downed brandies, she felt the air leave her lungs and black dots appear in her vision. With a soft sigh, her knees buckled, but thankfully, with William's arms wrapped securely around her, she never reached the carpet.

CHAPTER 4

William scowled at the detective as he scooped his wife into his arms and left the dining room. "I hope you are happy that your flippant words caused Lady Wethington to faint."

"Perhaps it was the shock of just now realizing she had married you," the man said as he and Detective Marsh followed him to the library.

The doctor and Albert trailed behind them.

William laid Amy gently on the settee in front of the fireplace and addressed the detective, his jaw tight, "Dead body or no, if you continue with these caustic remarks, I shall have one of the footmen remove you."

His demeanor much more serious, Detective Carson offered a slight bow, his face flushed. "I apologize, my lord. You are correct: this is not the time or place for such remarks. I shall also apologize to Lady Wethington once she recovers."

William tapped Amy's cheek. "Wake up, darling."

Dr. Kindle nudged William aside and waved a small vial from his medical bag under Amy's nose. She began to cough and attempted to sit up, but the doctor placed his hand on her chest to keep her from rising. "Not yet, my lady. Give your body time to recover."

William glared at the doctor's hand. "You may remove your hand from my wife's person. I will take over now."

"Of course." Startled, the doctor stood and backed up.

One of the footmen handed William a glass of water. He placed it near her lips. "Here, sweetheart, take a sip of this."

Amy looked up at the men gathered around her. "What happened?"

"You fainted," William said as he offered her another sip of water.

She shook her head. "I do not faint."

Silence followed as the men merely stared at her. Amy huffed, moved the glass aside, and sat up. "Perhaps we should get on with it. We have dozens of guests in the drawing room, wondering what is happening."

Detective Carson waved to the three chairs grouped in front of the settee. Dr. Kindle and Albert took two chairs, and Detective Marsh the third one, flipping open his ever-present notebook.

William shifted so he and Amy sat next to each other on the settee, their hands clasped. Detective Carson took advantage of the lack of a seat to tower over the group. "Since I know Lord and Lady Wethington are familiar with unexpected death, perhaps its best if his lordship tells us, briefly, what happened."

"My warning about appropriate comments still stands, Detective," William snapped. Gathering his thoughts, he continued, "My stepfather, Mr. Colbert, had just offered a toast to my wife and me, and the footmen began service. Within minutes, there was turmoil at one of the tables. Then my cousin-in-law, Mr. Finch"—William gestured toward Albert—"remarked to the crowd that his wife, Mrs. Finch, was dead."

Marsh had been scribbling frantically during the short tale while Carson kept his eyes on Albert the entire time. The detective then directed his comments to Albert. "Tell me, Mr. Finch, what occurred from the time you and your wife arrived at your table from—" He glanced at William.

"The drawing room. All the guests assembled there once they had gone through the receiving line."

Carson nodded and turned his attention back to Albert. "Proceed, Mr. Finch."

Albert ran his palm down his face and spoke softly. "As Lord Wethington stated, Mr. Colbert offered a toast to the couple, and the footmen began the service. After only a bite or two, Alice stiffened in her chair and turned to me. She looked confused, disorientated. She mumbled something about everything being blurry, and then within seconds she fell forward, her face landing on her plate."

Albert was panting by the time he finished his recitation. Beads of sweat had broken out on his upper lip and forehead, and he was gulping for air.

William waved at a footman who stood next to the door. "Please bring Mr. Finch a glass of water."

Marsh continued to write while Carson placed his hands behind his back and paced until the footman returned and Albert had gulped down the glass of water.

He looked back at Albert. "Mr. Finch, before we left the police station, and in anticipation of an untimely death, I requested for the coroner to meet us here. He should arrive momentarily. As expected, I have more questions for you, so please remain in this room."

The detective then addressed Amy and William. "I will need to speak with all the guests who I believe you said were gathered in the drawing room?"

William nodded.

"I will also require an audience with each member of the staff. Please make whatever arrangements you need to have them assembled in another room. Separate from the guests." He looked over at Albert. "You will remain here, Mr. Finch."

Carson motioned to the footman at the door. "Please stay with Mr. Finch in the event he is in need of your services."

They all knew the footman had just been given the duty of guarding the man whose wife had suddenly died in the middle of a party.

William looked over at Amy. "Are you feeling well enough to do this, or shall I do it myself and let you return to one of the bedchambers to rest?"

Before she even spoke, Carson held up his hand. "No one will be permitted to leave any room without my permission. Lady Wethington has not been granted leave."

"Of course, Detective, I understand." Amy stood and shook out her skirts.

"I just remembered," Marsh said, looking up from his notebook, "you are that mystery write, E. D. Burton."

A slight flush covered Amy's face and she grinned. "Yes. I am."

Carson glared at her. "If I need to warn you and your husband once more to stay out of police business, I will find a reason to lock you up."

"Who is locking up whom?" Mr. Nelson-Graves, the barrister who had represented both Amy and William on two different murder charges the prior year, strode into the library.

"Detective"—the barrister nodded in Carson's direction—"I believe you sent for me?"

★   ★   ★

Amy still felt a bit lightheaded but refused to believe she had fainted. She did not faint. Well, there was the time William insisted she had fainted in the morgue, but the only proof he had was that she hadn't remembered him carrying her up three flights of stairs.

She really must shake off this lightheadedness. 'Twas so unlike her. It was probably the brandy. "I'm ready."

Mr. Nelson-Graves shook hands with William and bowed in her direction. Detective Carson waved at William. "After you, my lord." They all trooped from the room and headed to the drawing room. Before they entered, Mr. Nelson-Graves pulled Amy and William aside. "Is there trouble for you, my lord, my lady?"

William shook his head. "No. At least I certainly don't think so, but I am glad Detective Carson sent for you. Because this happened at our wedding, I'm sure there will be some legal ramifications for us."

"Perhaps." Then he smiled brightly. "Please accept my felicitations."

"Thank you," Amy mumbled as they moved into the drawing room. It was a tad hard to accept good wishes when there was a dead body sitting at her wedding breakfast.

Silence descended as the group arrived in the drawing room. Annabelle stalked forward, over to the two detectives, and stood next to the window. "Albert killed my sister!" Her eyes were swollen and red, and she twisted a damp handkerchief in her hand.

Showing a bit of gentleness Amy had never seen before, Detective Carson smiled softly at Annabelle. "That is to be determined, Miss—"

"Munson. Miss Annabelle Munson." She took in a shuddering breath. "Alice is—was—my twin sister."

Marsh flipped open his book, and Carson cleared his throat. "To address your concerns, Miss Munson, because Mrs. Finch passed away suddenly, this is, right now, a police matter. I am Detective Ralph Carson, and this"—he waved his hand at his partner—"is Detective Edwin Marsh. We are here from the Bath Police Department."

Lady Battenberg took another dive to the floor. Exclamations, gasps, and frenzy arose until the woman was revived and sitting on a chair with her husband's hand clamped firmly on her back, her head pressed into her lap.

Hopefully, she would not be smothered by his attentions, presenting them with another body to deal with.

Carson spent the time during which Lady Battenburg's situation was dealt with studying each of the guests. When all settled down, he said, "Ladies and gentlemen, Detective Marsh and I will be interviewing each one of you." He raised his hand as mumbling began. "It is necessary for all of you to remain here in this house until the interviews have been finished." He added when a couple men raised their hands, "Finished to our satisfaction, that is."

Mr. Prescott, a friend of William's not well-known to Amy, raised his hand again. At Carson's nod, he said, "Detective, have you any idea how long this will take? I have an appointment this afternoon that I cannot miss."

Carson shook his head. "I'm sorry to say, you will miss your appointment, sir. Everyone needs to stay put until we determine it is acceptable for you to leave."

The uproar could have easily removed the roof. It was Miss Gertrude O'Neill's turn for a repeat performance of sliding from her chair into a heap on the floor.

Ignoring the woman crumpled practically at his feet, Carson raised his hands. "Quiet, please."

William leaned toward Amy. "This is not good."

"No. This is not good. I'm certain Aunt Priscilla doesn't have enough rooms for all these people to stay here if the detectives determine no one can leave by the end of the day. Perhaps the interviews won't take as long as Carson believes."

Carson continued. "Once the coroner arrives and the death is officially confirmed, I will begin the interviews. Depending on how well you all cooperate, this might end in only one more day."

Her great-aunt walked up to Amy, looking askance at the police, raising her chin, and sweeping her skirts aside as she neared the detective. Amy hid her grin.

"My dear, there are not enough bedchambers for each guest to have their own room. In fact, last evening we were forced to double up, and that was with only about the dozen or so who stayed. Whatever will we do?"

Amy took her great-aunt's hands. The poor woman had depended on her husband to make all the decisions during their marriage. The fact that she had offered, and even succeeded, in hosting the wedding breakfast was a monumental accomplishment, even with a large staff to assist. Now the poor dear was faced with accommodating all these people for at least one more night, as well as suffering an unexpected death in her own dining room. "Have no fear, Aunt. There would seem to be no reason why those who live locally would have to stay overnight. I'm sure they can be trusted to return tomorrow. I shall handle whatever problems arise."

"Oh, my dear, I knew you would. You are so very strong." She shook her head. "Nothing like me." She whipped out a handkerchief and patted the corner of her eyes. "Do you think we should have lamb for dinner? Or perhaps a nice roast?"

Amy's stomach turned at the mere thought of all the food that still sat on the tables in the dining room. "I think perhaps a light repast of tea, sandwiches, and pastries would be nice right now while we all wait. Then we can discuss dinner later."

Aunt Priscilla patted her arm. "Yes. A very good idea."

With that epic problem solved, Amy turned her attention to William. "What did I miss?"

William frowned at her. "Aside from the fact that we might not have a wedding night and possibly a shortened honeymoon? Nothing."

"Oh dear. I hadn't thought of that."

He scowled at the detectives. "I did."

CHAPTER 5

Although confusion reigned among the group, the detectives efficiently, and with enough expedience to impress William, herded the group into small clusters throughout the large drawing room, which seemed to introduce some calm.

The approach they'd employed seemed simple enough. They asked the guests a few questions and directed them to an area of the drawing room to join one of the groups. William wondered if his growing interest in Amy's books—and possibly their own recent experience with murder investigations—had piqued his curiosity in watching the detectives' methods.

Apparently either Amy or Lady Granville had requested tea, because two footmen arrived with a collapsible table that they set up and on which they arranged trays of biscuits, sandwiches, tarts, and cheeses. Two large pots of tea, along with a stack of small plates, napkins, and silverware, completed the placement.

William stopped one of the footmen as he made to leave. "Please attend Mr. Finch, who is waiting in the library, and offer him refreshments." The man nodded and left the room.

William had just finished a short interview with Mr. Nelson-Graves, who assured him there did not seem to be any reason why he or Amy should be concerned. Shortly after, the barrister took his leave, with promises from William that he would contact him if anything happened of which he should be made aware.

William turned to see a line of guests filling plates, accepting tea from one of the maids who had accompanied the footmen, and chatting subduedly. He shook his head. Even a sudden and suspicious death did not stop one's appetite. Unless it was someone near and dear, he noted as Annabelle Munson sat listlessly with a cup of tea tilting in her lap, but no food.

Detective Carson moved to the front of the room and clapped his hands to gain their attention. "Ladies and gentlemen, we will now begin our questioning. We will commence with the groups who may be granted leave after answering a few questions. You will be told at the end of our query if you may leave or need to remain here."

Grumbling began, and an older woman near William, who looked vaguely familiar, said sotto voce, "Well, I never. We are to be treated like common criminals? I shall send for my barrister the moment I arrive home."

Amy walked up to William, holding a plate of food in her hand. "Are you not hungry?"

He waved his glass of brandy in the air. "I am more interested right now in easing the too familiar memories of past events."

"The coroner has arrived," she said between bites of a lemon tart. "He is with Alice now."

Although most times the coroner could determine if a death was suspicious with a brief examination of the deceased, there would still be a full autopsy. "Tell me again about this argument between Alice and Albert."

Amy shrugged. "There is nothing more to add. It was merely an exchange of differences of opinion, as most arguments are."

"Did you hear what it was they argued about?"

She popped the last of the tart into her mouth and contemplated his question. "The only thing I heard were the words 'never again.'"

"Who said that?"

"Alice."

"Given what everyone knew about Mrs. Davis, I can imagine to what she referred."

Amy nodded. "I really need a cup of tea." She started toward the table with the rapidly diminishing foodstuffs. "Can I get you something?"

William grinned. "My goodness, aren't you turning into the solicitous wife?"

"Enjoy it, my lord." She smirked. "I do not intend to continue; it was merely my intention to impress our guests."

He took her hand in his, and they walked across the room, headed for the tea table. They had not been questioned and assigned a group yet, but the detectives were diligently working their way around the room.

"Can you guess what they are asking to move people into various groups?" William asked.

"Ah, you are counting on my superior knowledge of police tactics?"

He bent down so he could speak in her ear. "You forget I am slowly reaching the point where my knowledge and experience will soon match yours."

"Just so." She studied the various groupings. "I am thinking those who have a very loose connection, more so with Albert than with Alice, will be dismissed. However, I am sure the police will not allow them to leave without obtaining as much information as needed to contact them in the future."

Amy looked around. "For example, Lady Pritchard"—she gestured to the woman William had heard complaining about being treated as a criminal—"is a far-removed cousin who is only here because if she is ever left out, her harping and bitterness spoils the next several family gatherings."

"How are you holding up, dearest?" Amy's aunt Margaret walked up to them and placed her hand on Amy's forearm.

"Based on our relationship with the police thus far, it seems almost fitting," Amy said. Then she quickly added, "Not that I wished something like this to happen, and I feel very sorry for Alice and Albert both."

Amy's father, brother, and Eloise joined their little clique. "Nasty business," William's father-in-law said. "With the way those two fought the few years they were married, I must say I am not surprised one of them met a regretful end."

Surprised, William said, "Are you suggesting Albert had something to do with Alice's collapse at the table?"

Lord Winchester nodded toward Amy. "Just ask my daughter—your wife—who knows all about these things, what with her writing." He looked at Amy. "Isn't it widely accepted that if a person leaves this earth in a rather unexpected manner, it is oftentimes the spouse who helped him or her along?"

★ ★ ★

Amy was both amazed and flattered by her father's question. Firstly, he had acknowledged her as an author, within hearing distance of several people, then actually bowed to her expertise on a point. And waited for an answer. He had rendered her almost speechless.

Almost.

"Yes, Papa, that is the general thought. But I don't think it is fair to Albert to think along those lines. Nothing has been proven yet, not even whether or not it was something natural that happened to Alice."

Lord Winchester snorted and took another sip of his brandy. "I am surprised one of them did not do away with the other before this."

In perfect harmony with their discussion, the coroner entered the drawing room and walked directly to Detective Carson. Detective Marsh joined them as the coroner bent his head and said something that had Carson shaking his head, his lips tight.

"I don't suppose they would share that information with us?" Amy nodded toward the men in deep discussion.

Michael shrugged. "I doubt it. From what I remember, you two are not in the best graces with the Bath Police Department."

Eloise nodded her accord and grinned at Michael.

Amy scowled. "We should be. We handed them the murderers in both Mr. St. Vincent's death and Mr. Harding's. One would think they would be appreciative of our help."

"If I recall correctly, daughter, they did not see it as help, but more as a hindrance." There was a slight twinkle in Papa's eyes as he downed the last of his brandy.

Amy waved his comment off as Detective Carson walked up to their group. "There are certain people we do not want to leave the house just yet. We require more time to speak with them at length, but we also need to do a close examination and survey of the dining room. Therefore, I am advising you that roughly twenty people will most likely need to be detained overnight."

Lady Granville joined their group just as Carson finished his comment. "Twenty people to accommodate? Oh dear. We were quite pressed last night—I can't imagine squeezing in more. This home is not as large as my country estate, where this sort of adaptation could be handled."

"Detective, I do not see why those who live locally can't return to their homes and present themselves tomorrow," Papa said, quite disgruntled.

Detective Carson shrugged. "I have learned to trust no one, and I have found those who do not wish to be involved in a police investigation tend to 'forget' they were supposed to be at a certain place at a certain time. Prior appointments and all that. Until a case is solved, most everyone present today is under suspicion except for those can prove they were only remotely connected to Mr. and Mrs. Finch.

The detective turned his attention to Aunt Priscilla. "If there is a problem, my lady, I think the easiest way to accomplish this would be to have women double up and share rooms, and the men do the same," Carson said.

"What!" William looked as though he would lose his brandy. "That is not acceptable, Detective. No, not at all acceptable."

All those in their group turned to William. Michael and Eloise grinned, Papa flushed, and Aunt Margaret flat out laughed. Lady Granville looked befuddled.

Assessing all the reactions to William's words, it soon dawned on Amy that if the men were separated from the women, she and William would have no wedding night.

William placed his fisted hands on his hips. "Besides, despite your concerns, I see no reason why my wife and I need to stay here at all. We are heading off to our honeymoon in the morning to Brighton Beach."

Carson merely shook his head. "No one will be allowed to leave Bath until this matter is cleared up to our satisfaction."

Amy groaned. She'd been so looking forward to a couple weeks of relaxation and spending time with her new husband without the distraction of wedding plans and publisher's deadlines.

She glanced over at William, who looked as though he wanted to punch something. Most likely the detective's face.

"And," Carson said, pointing his finger at William, "I intend to keep a close eye on you two. I want no interference."

Papa cleared his throat and glared at the detective. "First of all, Detective Carson, I resent the manner in which you are speaking to my daughter and son-in-law. Next, if you are concerned about their interference, I see no reason whatsoever to prevent these two from a well-deserved honeymoon. I can vouch for them both."

Carson's smirk had Papa looking as though *he* wanted to punch something. "It matters not, *my lord*, what reasoning you see. The coroner has just confirmed that, pending an official autopsy and based on his initial examination of Mrs. Finch, he is quite sure the woman was poisoned."

Even though Amy had suspected the same, she still felt a jolt of surprise at the detective's words. *Poisoned.* And Alice had sat right next to her husband, who was now cooling his heels in the library, apart from everyone else. And guarded by a footman. It didn't take years of writing murder mysteries to conclude that he was the prime suspect.

Aunt Priscilla waved her arms around, obviously in a tizzy. "Goodness." She fanned her face with her hand and grabbed Amy's arm. "You must help me see to the arrangements." She nodded toward Aunt Margaret. "I would appreciate your assistance as well, Lady Margaret."

Aunt Margaret nodded. "Of course. I will be happy to assist in any way I can."

"Aunt Margaret is an impressive planner, my lady." Amy patted her great-aunt's shoulder. "I am sure all will be well. This entire matter could very well be cleared up in a matter of hours."

Of course, she knew it would not be cleared up so quickly unless Albert confessed to the murder. Which she doubted. She wasn't even certain that Albert had killed his wife. He seemed to have been in shock when it happened—a reaction she would not use in one of her books if he were the killer. Surprise would be a better response.

William leaned down to speak in her ear as Detective Carson verbally sparred with Papa over the honeymoon and who held more status, a combination of a marquess—her father, an earl—her brother, and a viscount—her husband, or a detective of the Bath Police Department.

Based on past experience, Amy had no doubt who would win.

"When you help your great-aunt with doling out rooms," William whispered, "make sure you keep one open for us. I do not plan to spend my wedding night alongside a bunch of snoring men."

"How about alongside a snoring woman?" She smirked.

"If it's you? Gladly."

CHAPTER 6

Amy lay on her stomach in her great-aunt's bed, dressed in a comfortable cotton nightgown borrowed from Aunt Priscilla, a far cry from the lovely confection she and Aunt Margaret had spent time choosing for Amy's wedding night. There was no point in wearing it for Aunt Priscilla's benefit. The only sound in the room was her bed partner's snoring and the ticking of the small porcelain clock on the dresser across from them.

She sighed and rolled over, placing her hands on her stomach and staring at the overhead canopy. Despite William's insistence—and then downright pleading—the detectives had insisted those they had designated remain overnight, and there was simply no way for her and William to have their own room.

Her great-aunt had been nice enough to offer them the use of her room, but Amy didn't feel comfortable knowing the poor woman who had done so much for her would be squeezed in with two other women.

Truth be known, no one could convince her that the detectives weren't doling out a punishment as retribution for the part she and William had played in solving the prior murders. She could envision them having a hearty laugh at the couple's predicament.

Her thoughts came to an abrupt halt at the sound of scratching at the bedchamber door. She held her breath and listened. Yes. Someone was scratching at the door. It wouldn't be her dog, Persephone, who was resting comfortably at Aunt Margaret's house, where she would stay while they were on their honeymoon.

Amy threw the covers off and padded across the room.

More scratching.

She slowly opened the door only to have an arm reach out, grab her, and pull her from the room. Before she could scream, William's large, warm hand covered her mouth. "Shh."

Amy yanked herself free. "William, you scared me to death! Whatever are you doing?"

He was still dressed in his wedding clothes, with his jacket, waistcoat, and ascot removed. The sleeves of his shirt were rolled up, revealing muscular forearms with a light dusting of brown hair. She gulped and returned her attention to his face.

"We are going to solve this murder. I am determined to have a honeymoon."

Amy flushed bright red at the look in his eyes. "I agree, but do you have a plan?"

He nodded. "First we have to examine the dining room. I know the detectives have already done that, but knowing them as we do, they won't move fast." He crossed his arms over his chest. "In fact, I believe they are having a great deal of fun in keeping us separated."

She sighed. "I'm afraid I came to that same conclusion."

He glanced at her feet. "Go back inside and put on a dressing gown and some slippers. It's chilly, and I don't know how long we will be downstairs."

Amy slipped back into the room, keeping an eye on her great-aunt as she shrugged into a dressing gown, tied it tight around her waist, and then bent to slide into borrowed house shoes, two sizes too large. She caught her breath and stopped when Aunt Priscilla rolled to her other side.

Once she was certain the woman would not awake, Amy padded to the door and left the room.

William had brought a lantern with him, which gave off enough light for them to see where they were going. There were also gaslights along the corridor, which helped keep them from awakening the household by tripping over something.

Holding hands, he led her downstairs to the first floor, where the dining room was. The silence in the house was eerie and unfamiliar. Not that Amy was in the habit of wandering around in the dead of night, but knowing a woman had died in the house only several hours before, and possibly by someone else's hand, caused her to shiver with trepidation.

"Are you cold? I can return to my room and get my jacket." Amy shook her head. "No. I'm fine."

With a curt nod, William turned and grasped the door handle. He cursed softly under his breath. "It's locked."

"Surely you are not surprised?"

"No. I just hoped they would forget to lock it." William looked around. "Is there any other way into the room?"

"I believe so. If I remember correctly, when we were working out the seating arrangements, I saw that there is a French door at the back of the room. I believe it opens to a small patio, but I am certain that would also be locked."

"No doubt. Leave it to those detectives to remember such a thing while they bumble along in every other way."

Amy tapped her finger on her lips. "Wait! I just remembered there is also a wooden door on the west wall that isn't actually visible unless you know it is there. It's used for the servants going in and out with food and drinks. There is a short corridor linking the kitchen and the dining room."

"How do we access that door?"

She grabbed his hand. "Come with me."

William handed her the lantern, and holding it up, she led him from the dining room past several closed doors. Amy made a quick turn, and they continued until they reached the kitchen door. Holding her breath and closing her eyes, she turned the latch and the door opened.

She let out a deep breath and turned to William. "We are halfway there."

He nodded and she continued down another corridor until they reached the door to the dining room. Again holding her breath, she moved the latch and the door opened.

They made their way silently into the room. Amy held the lantern up to make certain the detectives hadn't left someone in the room to act as guard.

Tears quickly came to her eyes when she viewed the room. Not all the food had been cleared away. Napkins lay alongside partially filled plates. The beautiful wedding cake that Aunt Priscilla's cook had made for them still rested in the middle of the table where she and William, along with Eloise and Mr. and Mrs. Colbert, had sat.

"It's so sad," she said, squeezing William's hand.

"I know, love," he said, "but we must get on with it."

Amy swiped the tears from her cheeks. "Yes, you are right." She wandered over to where the Finches had sat, William following in her wake. Alice's plate had been removed, along with her champagne glass.

She and William stood staring at the table, then turned to each other at the same time. "They left Albert's plate but took his champagne glass too," Amy said.

★ ★ ★

The next morning, William crawled out from the bed he'd shared with his father-in-law and brother-in-law. He'd tried his best to convince Amy after they had left the dining room the night before that the sofa in the drawing room would be sufficient for them to sleep on rather than returning to their assigned bedchambers.

She was both scandalized and amused by his suggestion, and unfortunately, they had gone their separate ways.

Luckily for him, his bed partners had turned out to be heavy sleepers and never woke when he'd left the room nor when he'd returned. If Lord Winchester got wind of the fact that William and Amy were again attempting to solve a murder, William had no doubt that the man would banish the two of them to his country estate.

William sighed. If he thought for one minute the detectives would allow that, he would shout from the rooftops that he and his new wife were again playing detective.

Since the other two continued to snore away, William used the time to wash and complete his dressing in silence. And to think about what he and Amy had discovered during their nighttime foray.

It appeared the detectives had some suspicion of Albert, as they had removed both glasses. He assumed they considered the poisoning might have come from either her food or one of the glasses. No doubt they were awaiting the results of the autopsy, which was to be conducted that day to determine what poison Alice had ingested.

It would have been quite easy, during all the confusion of everyone taking their seats, for Albert to have slipped something into his glass and then offered it to his wife when she finished hers. Or to switch glasses with her during the seating.

"Well, it appears the groom hasn't suffered for spending his wedding night away from his new wife." Michael swung his legs over the bed and stood, stretching his lithe body and scratching his chest.

William snorted. "Just because I'm standing doesn't mean I haven't suffered."

Michael laughed and slapped him on the back. "You will survive."

"I would prefer not to hear this conversation," Lord Winchester said from the bed. "We are speaking of my daughter, you know."

William found his father-in-law difficult to read, and he wasn't quite sure if his comment was meant in jest. Because he decided the better side of caution would be to take him seriously, he said, "I apologize, my lord."

"Now, now, William. We mustn't have any of this 'my lord' stuff. You may call me Franklin."

Without too much stumbling over each other, the three men finished their morning ablutions and made their way downstairs. "I imagine the dining room is still off limits. I guess we should see if the others have gathered in the drawing room," Michael said as they reached the bottom stair.

The minute they entered the drawing room, William's eyes scanned the room to settle on Amy, chatting away with Lady

Margaret. They both held teacups. Amy had apparently borrowed a frock from her great-aunt, he assumed, given the color and style of the dress.

A lengthy table took up almost an entire wall of the room, filled with breakfast offerings: eggs, bacon, tomatoes, sausages, smoked eel, rolls, toast, and tarts, along with pots of coffee and tea.

Lord Winchester—Franklin—rubbed his hands together. "This looks grand. I find myself quite hungry." He headed toward the table along with Michael while William sauntered over to Amy and Lady Margaret.

"Good morning, ladies. You slept well, I hope?"

"It has been quite some time since I shared a bed with other people," Lady Margaret said, a slight grin gracing her face. "And surely not something I wish to do on a regular basis."

William took Amy's empty hand and raised it to his lips, kissing the back of it. "And you, my dear? Did you sleep well?"

Attempting a serious demeanor, but with mirth in her eyes, she said, "I had some trouble settling down at first, but after a while I was able to sleep."

He grinned back and moved past the ladies to fix a cup of coffee. Tea was fine, and like every proper Englishman, it was his beverage of choice, but the Americans had it right, and there was something to be said for a cup of coffee first thing in the morning.

Guests continued to arrive in the drawing room, speaking in subdued voices, looking a bit rumpled since none of them had expected to spend the night. They filled plates, balancing them as best as they could while trying to eat. Footmen began to set up small tables and chairs in various spots throughout the generous room.

Albert Finch was noticeably absent.

Lady Granville barely made it across the doorway when she was accosted by Lady Pritchard. "I demand to know when I will be permitted to return to my home. I am certainly not used to being treated like a prisoner."

Amy's great-aunt sighed and attempted to walk past the woman. "I do not know, my lady. I am in much the same predicament as the rest of you. Perhaps you believe it easier on me because I am in my own home, but I am also not permitted to go about my usual life."

Franklin walked up to Lady Pritchard and extended his arm to the woman. "Allow me to accompany you to a table, my lady. I am sure one of the footmen will be delighted to fill a plate for you."

William and Amy exchanged mirthful glances. "It appears your father would do well as an ambassador for the Crown."

Once Lady Pritchard had been settled, and with a footman hovering over her to listen to her demands and complaints, the entire group took in a collective breath as silence reigned when Detectives Carson and Marsh entered the room.

They studied the occupants of the room for almost a minute, raising the level of tension among the guests. "Any news, Detective?" Franklin finally asked.

Detective Carson nodded. "Yes. It has been decided based on a thorough examination of the deceased that Mrs. Alice Finch was poisoned with belladonna."

With a sharp cry of agony, Annabelle burst into tears.

CHAPTER 7

"What does this mean for us?" Lady Margaret asked the detective. "Has a suspect been identified?"

Detective Carson didn't speak for a moment, almost as if he awaited the complete attention of the room. "Perhaps. But now I would like to have one more session with each of you, and most likely after that you will all be able to return to your homes." He looked directly at Aunt Priscilla. "My lady, I am sorry to continue to inconvenience you, but most likely the final interviews will take all day. I think you should have your staff prepare for another overnight stay for those who traveled a distance to be here."

Her great-aunt nodded and left the room in a tizzy to advise her servants of Detective Carson's directive.

William raised his hand. "Detective, may I request that my wife and I be questioned first so we may leave for our honeymoon?"

Amy was certain there was a sense of glee in the detective's demeanor when he answered. "I am very sorry, *my lord*, but you and your wife will have to postpone your trip as I cannot allow anyone to leave Bath until the matter of Mrs. Alice Finch's murder is resolved."

Amy quickly squeezed William's arm, attempting to calm him. "'Tis no matter, William," she whispered. "'Tis obvious the detective is attempting to pay us back for prior snubs we have caused him. Brighton Beach will still be there when this is over."

William looked at her in surprise. "The *beach* is not my main draw."

Detective Carson cleared his throat. "If you will all finish your breakfast, Detective Marsh and I will retire to the library, where we will conduct the interviews." He waved a piece of paper. "We will summon you according to this list."

"I guess that answers one question. Albert is no longer in the library. I wonder where he is?" Amy asked.

William shrugged. "With the discovery we made last night and how things look at present, I wouldn't be surprised if he is sitting in gaol." He took her hand. "Come, let us get some breakfast and spend time talking to the guests ourselves. We might learn a fact or two that solidifies the case for Albert or perhaps raises other questions."

"I agree. This is probably our best opportunity since all these people were present at the time of the poisoning, and I doubt we will have access to them once the detectives dismiss us all."

Plates brimming with breakfast items, Amy and William sat at one of the temporary tables with Alice's twin sister, Annabelle, who still looked ghastly.

Amy shook out her napkin and placed it on her lap. Then she reached over and patted her cousin's hand. "I am so sorry for your loss, Annabelle. I am sure you are devastated."

Despite the woman's near hysterical accusation the day before and her recent response to the confirmation of how the woman had died, she seemed almost composed. She'd apparently decided wine, instead of coffee or tea, was the best way for her to greet the morning. "Thank you, Amy. I have confidence that the detectives will find the necessary evidence to convict Albert."

Amy and William glanced briefly at each other. William cleared his throat, "I do not believe the detectives have decided just yet who gave your sister the poison."

Annabelle's eyes flashed. "It is quite obvious, *my lord*. My sister used belladonna to help with her breathing issues for years. A little bit in hot water and then inhaled worked wonders for her asthma. However, in heavier doses it is quite dangerous. Small doses help; large doses kill." Her voice rose as she ended her tirade.

The three guests at the table near them shifted in their seats and looked everywhere except at Annabelle. Amy took a deep breath and broke the uneasy silence. "That is true. *Atropa belladonna*—which stems from nightshade—can kill or help."

William took a sip of coffee. "I assume anyone who knew your sister well enough would be aware of this treatment that she used? And that she carried it with her at all times?"

Annabelle waved her wine glass around, bits of liquid sloshing over the edge, landing on her dress. "And we are all aware of who knew her best, aren't we?" The woman sounded nearly possessed.

The meal continued in silence, with Annabelle furtively wiping her eyes. A few times Amy attempted, in vain, to raise an innocuous subject to discuss, but Annabelle always managed each time to bring Albert into the conversation by insisting that he was the one who had poisoned her sister.

Once they finished their food, William stood and pulled out Amy's chair. "If you will excuse us, I believe it is our duty to speak with the other guests, as they are here for our wedding."

William took Amy's arm, and they wandered to a small group of guests gathered near the fireplace. "That was painful," Amy said.

"Indeed. Yesterday your cousin was clearly overcome with grief, and today she is almost hysterical."

Amy laughed. "She is furious, which is understandable. She is also well on her way to being totally inebriated and is not making much sense."

"Grief?" William said.

"Perhaps. People do grieve in different ways, and I imagine losing one's twin must be devastating."

"Had they shared a close relationship?"

"Extremely close. In fact, we were all surprised when Alice married Albert, because we never expected the twins to live apart."

"So, the investigation goes forward?"

"Of course."

"Excellent. Maybe we can squeeze in a honeymoon after all."

Amy sighed. "Can you not think of anything else, my lord?"

William seemed to consider for a moment, tapping his chin with his fingertip, then shrugged. "No."

She held in her grin as they moved on to a group of guests standing by the fireplace, two men who were related to her through her mother. Cousins. Lord Berger and Mr. Staunton.

"Nasty stuff," Lord Berger said, shaking his head.

Mumbled agreements followed. "I understand that you are a murder mystery author, Lady Wethington," Mr. Staunton said.

Amy appeared startled at being addressed by her new moniker. However, she quickly recovered. "Yes, indeed. I pen mystery novels under the pseudonym E. D. Burton." Amy glowed with the pride she always felt when someone acknowledged her work.

"Totally inappropriate thing for a sweet young lady to waste her time with," Berger repeated, frowning in such a way that reminded Amy of her father and his initial displeasure when she had shown him her first publishing contract.

Lord Berger's words had certainly taken some of the wind from her sails. Here she was gloating in her notoriety, and her cousin made no effort to hide his censure at her efforts. A typical male.

William drew in a deep breath and his shoulders stiffened. "I must disagree, my good man. My wife is an outstanding author. She has received awards for her work and has a rather large and loyal fan base. In fact, she attracted quite a crowd at a book fair held earlier in the year at Atkinson and Tucker bookstore—all anxious to meet her."

Were they not standing in public, Amy would have kissed William right there. At least *he* had no qualms about her writing.

"Yes, yes," Lord Berger said, "but a woman should not be writing about evil and unseemly goings-on." He pointed his finger at her. "Now that you have been rescued from such a life, you can forget all that nonsense and see to the needs of your husband. Soon there will be children to take up your time. They would be embarrassed if anyone knew their mother wrote such things."

Amy gritted her teeth, trying exceptionally hard not to insult one of their guests. Before she was able to compose in her mind something that would not be considered rude, William said, "Actually, my lord, I would never assume my needs are such that my wife would have to devote all her time to them.

I have numerous employees who see to the running of my household."

After a slight pause, he added, "Many young married women spend their time shopping and making numerous visits to gossip and drink tea, but I imagine Lady Wethington will instead spend her time using her brain. The wonderful brain that the good Lord has given her and she has put to good use."

"Bravo," Aunt Margaret said as she joined the group. "William, I am proud to call you nephew-in-law."

William bowed. "Thank you, my lady."

"Bah. You young people have no sense of propriety. In my day, women knew their place and stayed there." With those words, Lord Berger pounded his walking stick on the floor and left them.

"Well. That was interesting," Aunt Margaret said as she watched the man hobble off.

"I, for one, Lady Wethington, think it is quite modern for you to write these stories." Mr. Staunton looked over at William. "And I congratulate you, my lord, for being so open-minded."

"Can I steal these two away, Mr. Staunton?" Aunt Margaret said as she linked her arms with William's and Amy's. "There is something I must discuss with them."

Mr. Staunton nodded. "Of course. I am in need of another cup of tea myself."

The three of them strolled away, and Aunt Margaret offered a smug smile. "I have some information for you."

"What?" Amy and William said at the same time.

Her aunt nodded at the Misses O'Neill as they strolled by, then lowered her voice, most likely not wanting the ladies who loved gossip to hear her. "We all knew about Mrs. Davis and Albert, but because, as far as I know, no one has ever met her, you can imagine my surprise when I discovered she is here."

"Who?" Amy asked. She'd done the invitations herself with Aunt Priscilla.

"Mrs. Madeline Davis," Aunt Margaret said, gesturing toward a woman who sat between Michael and Amy's father. "The one in the light blue gown, with the dark hair."

"I don't remember her on the invitation list." Mrs. Davis was pretty in a striking sort of way. Her features were sharp, but when she smiled, her face transformed into something lovely.

Her curly hair was drawn back in a knot at the back of her head. Like that of every other woman present, her gown was wrinkled, but she still looked attractive.

Aunt Margaret shrugged. "Whether you remember adding her or not, there she is."

Michael seemed to be enjoying himself, bantering with Eloise on one side, and the lady Amy had just learned was Mrs. Davis, on the other. From the look on their faces, they were all having a grand time despite the somber event.

Studying the three of them, Amy said, "I was unaware of a connection between Eloise and Michael. I thought they barely knew each other."

"They look quite friendly to me," Lady Margaret said.

William bent toward Amy and Aunt Margaret and lowered his voice. "Mrs. Davis certainly doesn't look as if she is anticipating the loss of a lover if Albert ends up swinging from a rope, found guilty of Alice's murder."

"The real question is how did she come to be at the wedding if she wasn't on the invitation list?" Lady Margaret asked as she, Amy, and William all looked in the woman's direction.

CHAPTER 8

William quietly closed the door behind him and joined the two detectives seated behind the large desk in Lady Granville's library. He had been summoned for his "interview" with the men. Several other guests had been through the process already. Two had been sent home: Lady Pritchard—for which everyone was most grateful—along with Mrs. Holland, with both ladies departing amid grumbling and threats of action against the Bath Police.

Annabelle Munson and William's mother and stepfather had all been asked to remain. William couldn't help but wonder if the detectives had done that just to annoy William, as there was absolutely no reason to assume his mother and her husband had anything to do with Mrs. Finch's demise. They hadn't even known her until the wedding.

"Ah, Lord Wethington. Please, have a seat." Detective Carson waved at the chair in front of the desk. Which, of course, would put William at a disadvantage.

"How can I help you, Detective? I am most anxious to get this matter cleared."

Carson leaned back and grinned. "Ah, yes. The anxious bridegroom. How did you survive your wedding night?"

Doing his best to tamp down his anger, William stood and leaned over the desk, almost nose-to-nose with the detective. "I have absolutely no intention of discussing my marriage with you, Detective Carson. Furthermore, if this ridiculous line of questioning continues, I will leave here and visit with your superiors."

He took a deep breath, attempting to control himself. "And if I hear that you have harassed my wife in any way with such rude and uncouth comments, I will do the same." He tugged on the cuffs of his coat and sat down. "Now, if you wish to question me about something having to do with the unfortunate death of Mrs. Finch, I will be happy to oblige."

Detective Marsh continued to write in his notebook the entire time William spoke, which left William wondering what part of his threat the detective considered noteworthy.

After a few moments of silence, Carson dipped his head, almost in regret. "I apologize, Lord Wethington. You are correct. And I can assure you Lady Wethington will be treated with the utmost respect."

In all the time William had known the two detectives, having dealt with them through two other homicide inquiries, he'd never seen the man grovel in such a way. He nodded at the detective. "You have questions?"

Now all business, the detective began his questions, which were no surprise to William:

"Where were you seated at the wedding breakfast?"

"How close were to you Mr. and Mrs. Finch?"

"Did you see Mrs. Finch drink champagne?"

"Did you see Mr. Finch drink champagne?"

"How far into the event did Mrs. Finch collapse?"

"How well do you know Mr. and Mrs. Finch?"

William gave his answers for the second time, since these were almost exact duplicates of the ones the detectives had asked the day before. He noted that Detective Marsh barked them out with very little expectation of hearing anything different.

A definite waste of time.

"That is all for now, my lord. However—and please don't take this in the wrong way—I must insist that you and Lady Wethington do not leave Bath." He held up his hand as William opened his mouth to speak. "I know you are looking forward to a honeymoon, and believe me, I understand, having been in that situation myself at one time, but because this happened at *your* wedding breakfast and it is assumed that between you and your wife all guests are known, I might need more information from you."

As much as William wanted to protest, he knew the detective was correct. "Are you telling me you would like assistance from myself and Lady Wethington?"

"God, no! I merely need someone who is familiar with all the guests." He pointed his finger at William. "We are back to this again, I see. Despite what you see as success with Mr. St. Vincent's and Mr. Harding's murders, you and Lady Wethington are not to involve yourselves in this matter in any way."

"I assume we do not have to remain in the house, though?"

Carson shook his head. "No. Even those I have asked to stay will be granted leave to return to their homes tonight."

"What about Mr. and Mrs. Colbert—my parents?"

The detective nodded. "You may advise them they can leave as well."

William rose to leave.

"One more thing, my lord."

"Yes." William sighed as he reached the library door.

"Am I correct that Mr. and Mrs. Finch are connected to your wife and not you?"

"That is true."

"Was this event the first time you met them?"

"No. I met them at one or two other family events, including our betrothal ball back in May."

"Thank you. Will you please ask Lady Wethington to step into the library?"

★　★　★

Amy broke off her conversation with Michael and Eloise as William entered the drawing room. "Excuse me," she said and hurried off.

"Did you learn anything?"

William chuckled. "You do understand that the detectives are questioning us to acquire information from us, not provide it?"

She dismissed his question with a wave. "Yes, I know that. But I was hoping they might have perhaps slipped up in some way, to help with our investigation."

"Amy, there is no need for *our investigation*. This appears to be an easily solved crime. Everyone was given a glass of champagne. The detectives saw fit to take both glasses from the table where the Finches sat. Alice carried an asthma treatment wherever she went, which contains belladonna. She was found to have been poisoned by belladonna. No one would know better about where the poison was kept than her husband."

Amy shook her head slowly. "I am so disappointed in you, my lord. I thought I had trained you better."

"Oh?" He leaned back and crossed his arms over his chest. "And how is that, my love?"

She began to tick off on her fingers. "If Albert was deter-mined to kill his wife, why use a champagne glass while she sat right next to him? That would make the drug so easy to identify once her manner of death was established. Why use something to poison her that was so easily traceable to him? And there still remains the mystery of Albert's lover being a guest whom I don't remember inviting."

William grinned. "You make valid points, Lady Mystery Writer. However, right now you are wanted in the library for your questioning."

Amy raised her chin as she sailed away, speaking over her shoulder, "I am certain I will return with information."

The two detectives stood as she entered the room. Detec-tive Carson nodded. "Good morning, my lady. If you will take a seat, we would like to ask you a few questions."

Amy chose to sit on the settee, forcing the detectives to shift in their chairs. It was best to start off in control. However, she offered them a bright smile as recompense. "What can I do for you, Detectives?"

"Perhaps you can start by assuring us that you and your hus-band have no intention of interfering with our investigation."

Amy blinked as if surprised, placing her hand on her chest. "Of course not, Detective. We are newly married and looking forward to a honeymoon—"

Carson groaned.

"—so we have no intention of interfering with your inves-tigation." There was no reason to advise him that she and William had their own investigation to conduct. She was not convinced that her cousin-in-law had killed his wife. As she'd explained to William, there were simply too many other things to take into consideration.

"What connection do you have to Mr. and Mrs. Finch?"

"I believe you asked me this question the last time we spoke. Or rather the last time you interrogated me."

"Now, my lady, certainly we did not interrogate you. We simply asked a few questions."

Since that was not a question, she merely sat politely and continued to stare at the detective. Detective Marsh held his pencil at the ready, and Detective Carson cleared his throat. "Is it true, to your knowledge, that Mr. and Mrs. Finch engaged in an argument the night before your wedding?"

"Yes. That is true."

"What was the argument about?"

"I am not sure. They were speaking in muted voices."

"You did not hear any of the conversation, then?"

"I did hear Mrs. Finch snap, 'Never again.'"

Detective Marsh scribbled, never looking up.

"Are you aware of your cousin's involvement with . . ." Carson looked over at Detective Marsh, who flipped a few pages, then said, "Mrs. Madeline Davis."

"Cousin-in-law, Detective. Alice is my cousin, and yes, I had heard rumors."

The questions continued, Amy learning nothing new except that the detectives were definitely leaning toward Albert having done away with his wife, which Amy did not agree with. It just didn't feel right.

"Are my husband and I permitted to depart today, Detective?"

"Ah, yes. The honeymoon," Detective Carson said. "You and Lord Wethington may leave Lady Granville's home. However, I am sorry to inform you that leaving Bath will not be permitted."

Because there didn't appear to be any reason to appeal to the man's better nature—which Amy had her doubts even existed—she merely nodded and stood.

Detective Carson rose also and stretched. "Please ask Lord Winchester to step into the library."

William was speaking with Papa and Michael, and they all looked over at her as she entered the drawing room. "Papa, it is your turn."

"Good. I need to get this over with. Michael and I have business to attend to that cannot be put on hold."

"Will we be able to leave?" Michael asked as Papa left their group to attend the detectives.

"I believe so. They told me William and I will be able to leave here, but we cannot leave Bath."

William nodded at her comments, not looking very happy.

"Sorry, old boy," Michael said. "But at least you won't have to spend the night listening to me and my father snore."

"Yes. There is comfort in that." William turned to Amy. "Are you packed?"

"I am. I had expected to leave here and go directly to the railway to travel to Brighton Beach."

William sighed. "Well, Brighton Beach it will not be. We can either go to my house—rather *our* house—or a hotel if we want something special."

"Anywhere we can be together will be special," Amy said, taking William's arm.

Michael groaned. "If you will excuse me, I fear I will be so sugar-coated I may never recover." He leaned over and kissed Amy on her cheek. "I am sorry for how your wedding turned out."

Amy gave her brother a hug. "The most important part went well."

Aunt Margaret joined them from where she'd been speaking with another guest. "I assume you've been given permission to leave?"

"Yes, but we cannot leave Bath, so our trip to Brighton Beach is out."

Her aunt hugged her. "I'm sorry, but Brighton Beach will always be there."

Amy murmured, "Don't say that to William."

There was no great distance between Lady Granville's house and William's townhouse. Once they knew they would be returning there instead of traveling to the railway, William had sent word to his housekeeper, Mrs. O'Sullivan, that he and his new wife would be spending the night, and possibly several days, at home. No doubt the woman was in a tizzy preparing for their arrival, Amy thought, feeling sorry for the short notice she'd been given.

The carriage rolled to a stop in front of Wethington House. Amazingly enough, the staff was ready to greet their new mistress, lined up outside as was the custom. A slight breeze blew the caps and aprons of the female staff members.

William and Amy made their way up the steps, with Mrs. O'Sullivan introducing the maids, and William's butler, Filbert, presenting the footmen. Once inside, Amy pulled off her gloves, and the butler assisted her and William out of their coats. "My lord, a missive arrived for you early this morning. The young lad who brought it said it was urgent."

William took the letter from the salver and opened the envelope. His brows rose as his eyes moved back and forth over the writing.

"What is it?" Amy said.

He handed the paper to her. She looked at what appeared to be a quickly scribbled note.

My Dear Lord Wethington,

I beg you to come to me at the Bath gaol as soon as you are able. I have been arrested for Alice's murder.

Mr. Albert E. Finch

CHAPTER 9

William opened the battered and scarred wooden door of the Bath City Police building and ushered Amy inside. A young man in a city police uniform sat at a desk near the west wall of the room, snapping a rubber band, his feet resting on the desk in front of him. He jerked his feet off the desk and looked up as they entered. "May I help you?"

"I am trying to locate a Mr. Albert E. Finch, whom I believe is being held either here or at possibly another location. He would have been brought in most likely today."

The man studied them for a minute, then broke into a bright smile. "I believe I know you. Aren't you Lord Wethington and Lady Amy?"

"Lord and Lady Wethington now," William said.

The young man leaned back in his chair, a wide smile on his face. "So you married, eh? No surprise to me. I remember being with the two of you when you had to carry the lady up three flights of stairs because she fainted in the morgue. 'Twas quite an accomplishment, I must say so myself. I'm not sure if I would have had the strength to—"

William cut in. "If you will please assist us in locating Mr. Finch?"

The police officer flushed. "Of course. Just give me a minute to check the list." He stood and bowed to them. "I will be right back." He waved his finger at them. "I knew it was you."

"Amy, I am so sorry—"

She shook her head. "No need to be sorry. I told you at the time how amazed I was that you carried me three flights of stairs." She sniffed and tugged on her dress, as if the garment had suddenly grown too snug.

He cupped her chin. "Don't start that again. I think you are fine just the way you are."

She offered him a slight smile, but he wasn't sure he'd convinced her. Amy was certainly not plump. She simply carried perhaps a stone more than most women of her height, but her short stature probably made it difficult for her to enjoy her food and still maintain what she thought was a perfect weight.

Oftentimes she had mused to him about how she wished she had her Aunt Margaret's frame, but truth be known, although willowy and slender Lady Margaret was attractive, she was too slight for his taste. He would be worried that he might crush her bones in a proper hug.

They waited in silence until the officer returned, carrying a slip of paper. "Mr. Finch is being held at the city lockup, but I suggest you visit with him as soon as you are able as it's quite likely he will be transported to Shepton Mallet shortly."

Shepton Mallet was a prison located in Somerset, about twenty miles from Bath. William was shocked and surprised that Albert would be taken there so quickly. Most likely the detectives thought their case was solid and there was no reason not to move him to a more secure facility while he awaited a formal trial.

He couldn't help but think again that the detectives had zeroed in on one suspect and would attempt to close the case quickly. It seemed to be a bad habit of theirs, and not an effective way to run a murder investigation. As he and Amy had proven twice before, the most obvious suspect was not necessarily the guilty one. That they had done so had a lot to do with the detectives' animosity toward them.

William thanked the officer, and he and Amy left the building for the short ride to city lockup.

While certainly better than Shepton Mallett, the city lockup was not exactly a warm, loving place to spend one's time. William had had a thankfully short stint in lockup himself earlier in the year, when he'd been accused of Mr. James Harding's murder—something he would never want to repeat.

The structure was built of old, discolored stone, and dankly cold. He thought his memories might have brought on the shudder he felt when they entered, but Amy shivered also.

"What a horrible place. I can't believe you were contained here." Amy looked around the bare room and rubbed her palms up and down her arms.

They approached an opening in the wall to another room. It could not be considered either a doorway or even a window, though it stood about five feet from the floor and was the size of a window. Steel bars much like those in a gaol cell prevented callers from accosting the man on the other side, who walked up to the opening. "What?"

So much for good manners and a dignified reception. Given what they'd experienced so far, he hated the fact that Amy was with him for this, but because he knew his wife quite well, there would have been no having her wait at the house for him while he spoke with Albert.

"I would like to have a word with one of your prisoners: Mr. Albert E. Finch."

Without answering, the man turned and walked away. William glanced at Amy. "Do you suppose the man is deaf? Or just rude?"

"I'm in favor of rude." She nodded toward the opening. "However, he is going through some papers. Perhaps he's looking for Albert's name."

After a few minutes the man sauntered back to the window and waved at a long wooden bench along the wall. "You can wait there. Someone will come out and get you." He nodded toward Amy. "Is she going with you too?"

William drew himself up, quite annoyed at the man's manner. "I will certainly not leave my wife out here with the likes of you. We have hardly been treated with any sort of respect."

Although he had the grace to blush, the man shrugged and once again walked away.

William took Amy's arm, and they made their way to the bench and took a seat.

"I don't like it here, William."

"Actually, I would prefer if you would wait in the carriage."

Amy shook her head. "No. I will just use this as research for an upcoming book." Once again she ran her palms up and down her arms and looked around the dreadful place. "How one feels to be locked in a dungeon."

★　★　★

About another five minutes passed, although it seemed much longer, when a man dressed in a uniform unlike that of a police officer walked up to them. "You here to see Mr. Finch?"

Amy and William stood. "Yes," William said.

"You have permission from Detective Carson?"

Before William could answer, Amy jumped in. "Yes. We are quite good friends with Detective Carson and his partner, Detective Marsh. We just left them a couple of hours ago."

There. It wasn't exactly a lie, although the comment about being friends could be considered a bit of stretching the truth.

The man looked at her as if she had jumped the queue at the greengrocer. She offered him what she hoped was an encouraging smile.

"Follow me." The man turned and walked back the way he had come.

They were led to a room that was just as dingy as the rest of the building. Someone had made a miniscule effort, possibly a hundred years before, to paint the walls, but the color was now unidentifiable. They sat side by side at a worn table. Somewhere in the distance she could hear shouting and foul language. She shuddered again.

"Are you sure I can't persuade you to return to the carriage? I feel like the worst of husbands to allow you to even see such a place."

Before she could speak, the door opened and Albert walked in, with a guard pushing him forward. The poor man looked horrible. His skin was pasty, and he appeared not to have slept since the night before the wedding.

"Are you well, Albert?" Amy asked.

He pulled out a chair and sat across from them. "Not well, I'm sorry to say."

The guard settled himself against the wall, his arms crossed.

"Are we not to be accorded privacy?" William asked the man.

"No."

Albert leaned toward them. "I did not kill Alice." He looked at the guard and lowered his voice. "I will admit there were times when I was tempted, but I did not poison her glass of champagne."

"Why did you send for us?" William asked.

He glanced again at the guard. "Because I remember Amy getting into some trouble last year, and from what I heard, between the two of you, the real killer was identified." He looked at Amy. "It was your fiancé if I remember correctly."

"Ex-fiancé."

Albert nodded. "Then there was the matter several months ago when you"—he waved his hand at William—"were under arrest for the murder of your man of business."

"Well, you certainly keep up with family news, don't you?" Amy said.

William cleared his throat and took out the pad of paper and pencil he had in his jacket pocket. "Can you tell us exactly what the police plan to charge you with?"

Albert shrugged. "Murder." He looked William in the eye. "I did not murder my wife."

William picked up his pencil. "Tell me what you told the police."

Albert ran his hand down his face in a familiar gesture, one that William had employed when he had been in Albert's situation many months before. "They asked me about the champagne that was served at the wedding breakfast."

"The one I assume the footmen poured into the glasses before my stepfather made the toast?"

"Yes." Albert leaned forward, a look of desperation on his face. "Anyone who knows"—he blanched, then continued—"*knew* Alice can tell you that, for as much as I dislike champagne, she loved it. So once the toast was over, I slid my glass in front of her. She must have consumed both drinks, because once she slumped over, I noticed both glasses were empty."

Amy had watched Albert's face while he spoke, as William was busy writing. If what he said was true—and she had no way at the present time to decide if he was lying or not—either one of the glasses could have contained the drug. He could have slipped the poison into his own glass and then given it to his wife. Or he could have even been the intended victim. "What you are telling us is you have no idea whose glass contained the belladonna?"

"That's right."

William stopped writing and asked, "Who knows Alice used the drug for her asthma?"

Albert shrugged. "Everyone. I mean, anyone who knew her must have seen her either use it at some point or speak of it. She was quite convinced that it was a great help when her breathing gave her trouble. She'd suffered from the illness since childhood."

"Was the belladonna in a liquid form?"

"Yes."

"Did she carry it with her?"

Albert shook his head. "No. She would put a few drops into very hot water, then place her face over it and breathe in the steam. If we traveled she would have it with her, but if she were out shopping or visiting, she wouldn't carry it."

"And I assume she had it with her when you journeyed to Lady Granville's house, where if I am correct, you spent the night before the wedding."

"That is correct."

William asked his questions, not looking up at the man, but busy writing. Amy used her common sense and research from various books she'd written to study Albert as they spoke.

He was nervous, no doubt about that. But anyone in his position would be. Sometimes when he spoke, he looked William or her in the eye, other times he fumbled with the cuff of his shirt and looked down at the table.

"I have a question for you, Albert." Amy thought for a moment. "If we are to help you, there are difficult questions that must be asked."

Albert nodded, his lips tight.

"Over the three years of your marriage, it was well known what you had 'associations' with other women. Most recently with Mrs. Madeline Davis."

Albert ran his palm down his face again. "Yes. I am embarrassed to admit that Mrs. Davis was my lover. We went our separate ways a few weeks ago."

Amy's muscles tightened. "Your choice or mutual agreement?"

Almost a full minute passed while Albert drew small circles on the table with his fingertip. "I had reasons to suspect all was not well with our relationship. I felt it was best if we moved on."

"Not well how?" Amy persisted.

Waving his hand in the air dismissively, he said, "Nothing important—just little things that disturbed me."

"Yet, she was at the wedding."

"I know," he said, slumping in his seat. "I was quite surprised that she was there." He looked over at Amy. "Why did you invite her?"

Amy glanced at William and shook her head. "I didn't."

CHAPTER 10

After about another fifteen minutes of questions and answers, William threw down his pencil and stretched. "You have given us enough to get started. I assume you've told the police all this?"

"I did. But they didn't seem too interested. They were more focused on the asthma treatment, where the medicine was kept, how she used it, that sort of thing." He lowered his voice. "They were also quite interested in my relationship with Mrs. Davis."

"Of course," Amy said. "Their method of solving crimes is limited to accusing the most obvious and, instead of looking for other suspects, focusing all their energies on proving themselves right." She shook her head. "It's a good thing they have William and me to help them."

William turned to her with raised brows. "I'm sure they're thrilled with our assistance."

She offered a smug grin. "I am without a doubt."

He returned to his notes. "I think the first thing we should do is get you out of here, or out of Shepton Mallet, if that is where your next stop is."

Albert blanched. "Shepton Mallet?"

William nodded. "However, there is a fine barrister that helped both Amy and myself when we had our difficulties with the police. I trust him implicitly. His name is Mr. Nelson-Graves. I will call upon him and have him start working on your release."

"And you will prove I am innocent of Alice's death?"

Amy jumped in, most likely because William had done most of the talking, and it was not like her to allow that. "You must give us some time. These things need to be investigated, and people at the wedding need to be interviewed."

"And most of all," William said as he tucked the pad and pencil into his pocket, "we must keep our involvement hidden from the police."

Albert nodded. "As long as I know someone believes me and is working on my behalf, I feel much better."

As William was not completely convinced Albert was innocent, he merely stood and shook the man's hand. "We will send word to Mr. Nelson-Graves when we leave here."

"Thank you." The man's voice shook, which William fully understood, having gone through the same experience himself.

The guard departed with Albert, and in less than a minute the same young man who'd brought them to the room appeared and led them out without saying a word.

Once they settled into the carriage, Amy said, "What do you think?"

William shrugged. "He seemed sincere in his protestations that he had nothing to do with the murder, but all murder suspects say that. The evidence is certainly overwhelming against him. He was sitting right next to his wife, she drank both glasses, and one of them had poison in it."

Amy thought for a minute, then said, "On the other hand, as I've mentioned before, if he intended to kill Alice, it was sloppily done. He had to know he would be the prime suspect, so why do it that way? Why not remove the poisoned glass during all the confusion?"

"True."

Amy pushed the curtain aside and studied the passing traffic and townhouses. "Where are we headed?"

"I told the driver to take us back to Lady Granville's home. Hopefully, the police are finished and gone. I wish to speak to her without their presence. While we are there, I will send an urgent missive to Mr. Nelson-Graves to begin the process to have Albert released."

"Do you think they will release him? The detectives think they have a good case this time."

"They always think they have a good case."

Amy was silent for a couple of minutes, then raised her chin and cleared her throat. "My lord?"

William's stomach dropped. It appeared he was in trouble, although he wasn't quite sure for what. Women—and more specifically, wives—had a way, he'd been told, of saying simple words that meant a great deal more than they seemed. However, there was no doubt he was about to find out. "Yes, my love."

Her eyes narrowed, which told him she wasn't falling for any diversions from him of soft, loving words. "It appears to me that you have assumed the position of lead investigator." Her cute little chin rose even farther.

"Oh?" He knew precisely what she meant, and had been waiting for this confrontation.

"Yes." She waved her hand between them. "*We* are in this together. *We* have always been in this together. While I have no objections to your methods so far, I do intend to be treated as an equal. Marriage has not changed that."

William reached out and pulled her across the space, to sit next to him, wrapping his arm around her shoulders. "Have no fear, dear wife. I do not intend to ever treat you as anything but my equal and partner. In all things." To solidify his statement, he tugged her closer for a kiss.

Just as things had become interesting, the carriage came to a rolling stop in front of Lady Granville's home.

William released her and sighed.

★   ★   ★

Amy adjusted her clothing, which had become mussed after the ride and William's kiss. He climbed out first and turned to take her hand and help her down.

Although she had felt quite like a bride the day before, she had yet to feel like a wife. Hopefully, nothing would prevent them from a nice quiet dinner and time together that evening. If she was becoming frustrated, she could only imagine how William must feel.

The same butler who had been at the door the day before greeted them and bid them wait in the front parlor until he learned if Lady Granville was receiving guests.

William retrieved his pad and pencil from his pocket and wrote a note. He tore the sheet from his notebook and stood. "I will ask the butler to see that this note is delivered to Mr. Nelson-Graves immediately."

About fifteen minutes after William had given the note to the butler, Lady Granville's voice drew their attention from discussing Albert's interview.

"Oh, my dears." She entered the room, her arms extended, a lace handkerchief clutched in her hands. "I am so very happy to see you."

William stood and Amy joined him, ducking her head to hide the smile at her great-aunt's histrionics. They'd only left her mere hours before.

"'Tis nice to see you also." She hugged her great-aunt and leaned back to study her. "Have the police finished?"

"Yes. All the guests have been dismissed, and the detectives left some time ago with instructions that the dining room could be cleaned up. For which I am most grateful." She lowered her voice. "I believe the room was beginning to have a certain, shall we say, 'aroma' about it?"

"Are you well?" Amy asked.

"Yes, my dear." She waved her handkerchief around. "That is, as well as one could be after a murder takes place in one's home." She inhaled deeply and placed her hand on her chest. "Oh my goodness. I must sit down. I don't believe I have recovered quite yet."

"Shall I ring for tea?" Amy asked.

Again the handkerchief fluttered. "Yes, do."

Once Amy had done her duty and was seated next to her great-aunt, the woman gripped her hands. "How are you holding up, my dear? Such a dreadful event." She shook her head and patted the edges of her eyes. "Dreadful."

William took the seat across from them. "Lady Granville, might we ask you a few questions?"

The trembling, tearful, frail, dramatic woman disappeared in a flash. Aunt Priscilla sat up straight and looked William in the eye. "Of course, nephew. How may I help you?"

"Do you remember the footmen who poured the champagne right before Mr. Colbert offered the toast?"

"Let me think." She tapped her lips with her fingertip.

Amy leaned forward. "Did the police not ask you that question?"

She shook her head. "I don't believe so, dear. In fact, I'm quite sure, because I would have had to find the list of servers to recollect who worked where." She stood. "That is precisely what I have to do now. If you will excuse me, I have all the papers with the information relating to the wedding breakfast in the top drawer of the desk in my sitting room."

Her great-aunt left in a whirl of taffeta skirts just as a footman arrived, pushing a tea cart. While they waited, Amy poured tea for William and herself and filled small plates with tiny sandwiches, biscuits, fruit, and cheese.

"I find I am quite hungry. Did we have lunch?" Amy asked as she took a sip of tea.

"No. We did not. In fact, we haven't done anything normal since yesterday. A guest was murdered at our wedding breakfast, we slept apart on our wedding night," he growled. "I believe we had breakfast here, then went home, were immediately summoned to the gaol, and now we're back here again. No, no lunch."

"Or wedding night." Amy repeated.

"Indeed."

They ate in silence, and Amy was just beginning to wonder if she should go upstairs to her great-aunt's sitting room to see if she was all right, when the woman appeared, a sheaf of papers in her hands. She looked up at them with a puzzled expression. "How very odd."

"What is odd?"

She sat alongside Amy once again. "These are all the papers that I had in my drawer." She began to shuffle them. "Flowers, menus, room assignments, wines and champagne, furniture placement—to allow more space—lighting, and staff on duty for the dinner the night before and the wedding breakfast after the ceremony." She shook her head and looked up. "All the papers are here except for the list of those working at the dinner and then at the wedding breakfast. Mostly my own staff, but a few extra servants were hired for the event."

William frowned. "Do you generally keep a list of staff members when you have a party, ball, or other event?"

"Goodness, it's been so long since I entertained, 'tis hard to remember. But this was such an important event"—she leaned over and patted Amy's knee—"that when I decided we needed to hire outside help, I thought it would be easier on my housekeeper, Mrs. Fletcher, with everything else she had to do, if I assumed that task. I believe I gave her the list of servants."

"I suppose you used an agency to hire the temporary staff?" Amy asked.

"Yes. Is that important?"

William nodded. "It might be. Can you provide us with the name of the business you used?"

"Of course." Lady Granville stood. "Mrs. Fletcher gave me the name so I could make the arrangements and interview the potential staff. It will only take a minute to fetch that from her."

Heading to the door, her great-aunt stopped in her tracks and turned back. She frowned. "Is there some reason you need all these things? Shouldn't you be on your honeymoon?"

"If only," William mumbled.

Amy cast him a like-minded look before addressing her great-aunt. "Mr. Finch has requested that we assist him in finding his wife's killer."

Aunt Priscilla's hand went to her throat, and she paled. "I thought it was determined that he was the one who poisoned Mrs. Finch?"

William shook his head. "Although it appears to be him, Amy and I have learned—the hard way, I might add—that the most obvious suspect is not always the true culprit."

"Are you conducting your own investigation, then? Do the detectives know this?" The poor woman looked distraught. Truth be known, she had every right to feel discombobulated. Learning that her great-niece, whom she'd known since her birth, and her new husband were trying to solve a murder instead of frolicking on the beaches of Brighton must have been quite alarming for a woman who had never been touched by lawbreaking of any sort in her well-protected life.

"We are not precisely 'investigating.' We merely promised Mr. Finch that we would ask a few questions." There, that sounded elusive enough, which Amy hoped would calm her great-aunt. And prevent her from notifying the police or, worse yet, her papa.

"I don't know if I like this, Amy. It could be quite dangerous."

"Why? If you believe Mr. Finch is the guilty party and he is in gaol right now, there would be no danger to us."

Aunt Priscilla placed her hands on her hips and glared at her. "But what if you discover Mr. Finch is not guilty? The actual guilty party could do you harm."

Before Amy could think of a clever answer to assuage her great-aunt's concerns, the butler entered the parlor. He offered a stiff bow, his lips curled in distaste. "My lady, Detectives Carson and Marsh from the Bath City Police have arrived and asked for a few minutes of your time."

The two detectives, never ones to bow to proper procedure, entered right behind the butler.

"Well, look who is here having tea with Lady Granville." Detective Carson grinned at Detective Marsh. "And the day after their wedding. And Lord Wethington so anxious to be granted leave to depart the premises merely a few hours ago with his new wife. One would imagine they would have better activities to occupy their time."

"Shite," William mumbled.

CHAPTER 11

Apparently picking on up on his and Amy's angst with the arrival of the detectives, Lady Granville raised her chin and regarded the men with all the dignity of her station. "I believe you only left us little more than an hour ago, Detectives. What may I help you with"—she hesitated—"now?"

William hid his smirk and watched the play between the detectives and Amy's great-aunt.

Carson fumbled a bit while Marsh avoided the entire thing by pulling out his notepad and licking his pencil.

"We don't mean to inconvenience you, my lady, but there are just a few minor things we need to clear up."

"I do hope this is the last time I need to see you." Lady Granville nodded, flicking her fingers, like a queen barely tolerating her subject. "Go on."

Carson cleared his throat. "Was there a Mrs. Madeline Davis at the wedding breakfast?"

Lady Granville sniffed. "I believe you interviewed all the attendees, so I assume this is a rhetorical question."

He sighed. "Yes, my lady." He then turned his attention to Amy. "Do you know Mrs. Davis?"

"I do not know her. I know *of* her."

He smiled as if he'd finally uncovered a boon. "Yet she was on your invitation list."

"No, Detective. She was not. I sent my list to Lady Granville, who, I believe, had her companion use that to send out the invitations. Mrs. Davis was not one of the anticipated guests."

Carson looked surprised. "Yet she was in attendance."

Amy merely nodded.

"Then how did she get in?"

She raised her brows. "Through the front door, I imagine."

A soft cough from Lady Granville was the only sound as Detective Carson glowered at Amy. "Let me rephrase that question. Is it a general habit of the upper crust to attend events they were not invited to? Would there have been a way that uninvited guests were identified?"

Amy nodded to her great-aunt. "I am sure Lady Granville can answer that better, as Lord Wethington and I were busy getting married when the guests began to arrive."

The detective looked confused. "Did not the people who attended the wedding breakfast also attend the ceremony?"

"No," William answered. "Traditionally, only close friends and family attend the church service, but many others are invited to the wedding breakfast."

As he continued to scribble in his notepad, Detective Marsh shook his head and mumbled, "Odd bunch, the aristocracy."

William decided not to challenge the man because he wanted this over with as quickly as possible.

"Lady Wethington, if you don't know Mrs. Davis, but know of her, can you confirm that she and your cousin-in-law, Mr. Albert E. Finch were involved in an adulterous affair?"

Amy drew in a sharp breath. "I hardly think I am in a position to answer that question, Detective. I certainly do not follow my cousin-in-law about, watching whom he meets and where they go. 'Twould be quite tiresome to climb in and out of bedroom windows all the time to see what they were doing. However, I can confirm that there have been rumors amongst family members of an association between Mrs. Davis and Mr. Finch."

The detective looked from William to Amy, to Lady Granville. "Can anyone confirm where Mrs. Davis sat during the breakfast? In relation to Mrs. Finch, that is."

No one spoke. Then Amy said, "I did not know her except by name before our wedding, so I cannot say where she sat."

Carson nodded at Detective Marsh, who flipped his notepad closed. They both stood. "Thank you for your time, Lady Granville. I hope this is the last time we need to disturb you."

She nodded and Detective Carson looked at William. "A word, my lord?" He waved toward the doorway.

William followed the two men out of the room to the entrance hall. Carson stood with his hands on his hips. "I sincerely hope that you and your new wife are not wasting time following in our footsteps."

"I can assure you, Detective, we are not following in your footsteps." A true statement since he and Amy had always gone their own way and arrived at the necessary places *before* the detectives did.

"That's good to know. Because we will not tolerate interference again." Carson slapped William on the back as if they were old friends. "You have more important things to attend to, lad." He winked. "I'm sure you know what I mean."

Considering that an insult to his wife, William drew himself up and glared at the man. "If you are finished here, Detective, I wish you a good day." With those words he turned on his heel and left them.

Amy and her great-aunt were huddled together on the settee when William returned to the front parlor, the older woman flipping through the papers she held, Amy waving her arms around as she spoke. They both looked up as he entered.

"What did he want?" Amy asked. "Or should I assume it was the same old warning?"

"Yes." He reached out and took her hand. "I think it's best if we leave her ladyship to enjoy a bit of peace after a couple of harrowing days."

"First, allow me to obtain the name of the agency from Mrs. Fletcher and see if she still has the list of servants used for the affair, as we were distracted by the arrival of the police." She handed the papers she held to Amy and left the room.

Within minutes she returned with a slip of paper, a name scribbled on it, that she passed along to Amy. "I don't wish to keep you, as Mrs. Fletcher needs to search for the servant list, but here is the name of the agency." The two ladies stood, and Amy turned to hug her great-aunt. "Thank you again for all you have done for us, Aunt. I am so sorry things turned out the way they did."

Lady Granville patted Amy on the arm as they strolled from the room. "Do not concern yourself, my dear. Things have settled down now, and despite your idea that Albert played no part in poor Alice's demise, I think the detectives have assured themselves of his guilt. No doubt it will all be over soon."

Rather than dispute the woman, Amy merely nodded. William took Amy's arm, and they made their way down the steps to his waiting carriage.

Once they settled into their seats and William tapped on the ceiling for the driver to move ahead, he turned to Amy.

"I think we have spent enough time on this matter for the day. I propose no more talk of Mrs. Finch, Mr. Finch, Detective Carson, Detective Marsh, or Mrs. Davis and that we head home and have a nice quiet dinner in our bedchamber. In more comfortable clothes. With a bottle of wine."

"And . . .?" Amy said, eyebrows raised, with a slight smirk on her plump lips, and a deepening blush on her lovely cheeks.

He drew his fingers around the inside of his neckcloth and tapped on the ceiling once again as a signal to the driver to move faster. "Exactly."

★   ★   ★

Amy took one final look in the looking glass, assured that all was in place. Her black dress, gloves, and straw hat were fitting attire for Alice Finch's funeral. After the funeral, the family had been invited to Annabelle's house for refreshments and the reading of the will. She assumed they'd been invited to the reading not because of any inheritance, but merely as members of the family.

"Are you ready, Amy?" William strolled into her dressing room, also well suited up for a funeral.

"I am. Frankly, I am not looking forward to this, even though I am curious."

William straightened her hat and adjusted the collar of her dress. "Why so?"

"The other murders we were involved with—goodness that sounds terrible!—we did not go to the funerals. This time we will be able to watch all the attendees. It has been said that the murderer always returns to the scene of the crime."

"Alice was not killed in the funeral parlor." William took her hand and led her out of the room and down the stairs.

She waved her hand around. "I know that. But it is also said that oftentimes the murderer attends the funeral."

Filbert opened the door for them and nodded as they passed by and descended the steps to the waiting carriage. William helped Amy in and climbed in after her.

"I don't like funerals," Amy said as the carriage rolled away. "This one especially because it's a family member—and a murder victim." She shook her head.

"I assume Lady Margaret, your brother, and father are attending?"

"Yes."

Silence reigned for the rest of the trip. Several carriages were parked next to the small church where the funeral was to be held. It made Amy wonder why Annabelle had chosen to hold the funeral there instead of at St. Swithin's, which both she and Alice had attended on a sporadic basis.

Once the vehicle stopped, William opened the door, not waiting for the driver to jump down. He turned and held out his hand. "Goodness, Amy, your hand is shaking."

"I know. Isn't it silly? For some reason this has unnerved me. Even having dealt with unexpected deaths before."

William tilted his head and studied her. "You do not have to attend if you don't wish to."

"No. I will be fine." She straightened her shoulders and took William's arm. "Yes, I will be just fine."

The fifty or so mourners just about filled the tiny church. She and William took a seat near the back. Within a few minutes, Amy felt a nudge and looked up to see Papa, Michael, and Aunt Margaret standing there. She slid over and the group joined them in the pew.

It was a brief service, the pastor giving the eulogy. Since Alice's husband was in gaol and her sister so very distraught, apparently no one else was willing to do it.

Afterward, they trekked from the church to the small cemetery behind the building. The mourners gathered together, shifting uncomfortably as a few mumbled prayers were offered. Then it was all over. Amy took the time standing over the gravesite to examine the crowd. There were a few people she did not recognize, most likely Alice's friends.

The rest were family members, most of whom lived locally and had attended the wedding only a few days before.

A young man placed his hand on Annabelle's shoulder and addressed the gathering. "My aunt would like to invite all of you back to her house for refreshments." In a solicitous manner, he took Annabelle's arm and led her from the gravesite. She leaned her head against his shoulder, her muffled cries swallowed by the handkerchief in her hand.

William bent toward her ear. "Who is the young man?"

"He is Annabelle's nephew, Jared Munson, son of her older brother, Adam. Adam passed away a few years ago, and Jared's mother the year before that. I haven't spent a great deal of time in Jared's company, but I understand he was a bit of a problem for his parents.

"He was close to Alice, from what I heard. She was forever giving him money, and she kept him from a serious beating one time by covering a gambling debt." She shook her head. "The young man truly is a wastrel."

Before they entered the carriage, Papa walked up to them. "Daughter, Michael and I are not returning to Alice's house. We expressed our condolences again and will be on our way."

"What about Aunt Margaret?"

"I believe she is returning home with us."

"Very well." She kissed Papa on the cheek and climbed into the carriage, William following her.

Now to spend some time closely studying the attendees.

CHAPTER 12

Annabelle's house was quite large, considering the woman lived alone. But then, if one had the means to purchase a large, lovely house, who was William to question it?

Again, Jared Munson walked with his aunt Annabelle, his arm around her shoulder, murmuring what must have been comforting words into her ear. She did not look pleased. Perhaps she was not as enamored of the young man as her sister had been.

The guests shared small sandwiches, biscuits, and tea. Most of the mourners left after only about twenty minutes. William placed his empty plate on one of the tables and walked to where Amy stood speaking with another woman he did not recognize.

"Mrs. Albright, may I present to you my husband, Lord Wethington?" She turned to William. "Mrs. Albright was Alice and Albert's housekeeper."

"How do you do, Mrs. Albright? I wish we could have met under better circumstances."

The woman nodded and said, "I agree, my lord. 'Tis a terrible thing what happened to Mrs. Finch." She turned to Amy. "I will be leaving now. I have much to do at the house before Mr. Finch returns home."

Once she moved away and headed toward the front entrance hall, William said as he studied her slow gait, "It sounds as though she doesn't think Albert will be hanged for the crime, if she is preparing for his return."

"I think the poor woman doesn't know what to do. Her mistress has just been buried and her master is in gaol, possibly never to return to the house at all. I imagine doing work keeps her from worrying too much about her situation."

"Ladies and gentlemen, if you are staying for the reading of the Last Will and Testament of my aunt, Mrs. Alice Finch, Mr. Stanford Lawton is ready to proceed." Jared stood at the entrance to the library, addressing the group. Once again he wrapped his arm around his aunt's shoulders and led her into the room.

William and Amy followed the others. About twelve people took seats in the library, where rows of chairs had been set up. An older man with white hair and deep blue eyes behind a pair of wired spectacles stood at the front of the room, holding a document in his hand.

"Are these all relatives? It's quite a crowd," William whispered in Amy's ear.

Amy smirked. "A *wealthy* relative, my lord." She looked around. "Most of them are family members, and there are a few I don't know and assume might be household staff or friends. I was never really close to either Alice or Annabelle once we left our childhood behind."

"One would assume Mrs. Finch left most of her wealth to her husband. I mean, that is generally how these things are done."

"Yes. And I doubt she left anything to Annabelle because she is just as wealthy as Alice was."

Just then the man cleared his throat, and everyone in the room shifted in their seats to give the older man their notice.

"If I may have your attention, ladies and gentlemen, I should like to introduce myself. I am Mr. Stanford Lawton of the firm of Melrose and Lawton, solicitors for Mrs. Alice Finch. I drew up her will, and I shall now begin the reading." He removed his spectacles, polished them with a snow-white handkerchief he withdrew from his pocket, put the glasses back on, and cleared his throat.

"*In the name of God, Amen. I, Mrs. Alice Marion Munson Finch, being of sound mind and body, do declare this document to be my Last Will and Testament. I do this of my own free will and with no coercion from any party.*

"*On the day this document is signed, I am married to Mr. Albert E. Finch. There are no children from the marriage. Attached to this paper is a separate list of personal items and monetary amounts I leave to family members and staff members of my household. Mr. Lawton will see to the distribution of such.*"

The solicitor then proceeded to read from the list, mentioning various people and what item was being bequeathed to them. Sighs of happiness, gasps of shock, and soft weeping ensued as he continued with the inventory. Alice had also left nice sums of money to each of her servants.

He then flipped the page and continued with the reading:

"*The rest of my estate, including bank accounts, investments, cash, jewelry, my two homes, and all their contents—except for those on the list of bequests—I leave to my husband, Mr. Albert E. Finch.*"

"No!" Jared jumped up from where he sat next to his aunt. "That cannot be. Albert killed her." He looked around frantically. "You all know this."

"Mr. Munson, please," Mr. Lawton said, quite pale, "I beg you to take your seat. I have not finished with the reading."

Red-faced and obviously angered, the young man sat. Annabelle leaned over and said something to him. He gave her a curt nod.

Mr. Lawton cleared his throat once again and continued. *"In the event my husband, Mr. Albert E. Finch, predeceases me or we both die at the same time, all that I possess, except for the previously mentioned bequests, will pass on to my nephew, Mr. Jared Munson."*

Stunned silence enveloped the room. Then, within seconds Jared erupted once more. "He cannot inherit from her." He waved his arms in the air. "He killed her!" He turned to the others, still sitting in shock. "Is there not a law that if someone murders another person, they cannot benefit?"

When no one answered him, he swung around and asked the same question of Mr. Lawton.

Obviously uncomfortable, the solicitor said, "Mr. Munson. I suggest we let the rest of the group leave, and I shall consult with you privately as to your position in the matter."

Slowly and quietly, those others in the room rose and made their way to the door. Jared continued to speak forcefully but inaudibly with Annabelle. Mr. Lawton patted his forehead with his handkerchief.

William took Amy's arm and led her from the room to the entrance hall, where they requested their carriage be brought around.

They listened to the murmurings of others that waited as well, but he was unable to hear anything distinct. He helped Amy into her coat, readjusting her buttons after she finished, and left the house, hurrying to their vehicle, the wind having picked up since the morning, and the clouds overhead threatening rain.

It would be good to get home after the long, trying day and have a peaceful dinner and a quiet night.

Once they settled in, Amy turned to William. "What did you think of that, my lord?"

"I believe Alice's will offered Jared Munson a reason to hope Albert will be hanged for his wife's murder."

Amy studied him for a minute. "Or she left her husband with a death sentence hanging over his head."

★ ★ ★

The next morning, Amy arrived at the breakfast room, ready and eager to face a day of investigating. She and William had spent a great deal of time the night before discussing the situation with Alice's will and Jared's reaction to the reading. They had agreed there was no doubt the young man had been quite surprised and disappointed at losing the benevolence of his aunt.

Amy wondered if Albert would be as generous to the nephew as Alice had been. Because she had left her husband everything, it was expected that Alice had assumed he would continue to support the young man.

If that were the case, then it seemed Alice did not trust the nephew to inherit a large sum of money, believing he would waste it all.

William stood as she entered, offering her a bright smile. "I didn't realize you would be joining me for breakfast. You were in quite a slumberous state when I left you earlier."

After receiving a light kiss on the cheek from her husband, she slid into the seat across from him that the footman pulled out. With a flair, the man immediately placed silverware and a snowy white napkin in front of her. She picked up the serviette and shook it out, placing it on her lap. "As we will now be sharing our living space, I guess all these little habits will soon be discovered. I always have an early breakfast, and generally in the breakfast room."

"Excellent. I do the same. I shall have hot food brought in." He signaled the footman and touched the pot of tea on the table. "I believe this is warm enough, if you would like a cup."

"Thank you. I would enjoy some tea." Amy poured the steaming liquid for herself and fixed it with one sugar and a bit of milk. "What are the plans for today besides retrieving Persephone from Aunt Margaret?"

William pushed away his empty plate. "I was hoping you would forget that dog."

"Not at all! I've had her for years, and you know she is so very special to me. I did grant your request that she not attend our wedding or honeymoon."

The sweet little Pomeranian had given birth to puppies a few months before, and she'd become even more temperamental since then. But Amy treasured her just the same, even though her new husband and her beloved pet did not see eye-to-eye on most things.

Skipping over the dog issue, William said, "To answer your question, I have nothing scheduled because I cleared my calendar in anticipation of our trip to Brighton Beach. What does the time frame for your next book look like?"

"Nothing to be concerned about. I haven't anything due to my publisher for a while. But I believe you misunderstood. What are we doing today for our investigation?"

"Ah, the investigation. You are still convinced Albert is innocent?"

"Not necessarily. I merely present the idea that more effort should be put into identifying other suspects. As I've said many times before, a man who is planning on killing his wife in front of dozens of witnesses must have it well planned out. And handing her a poisoned glass of champagne while sitting right next to her doesn't make sense."

"Maybe Albert is an idiot."

Amy shrugged. "That may be true, and in the few years I've known him, he hasn't given me a great deal of faith in his intelligence, but I don't believe anyone would be that imprudent."

"I bow to your superior knowledge of all things felonious." He took the last sip of coffee and placed his cup carefully in its saucer. "Was Jared Munson at our wedding? I don't remember. It was a confusing day."

"Yes. He'd been invited, and I remember seeing him."

William nodded and pointed to a piece of paper sitting alongside his plate. "I am doing my part. I have a—very short— list of suspects." He crossed his arms over his chest. "Do you think we should add Jared to the list? Apparently, his expectations were quite high as to what he would gain by Alice's death."

"But she had always been quite generous with him. *Don't kill the goose that lays the golden eggs*, and all that."

William shrugged. "Perhaps she had threatened to cut him off."

"Perhaps." Amy nodded and thanked the footman who placed a hot platter of eggs, bacon, tomatoes, toast, and hot rolls in the center of the table. She began to fill her plate. "I would assume he wouldn't expect to inherit over her husband."

"No. But he might have thought he would get at least half her fortune."

Amy would give that some consideration. "Who else is on the list?"

"Despite our reservations—well, at least mine—Albert is, of course, at the top of the list. It would be foolish to leave him off. I have also included Mrs. Madeline Davis."

"Yes, that is indeed a short list. What do you suggest we do first?"

William held his hands up in surrender. "I have my suggestions, but as you are the expert, I would like to hear your ideas first. I would not want to be accused of taking over." His grin softened his words.

Amy thought for a minute as she chewed. "I believe we need to expand our suspect list, so I suggest we visit with the staffing agency and see who was on the list of temporary employees at the wedding breakfast since we haven't heard from Aunt Priscilla about the list Mrs. Fletcher was to locate."

"Is there anyone in your family who might have more information on Mrs. Davis?" William asked. "You say she has been Albert's most recent paramour. Someone might know about her."

"I doubt it. Aunt Margaret is the keeper of family secrets and non-secrets, and even she didn't know what the woman looked like until she found out from a guest at the wedding who had occupied the seat next to Mrs. Davis." Amy frowned. "What I would really like to learn is how Mrs. Davis even managed to be there. I know the announcement and location of our wedding breakfast appeared in the newspaper—as Detective Carson mentioned—so it would not be impossible for her to know all that."

She considered her thoughts for a moment. "I guess there really was no way for an uninvited guest to be recognized.

One could just show up at an event, and act and dress as if one belonged there, and no one would question it."

"Did you notice the night before, at the pre-wedding dinner, if Mrs. Davis and Albert spent any time together?"

Amy tapped her lips with her fingertip. "You know, I don't believe she was there Sunday night for the dinner. I certainly don't remember seeing her, and it was a smaller group for that event."

Before William could comment, Filbert entered the room and held out a salver with an envelope on it. "My lord, a note has just arrived for you."

"Thank you." William studied the envelope before he opened the missive, his eyes scanning the page.

"What is it?"

He looked up at her. "It's from Mr. Nelson-Graves. It didn't take him long to start work on Albert's case. The barrister has spoken with the detectives and was advised that Albert will be formally charged today for the murder of Mrs. Alice Finch."

Chapter 13

Amy continued with her breakfast as William poured another cup of coffee. "I am not surprised that Albert has been formally charged. It was inevitable since our detective friends are using their usual method of solving a murder. Look at the most likely suspect and spend all your time and efforts gathering evidence against him."

"I agree," Amy said. "No doubt that means Albert will be moved to Shepton Mallet sometime soon." She shuddered. "Heaven knows city lockup was bad enough."

William had some reservations about the time they'd spent with Albert at gaol. Although certainly not as adept at solving murders as his wife, with her extensive research and her many books on the subject, he had still left there with a nagging feeling that he hadn't yet been able to put into words.

"Maybe I'm looking for an easy investigation myself this time, because our honeymoon trip is on hold until this is all resolved, but I do have a strong feeling that Albert, while maybe not guilty of this crime, is hiding something," William said.

"Are you referring to his lack of frankness on what it was that caused him and Mrs. Davis to part ways?"

He nodded. "Yes. He was quite evasive. But something else too. What do you know of the man? They'd been married, what, three years?"

"I truly don't know all that much. I believe Alice met him at the Assembly here in Bath one Saturday night. She was immediately smitten, and despite Anabelle's dire predictions that Albert was marrying her for her money, they eloped within a few weeks of meeting."

"How wealthy were the twin sisters?"

"Very. Their father owned a fortune in stocks and a shipping company, among other businesses, and when he died, the businesses were all sold and the money put into trust for them and held by a board of trustees. They were mere girls at the time. Their mother died shortly after their birth. My memory of them, during the few visits we made over the years, was that they always had a nanny or other servant hovering around them."

"It sounds like a lonely life. No wonder the girls were so close."

Amy nodded. "My mama and I visited them occasionally before she died. Then those visits dwindled once Aunt Margaret took over my rearing. I don't really know why. My cousins gained full control of their money on their twenty-first birthday."

William frowned. "Considering the way Albert treated his wife, with his various dalliances, I believe it is fair to assume he most likely did marry her for her money."

"True." Amy sighed. "However, Alice held tight to the purse strings. From what I've heard, she had him on an allowance that he was not too happy about." Amy stopped for a moment. "I guess that gives him a solid motive for killing her."

"That and his lover, Mrs. Davis."

"One of several over the three years, and one who he seemed to callously dismiss." Amy studied the wall behind her husband for a minute, obviously lost in thought. "He must understand that if we are to help him, he cannot hold anything back."

William shrugged. "What I'm considering is that, perhaps since you are related to his wife, he felt uncomfortable discussing the matter of his mistress with us. I can only hope he has no reservations when it comes to dealing with Mr. Nelson-Graves, who is the one to save him from either life in prison or a neck stretch.

"To switch to a more pleasant topic on this lovely sunny day, it occurs to me that I have lost track of the days with all that has been going on. I just realized this morning that today is Thursday, and we can attend the book club meeting tonight, if you wish."

Amy perked up. "That is true. We hadn't planned on going because we were to be in Brighton Beach right now, but it might lend some normalcy to our lives."

"We could use some normalcy." William sat back and crossed his arms over his chest, thinking on how the last few days, which he had been anticipating for months, had not turned out anywhere near as he had expected.

But the most important part of the plans had been successfully accomplished, and Amy, his friend and partner, was now his wife.

"As I had no intention of meeting with the others tonight, I haven't read our book for this week. Do you remember the title?" Amy asked.

"Yes. As a matter of fact, I purchased the book, *The Mystery of Edwin Drood*, and even read a few chapters."

"Yes, I remember now. That was the unfinished book by Charles Dickens. The one he was writing when he died. Now that I recall the history of the book, I am anxious to read it."

William viewed Amy's excitement with all the love for her he'd discovered over the last couple of years. Even though they'd been friends and belonged to the same church and book club for a while, it had only been when she had dragged him into helping her solve the murder of her ex-fiancé that things had begun to change between them.

After she had been accused of murder and started her own investigation, he'd agreed to become her partner. To his shock and surprise, she'd then revealed her secret identity as E. D. Burton, renowned mystery writer. Her father had insisted she assume a pseudonym because he was embarrassed by her writing.

"I suggest we visit with the temporary staffing agency this morning and then stop by Lady Margaret's house to see if she has any information on Mrs. Davis."

Amy pushed away her empty plate and drew her teacup closer. "And bring home Persephone. When shall we leave?"

"Very well." William gritted his teeth. The only drawback to marrying Amy had been the blasted dog. "And then we shall spend the rest of the day reading *The Mystery of Edwin Drood* in preparation for tonight's meeting. We can leave whenever you can ready yourself."

About a half hour later, William stood at the entrance hall and watched his wife hurry down the stairs. Her hat was on straight, her coat buttoned correctly, and her shoes matched. Hiring a maid for her had been the best of ideas.

Amy was anything but scatterbrained when one considered how she worked out murder plots, red herrings, weapons, and all the rest for her very successful books, but for some reason she found it hard to maneuver through the normal life processes.

Thankfully, he'd always had an excellent housekeeper, who had taken an instant liking to Amy when she'd visited before their wedding. Mrs. O'Sullivan kept the house running smoothly.

His wife had been happy to leave it all to her, allowing her the freedom to write her books, which he promised her she could continue once they married. Even as a man, it sometimes annoyed him that women were still treated like children in some respects, always under the control of their father, brother, or husband.

He took her arm as they made their way down the steps to the waiting carriage. "I consulted my business directory this morning and found the direction to the agency. It is, as your great-aunt remembered, on Broad Street, so it should not be a long ride."

On the way to the business, they discussed their investigation as their driver negotiated the numerous carriages, carts, and pedestrians, along with the ruts in the roads in dire need of repair.

"I hope Mr. Nelson-Graves can secure a bond for Albert, so he does not have to wait for long in that horrid place," Amy said, wincing and clinging to the strap alongside her head as the carriage bounced along the poorly maintained roads.

"Acquiring bond for a murder suspect is not an easy thing."

"Yet when Mr. Harding was shoved into the river last January, Mr. Nelson-Graves was able to have you released."

"Yes. But remember, I am a peer, and their evidence against me was nebulous at best." He grabbed the strap by his head. "Albert's case is a bit stronger."

"When we stop to reclaim Persephone, we must remember to ask Aunt Margaret if she has learned any more information about Mrs. Davis."

William nodded. "Yes. I think we should start making notes on what we need to do, along with information on the short list of suspects we have."

Amy pulled out a piece of paper from her reticule. "I already did," she said with a smug smile on her face.

"Of course. The murder mystery writer." William dipped his head. "I should have known." He nodded to the paper. "What have you written so far?"

"Visit with the staffing agency. Check. Visit with Aunt Margaret. Check." She looked up. "That's all."

They both burst into laughter as the carriage came to a halt.

The street was teeming with people, strolling in some cases, bustling in others, as they went in and out of shops lining both sides of the street. They found the door with the correct number on it. It appeared the agency was up one level from a haberdasher via a narrow door and equally slim staircase.

The boards under their feet creaked as they made their way up. "I can't imagine Aunt Priscilla coming here to request help."

William shook his head and grabbed Amy's elbow as she stumbled. "No. There must have been another way she made the arrangements."

There were only two doors on the floor, right across from each other. Both doors were wood paneled on the bottom with glass on the top. "Manor-Whitely Temporary Staffing Agency" was painted in black and gold on the one to their right.

"This is it," William said as he opened the door and ushered Amy inside.

* * *

Amy immediately scrunched up her nose at the smell of something odorous and not pleasant that instantly hit her as they entered the room.

The man sitting behind the desk in front of them stopped, his mouth open, ready to bite into something nasty. He was a big man with large facial features and meaty hands. He had removed his jacket and waistcoat. The sleeves of his wrinkled shirt were rolled up to his elbows, and his neckcloth looked as though he'd spent the past hour tugging on it. "What can I do for you?"

No standing in the presence of a lady, no introduction, no putting away his food, no offering them a seat. So far Amy was not at all impressed with this agency and again wondered how her great-aunt had ended up hiring staff from them.

William drew himself up, generations of nobility in his blood rearing up. "As a fellow businessman, I suggest that you put your food away, stand when a lady enters the room, introduce yourself, roll your sleeves back down, put your jacket on, and apologize for not doing so immediately."

The man's jaw dropped, and he quickly wrapped up whatever it was he was eating, shoved it into a drawer, and stood. "I apologize. I am Mr. Jason Manor, part owner of this business." He fumbled to lower his sleeves and put his jacket on, ignoring the waistcoat thrown over his desk. He waved to the two chairs in front of him. "If you will please take a seat, I will be happy to assist you."

They both sat, William's lofty demeanor continuing, much to Amy's delight, since she rarely saw him exploit the entitlement of his station.

William cleared his throat. "We are Lord and Lady Wethington." He paused when the man's face grew pale. "You provided temporary staff to Lady Priscilla Granville for a wedding breakfast Monday last."

Mr. Manor nodded. "Yes, we did. Are you in need of staffing?"

"No. We are in need of information."

Appearing a bit confused, the man frowned, most likely sorry he'd put away his food to provide mere information instead of gaining new business.

Amy jumped in, not to be left out of the conversation. "I assume you keep records of the people who work at various assignments?"

"Yes, of course."

"Then we would like to see the record of those who were sent to Lady Granville's home."

Mr. Manor studied them for a minute. "I'm not sure if I can do that. I mean, it might not be legal."

William stepped in again. "Have no fear, Mr. Manor, we have no nefarious designs on the list." His bearing had softened, switching to charming, friendly William.

"May I ask why you want it?" Apparently, Mr. Manor might lack manners, but he was no fool.

"Lady Granville is my great-aunt, and she wanted to maintain a list of those who served her well in case she needed temporary help again. She can be a bit scatterbrained and didn't think to ask for it at the time."

Now that the idea of new business presented itself, Mr. Manor was eager to help. "Of course. I will check my file." He stood and opened a cabinet drawer, going through various stacks of papers, then pulled one out. "Here it is."

Amy took from him the paper with four names on it. As she perused the list, Mr. Manor said, "You may keep that one. I have another one that I use for the employees to pick up their pay." He waved a piece of paper, then glanced down at it. "That's very odd."

"What?" Amy and William said at the same time.

"It appears one of the staff I sent there never picked up her pay." He looked up at them. "If I remember correctly, this was her first assignment with us, and I was a bit reluctant to send her, but I had two other requests for help the same day, so I had no choice."

Amy looked over at William, her brows raised. "And which employee was that?"

Mr. Manor looked down at the list. "A Mrs. Caroline Beaver."

Amy checked the list and removing a small pencil from her reticule, drew a circle around Mrs. Beaver's name.

CHAPTER 14

"Good afternoon, Lady Amy—excuse me, I mean Lady Wethington." Stevens, the butler who had manned the door at Winchester Townhouse for ages, smiled brightly at her and William. For as long as Amy could remember, Stevens had been opening doors and greeting family and callers.

"That is quite all right, Stevens. I am having a hard time adjusting to my new name myself. Each time someone says 'Lady Wethington,' I think they are speaking to William's mother."

"Except my mother is now Mrs. Colbert," William added.

This was true and one of the odd things about the peerage. Had the former Lady Wethington held the honorific 'lady' due to her father's title before she had married Lord Wethington, she would now be Lady Lily Colbert with her husband addressed as Mr. Charles Colbert. Since she had gained her honorific only when she married William's father, she lost it upon remarriage to a nontitled man and was now merely Mrs. Charles Colbert.

But from what they had all seen these past months, she was very happy to be so.

They were barely free of their outer garments before Lady Margaret came gliding down the stairs. "What are you two doing here? Aren't you on your honeymoon?"

"I have grown to detest that word," William mumbled as he handed his hat and gloves to Stevens.

Amy shrugged. "No, we have not yet been granted permission to leave Bath."

Aunt Margaret offered a sly glance. "You needn't be in Brighton Beach in order to enjoy a honeymoon."

"All right." William scowled, grabbing Amy's elbow. "Why don't we move upstairs and visit for a bit."

The three of them climbed the stairs to the drawing room, where Papa and Michael sat on the sofa, their heads together, studying a map on the table in front of them.

"Daughter!" Papa stood and opened his arms for a hug. "Why are you here? Shouldn't you be—"

"Good afternoon, Franklin, Michael," William said. Amy held in her laugh. The last thing her poor husband needed was to continually hear about the honeymoon they'd had to forfeit.

Amy took a seat in the chair across from the men. "What are you looking at there?"

Papa leaned back and crossed one leg over the other. "Daughter, your brother and I have made a decision we've been toying with for over a year now. We are selling our London townhouse and moving to Bath, where most of our new business ventures are."

"Papa!" Amy never thought she would see the day that she and her family were all together in the same city. "That is wonderful news!"

She looked over at Michael. "And you as well? You have no qualms about leaving the life of a young man in London?"

"None, minx. In fact, I have decided 'tis time to settle down and select a wife. Secure the title and all that by siring an heir."

Amy was stunned. Her brother, while not exactly a rake, since he worked too hard to have the time to pursue all the debauchery the moniker suggested, had oftentimes scoffed at the idea of leaving London. And the word "marriage" had always brought on a rash. She smirked. "Anyone particular in mind?"

She swore Michael flushed, though he quickly recovered. "'Tis none of your business, little sister."

"Now I am truly speechless. To think we will all be here in Bath together. This is extremely exciting. Perhaps we can help you get settled, Papa. William has many contacts in Bath. Why, he can introduce you to his solicitor and man of business, even help you both gain membership in his clubs. If you're looking for a house we can—"

"Stop." Papa held up his hand. "For someone who has been left truly speechless, you certainly have a lot to say, daughter." Papa offered her a warm smile.

"Oh, sorry. I guess I am just happy."

Although her parents had gotten along fairly well, for as long as Amy could remember Papa had lived in London, where he was involved in Parliament and managed all his businesses and investments from there.

Mama had detested the noise and smell of London and loved the uniqueness of Bath. So they had lived in separate cities but were quite cordial and even affectionate when they were together for family events and holidays.

Not the sort of marriage Amy had wanted, but it seemed to work for her parents.

"Will you be living here?" Amy glanced at Aunt Margaret but found it hard to read her thoughts. Although the house did belong to Papa, now that Amy had moved into William's townhouse, Aunt Margaret had the house to herself for the first time since Amy and her mother had moved in when Amy was a baby.

Papa and Michael had been staying at the Winchester townhouse while they attended Amy's wedding.

"For now." Papa tapped on the map in front of them. "I will be looking to purchase something eventually. Presently, Michael and I are more focused on setting up our offices."

Amy had always been amused by her papa and brother. Except for the slight wrinkles alongside Papa's eyes and mouth, the bit of silver streaks throughout his black hair, and the stone or so he'd gained over the years, he and Michael could be twins. Father and son rendered a remarkable resemblance to each other, walked the same way, and bore similar expressions, their tall, lanky frames exuding confidence and power.

"Will you stay for dinner?" Aunt Margaret asked.

Amy looked over at William, who shrugged.

"Thank you very much, Aunt, but since we are still in town"—she dared not mention the word *honeymoon*—"we decided to attend the book club meeting tonight, and neither one of us has competed the book we will be discussing."

After a short lapse of conversation, William cleared his throat and directed his attention to her brother. "Michael, when you and your father spoke with Mrs. Davis the day after the wedding breakfast, did she seem distraught at the possibility of Albert being charged and possibly hanged for Alice's murder? From what we observed, she appeared to be in quite good spirits."

The man thought for a minute. "Not as much as one would have expected, but she did mention remaining in Bath until the issue is resolved. I assume as a way to support Albert."

"Because Albert and Alice lived in Bath, I thought Mrs. Davis also resided here." Maybe Albert had the good sense not to have his mistress so close since the Bath community was somewhat cliquish.

Michael shook his head. "No. She mentioned that she lives in a small village outside Bath."

"Indeed? Did she mention where she was staying in Bath?"

"At the Francis Hotel in Queen Square."

Papa narrowed his eyes at William. "You two are not planning on getting involved in this matter, I hope. We've been through this before. Sticking your nose into places it doesn't belong can get you hurt. Or even killed."

"No, no, not at all, Papa," Amy quickly said. "We are just curious because we all knew about Mrs. Davis, but none of us had ever seen her before."

"Just curious, eh?" Something in his tone put her on alert. "Then if you are not seeking information to conduct your own investigation, and don't plan to stay for dinner, what brings you here when you should be on your—"

"We're here to pick up Persephone," William blurted as he hopped up.

Well done, William.

★   ★   ★

For the first time since he'd met Amy, William was grateful for the little beast Amy referred to as her pet dog. Franklin did not look as though he believed him, but without calling him a liar, he was forced to accept William's answer.

Not wishing to give Amy's father time to think of other things to ask, William turned to his new wife. "Well, my dear, I guess we should gather up our darling Persephone and be on our way."

Amy's brows rose. "No need to overstate it, my lord," she murmured.

"Never mind." He grabbed her elbow.

Aunt Margaret stood, a knowing smirk on her face. "I will get your *little darling* and be right down."

Amy went up on tiptoes to kiss her father on his cheek. "Really, Papa, I am so glad you are moving to Bath."

The frown on Franklin's face eased into a warm smile as he hugged his daughter and kissed the top of her head. "As I am as well."

"What about me?" Michael asked.

"'Twill be lovely to have you here also, Michael. I have numerous friends I can introduce you to. In fact, my best friend, Eloise—"

"Not that hoyden," Papa snapped. He turned to Michael, "Do not involve yourself with that young woman. She is trouble."

Michael raised his hands, palms facing forward, in an act of surrender. "First of all, my dear family, I am just now thinking about finding a wife; I'm certainly not ready to make a decision. And when the time comes"—he looked back and forth between Amy and Franklin—"I will make my own choice and will not have streams of young ladies dragged before me."

"Yes, you are right, brother."

Before she could continue, Aunt Margaret returned to the drawing room with Persephone snug in her arms. The dog took one look at Amy and leaped from Aunt Margaret's hold and began running in circles, barking like crazy. The Pomeranian with the missing tail ran to Amy, her little paws on her mistress's legs, hopping up and down, wanting to be picked up.

Amy laughed and scooped the dog into her arms. "Hello, my sweetie. Did you miss me?"

After giving Amy time to snuggle, speak nonsense, and act in other ridiculous ways with the creature, William bundled them both up and escorted them out of the Winchester Townhouse and into their waiting carriage.

Their arrival home was uneventful, with no new missives waiting to force them to dash out of the house again. "I suggest we send for tea and begin reading. I think a pleasant way to spend the rest of the afternoon would be for us each to take a turn reading aloud."

"That's a wonderful idea. I will send for the tea and get Persephone settled while you get the book."

William cleared his throat. "Get her settled where?"

Amy looked surprised. "In our bedchamber, of course."

He shook his head.

His wife raised her chin. "I insist."

William scowled. "As do I. I won't have a dog sleeping in my bed."

"She's always slept with me." Amy looked as though she wanted to stamp her foot.

"Now I have that privilege, so she no longer does." He immediately regretted the words and wished them back.

Amy glared at him. "I will not respond with the obvious retort to that statement, my lord."

Shite.

He ran his palm down his face. Then he realized marriage was a compromise. They were both older, Amy at six and twenty years and him at three and thirty, a bit set in their ways, for sure. "Very well. Would you agree on a compromise?"

"What?" She looked quite suspicious.

"That dog—"

"—Persephone." She sniffed.

"—can sleep in the room, but in a basket at the foot of the bed. Not *in* the bed."

She studied him for a minute, chewing on her lower lip. "Very well. I will compromise."

He nodded. "Good. You ring for tea, and I will ask Mrs. O'Sullivan to locate a basket for . . ." He waved his hand around in the general direction of the animal.

"Persephone."

★   ★   ★

That evening, William and Amy arrived at the Atkinson & Tucker bookstore just as his mother and stepfather—William was still not used to that appellation—also arrived. They all greeted one another, and Mr. Colbert, of course, mentioned the honeymoon again. 'Twas bad enough having to put the trip off without everyone constantly reminding him that instead of lounging on the beach and enjoying walks along the shore and quiet intimate dinners with his new wife, he was stuck in Bath.

He made a mental note to contact the detectives and insist they be allowed to leave since they seemed to think they had their murderer. He might have a time of it trying to convince Amy to leave without solving the murder, but they could certainly cut their trip short to ease her mind.

On the other hand, William had a strange feeling that there was more to Alice's killing than a husband trying to rid himself of a wife. Were that so, then the obvious question presented itself.

Who else besides the woman's husband would benefit if Alice were dead? Who would gain, or think to gain, her fortune?

Mr. Jared Munson.

CHAPTER 15

Eloise hurried up to Amy and William as they entered the back room of the bookstore.

"What are you two doing here? Why aren't you on your—"

Amy slapped her hand over her best friend's mouth. "Don't. Say. It."

Eloise's brows rose and she nodded. "All right. I won't say it. But can I ask why you are here at the meeting, at least?"

William snorted and moved away from them to join his parents, chatting with the two Misses O'Neill, Mr. Christopher Rawlings, and his friend Mr. George Davidson. Mr. Davidson had been a member of the book club for years and only earlier in the year had he introduced Mr. Rawlings, who she and William had accidentally discovered was apparently more than a friend.

Although she had found something odd about Mr. Rawlings comments to her upon their initial introduction, it had been weeks later, at the book fair where she had revealed her identity as the mystery writer E. D. Burton, that Amy learned Mr. Rawlings was the Somerset representative for her publisher, Chatto & Windus.

Amy sighed and took Eloise's arm as they strolled the room. "We still don't have permission to leave Bath."

"Has there been any news about Mrs. Finch's murder?"

"Mr. Finch has been charged."

Eloise sucked in a breath. "My goodness. So he did kill his wife." She shook her head.

"Um, we are not absolutely certain he did."

"We?" Eloise grinned. "Don't tell me you are becoming involved in another murder?"

They continued their stroll, Amy happy to have privacy to discuss the situation with someone other than William. "'Tis too easy, Eloise. Why kill your wife in front of dozens of witnesses when you have access to her in private settings all the time?"

"True. Except that in itself could be an alibi. Everyone thinking he wouldn't do it because it was too obvious."

"Then why choose a method that is easily traceable to yourself?"

"I see what you mean. I hadn't thought of that, but then again, you have a murderer's mind."

Amy drew back. "I don't know if that's a compliment or an insult."

"A compliment to be sure. You have a great mind and see things many of us do not." She stopped their movement forward. "Then I was correct. You and William have assumed your detectives' personae once again."

"You might say that." They remained silent for a minute or so, then Amy said, "Oh, I forgot. I have great news!"

"What?"

They had reached the front of the room, where a table had been set up with drinks and pastries. They each took a cup of lemonade. "My father and brother are moving from London to Bath."

Eloise's eyes grew wide. "Michael?"

"'Tis the only brother I have."

She nodded, but Amy noticed a slight smile and a tinge of pink to her friend's cheeks. Before she was able to comment on that, Mr. Colbert called the meeting to order, then solicitously escorted his wife to a chair in the front part of the room. Most likely so he could gaze upon her the entire meeting. The man was truly besotted.

Amy still had the urge to giggle every time she thought about how Mr. Colbert had been immediately smitten with William's mother from the first night she'd attended one of the meetings. Something that William had not been happy about, but he had eventually accepted that a man wanted his mother, and it had all turned out well.

"I must say that *The Mystery of Edwin Drood* is probably one of the most mysterious selections we've read," Mr. Colbert said once he had everyone's attention. "Because only six of the twelve planned installments were published before Mr. Dickens's death, the story has had many conclusions proposed by readers and amateur sleuths for years."

"Maybe we should ask our resident mystery writer how she would finish the book." Lord Temple, another long-time member bowed his head in Amy's direction.

"That isn't fair," Mr. Davidson said. "At least not fair until the rest of us have had a chance to do the same. We all know now, much to my shock, that she writes these things."

Mr. Davidson had always been a thorn in Amy's side, even though his close friend was her representative. Mr. Davidson had made cutting remarks about women that had brought the wrath of the female members of the group down upon his head more than once.

But since he had bowed to her expertise, except for the slight slur he no doubt could not leave off, she felt a tad kinder toward him.

"Perhaps Mr. Davidson is correct." She smiled in his direction and was rewarded with a scowl. She sighed.

"Then let us begin with this question," Mr. Colbert said. "It was obvious to me from the start that Edwin and Rosa were not well matched. Their betrothal had been arranged by their families. What do you think about arranged marriages? "

"Amy, as a new bride, why don't you offer your opinion on that?" Eloise said.

Before she had a chance to open her mouth, Mr. Davidson stood. "If the entire meeting is to be questions for the new Lady Wethington to answer, perhaps the rest of us can just leave."

"George, sit down," Mr. Rawlings drawled. "You are making a nuisance of yourself."

To Amy's amazement, Mr. Davidson sat down and even smiled at Mr. Rawlings.

Mr. Colbert studied what must have been his list of questions for the group's discussion. No doubt he was trying quite hard to find something that would not be construed as a link to her.

He cleared his throat and tried once more. "As so many of Mr. Dickens's main characters die in his books, should we assume the missing Mr. Drood's possessions found on the riverbank suggest he drowned? And if so, was he helped?"

Before anyone could answer, Mr. Colbert waved at Mr. Davidson. "What do you think, Davidson?"

And so the meeting went, with Mr. Davidson at least offering a few opinions. Amy tried her best to keep her remarks to herself, until William nudged her. "Please don't allow Mr. Davidson's comments to keep you from participating."

"I'm not. Well, not truly."

William leaned in, close to her ear. "If you like, I will play the offended husband and challenge him to meet in the morning on a field of honor."

Thinking he was serious, Amy's jaw dropped and her eyes widened. "No!"

He shook his head. "A mere jest, my dear."

"And a poor one at that," she returned.

The discussion continued, growing quite lively at times. After the group decided that the following week's analysis of the book would consist of each member offering their own ending to the story, Mr. Colbert closed the meeting, leaving Amy wishing more than ever that she and William were at Brighton Beach.

★　★　★

"I believe a visit to Mrs. Davis would be a good way to spend our time today," William said the next morning as he helped himself to a piece of toast spread with gooseberry jam.

They were seated at the breakfast table, enjoying breakfast together again since they were both early risers. The sun shone in a rare appearance, bringing brightness and light to the room, raising William's spirits after a few days of somberness.

"I agree. We must begin to move forward on this, or we will never have our trip." Amy stirred sugar and a bit of cream into her tea.

"I thank you very much, dear wife, for not using the 'h' word," William said with a smile.

"No one ever suggested I was stupid, husband. I am as sick of hearing that question as you are. As our trip has been postponed, I believe I will spend some time before our interview with Mrs. Davis, outlining my next book."

"An excellent idea. In fact, I have decided to send a missive to our favorite detectives, suggesting we be permitted to leave for our trip since they feel as though they have their murderer."

"But what about our investigation?"

"It will still be here when we return. Because of the delay, it's a shorter trip anyway. I'm sure nothing will change while we're gone."

William waved the footman over. "Please have Filbert send a message to my man of business, Mr. Wilson, and ask that he attend me this morning. I will also have a note to be hand-delivered to the Bath Police shortly if you will stop into my study in about ten minutes." William checked his timepiece. "See if Mr. Wilson is able to arrive at ten o'clock."

"What time do you want to visit with Mrs. Davis?" Amy asked.

Before he could answer, Filbert entered the room. "My lord, there are two detectives here who wish to speak with you and her ladyship."

William looked over at Amy with raised eyebrows. "This will save me sending a note."

"What note?" Detective Carson strode into the room with Detective Marsh right behind him.

"Detectives, do you not know that common courtesy dictates that when one arrives unexpectedly at another's home, one waits to see if he will be granted permission to enter?" Amy's voice could have frozen the Thames.

Making themselves at home, the two detectives pulled out chairs and sat as if Amy had not even spoken. "We only need a few minutes of your time."

Although William had the desire to have one of the footmen toss the detectives out on their ears, antagonizing the police was not a good idea if he wanted to escape to Brighton Beach before their twenty-fifth wedding anniversary.

"Very well, Detectives," William sighed, "you are here now, and my wife and I are captive. What is it you want from us?"

"Information."

Neither he nor Amy reacted to the man's statement.

"We've learned that you have no recollection of inviting Mrs. Madeline Davis, so I would like to know if there were any other surprise non-invitees at the wedding event, about whom either one of you were aware?"

William and Amy looked at each other. "No one that I remember," William said as Amy shook her head.

Detective Marsh flipped through several pages of his notebook. He cleared his throat. "You told us that the day of your wedding, not everyone who attended the celebration had also been present at the service." He stopped and looked up at them.

They both nodded.

"Think back, if you will, to the church. Was there anyone there who did not appear later at the breakfast?"

William was confused by their questions. If they were certain enough that Albert was the murderer to officially charge him, why use this line of questioning, almost as if they thought someone else might be guilty?

Or involved.

"No."

Detective Carson took over. "Were either Mr. or Mrs. Finch at the church?"

"No," Amy answered.

Tossed out nonchalantly, but with obvious interest, Carson said, "Was Mr. Jared Munson present at the wedding breakfast?

"Yes," Amy said.

"I don't suppose you remember where he sat in relation to Mrs. Finch?"

"No, Detective, I am sorry, I do not. It was my wedding day, I had other things on my mind besides where everyone was seated."

"One last thing." Detective Carson glared at William. "It seems a man and a woman presented themselves at the Bath lockup to see Mr. Albert Finch this Tuesday past."

When they didn't respond, he added, "Whoever these people were, they obtained permission to speak with Mr. Finch because they alluded to an association with Detective Marsh and myself."

"How very odd," William mused, then grunted when she kicked his shin from under the table.

"Indeed."

Marsh wrote a bit more in his notebook, then flipped it closed. Detective Carson stood and tugged on his jacket. He placed his hands on his hips and adopted a friendly, fatherly stance.

"I am happy to see the two of you married to each other. I cannot think of a better pairing in all my years, and I don't believe I need to say why. I'm sure you know. Please don't involve yourselves in this matter. We have already charged the correct suspect, and I believe shortly I will be able to grant you permission to leave Bath."

There went the need to send the note to make the same request.

William and Amy both stood. "Thank you, Detective," William said. Truth be told, he was ready to dispense with the entire mess and accept Albert as the guilty party and move on.

One look at his wife's face, though, and he knew they would be continuing the search for the person she believed was the true killer.

They left their unfinished breakfasts and retired to the library.

"I believe they only came to warn us again and let us know they were aware of our subterfuge in gaining access to Albert," Amy said as she settled into a comfortable chair near the window.

"Perhaps, but I was encouraged by their questions about Jared Munson."

"Yes. That was a nice surprise."

"I don't suppose you want to take Detective Carson's advice and forget this investigation? It sounds as though we can make our trip soon. As I said, we can continue the investigation when we return." She thought for a minute, then smiled. "If you give me just a few more days, I think there is something we're missing, but I can't put my finger on it."

William sighed. "I was afraid of that. As you wish, dear wife."

CHAPTER 16

The Francis Hotel at Queen Square was made up of several townhouses. The very clever widow of Mr. Solomon Francis, who had run a boarding house in one of the townhouses, had purchased additional residences and turned them into a hotel. Located across from the well-known Queen Square, the huge yellow stone building was elegant and impressive.

In full regalia, a doorman stood outside, as staunch and stiff as a Buckingham Palace guard, though lacking the signature tall black hat, of course.

A sense of unease washed over Amy. "Perhaps we should have sent a missive before we decided to visit this afternoon."

"I thought of doing that, but I believe catching her off guard might work better. She still remains a mystery woman whom I am sure has been questioned by the police."

"I wonder if she made it onto their suspect list."

William shrugged. "It is my belief that she only added to their certainty that Albert did away with Alice to be with Mrs. Davis. After all, he was the one sitting right next to her, and by his own admission gave her his glass of champagne to drink."

"Do you think he told the police that?"

"If he is guilty, no. If he is innocent, yes. But, I don't believe there was a way for the police to know whose glass contained the poison that Alice drank."

Amy stopped and looked at him. "You are correct. Therefore, it is quite possible that Albert, and not Alice, was the intended victim."

William stared back at her. "Or Albert put the poison in his own glass and gave it to Alice after she'd finished hers."

The lobby was quiet and elegant. A rich carpet covered most of the floor, with chairs made for comfort scattered around the space. The walls displayed rose and green silk wallpaper, with white wainscoting below. Elegant paintings of various scenes in Bath decorated the walls. Two men sat in chairs, reading the newspaper.

Amy and William approached the gentleman sitting at a desk in the lobby. Although elegantly dressed, he did not possess the demeanor of the doorman. The desk clerk was an older man with a white mustache concealing most of his wrinkled face. His bright hazel eyes belied his age.

"We are here to see Mrs. Madeline Davis, who, I believe, is a guest." William spoke in a friendly, casual way, but his bearing was one of nobility and a sense of expecting to be obliged.

"Is Mrs. Davis expecting you?"

"No. However, my wife is a relative," he said, nodding at Amy, "and it is imperative that we speak with her about an urgent family matter."

Amy never batted an eye at the flat-out lie. But then they had professed to be close acquaintances with the detectives, which had gotten them into gaol. She studied the man with an innocent expression.

He gave them a curt nod. "Mrs. Davis is in room forty-two. Go up to the level above the next one, and you will see numbers in gold lettering on the door."

"Thank you," William said as he took Amy's elbow and escorted her up the stairs. He tapped lightly on the door of number forty-two. They were both attempting to catch their breath when the door opened.

"I told you I do not wish to be disturbed!" The words seemed to come out of the woman's mouth before she even realized to whom she was speaking. "Oh, I apologize. I thought you were the maid whom I asked not to come back until later."

Since neither he nor Amy responded to her comment, but merely nodded, Mrs. Davis said, "May I help you with something?"

Uncertain whether the woman remembered them or not, but pretending she did, William said, "Good afternoon, Mrs. Davis. My wife is cousin to the late Mrs. Finch, and we would like to ask you a few questions."

She blanched for a second, then said, "Oh yes, of course. Please, come in." She moved back and allowed them to enter.

The space was pleasant, certainly not as elegant as the lobby, but nevertheless comfortable enough. A small arrangement of two chairs and a settee circling a low table was positioned near the fireplace, about twenty feet from the bed.

A tray with the remains of breakfast cluttered up the table, and clothing was strewn about the space. No wonder the maid wanted to enter the room and tidy up.

"I can send for tea if you would like," Mrs. Davis said reluctantly.

"No, but thank you," Amy replied.

They settled into the grouping, and Amy started. "Mrs. Davis, Mr. Finch has asked Lord Wethington and me to assist him in proving his innocence in poisoning Mrs. Finch."

Amy watched the woman carefully, to see her reaction. She didn't catch any sense of guilt, or of relief either, at hearing that someone was helping Albert.

Very strange.

"I'm sorry that some of my questions might be uncomfortable for you, but please understand we are trying to help."

Mrs. Davis nodded.

"We are aware of a relationship between you and Mr. Finch." Amy had no intention of passing along the information that Albert claimed they had gone their separate ways.

"Is that what Albert told you?"

Not a stupid woman, Mrs. Davis. Amy looked over at William, who she felt agreed with that assessment.

He cleared his throat. "Mr. and Mrs. Finch lived in Bath, but I understand you reside in Bristol?"

"Yes. Very recently."

"With your husband?"

Mrs. Davis hesitated. "I don't understand how asking me these questions will help Albert in any way. And no, there is no Mr. Davis. At least not for several years."

Sensing they were about to be shown the door, Amy stepped in, using her "we women have to stick together" voice. "Mrs. Davis, my husband and I, though not experts by any measure, have had some experience, and success, in solving two other murders of close acquaintances."

"Indeed? It sounds as though you are not safe people to be around."

Since Mrs. Davis did not say that with a smile, Amy had to assume she was not making a bad joke. Choosing to ignore her words, Amy continued. "We have found that the most innocuous answer can lead to important discoveries."

After no response from Mrs. Davis, and apparently wanting to get down to business, William said, "It has come to our attention that your name was not on the invitation list for our wedding breakfast. Can you tell me why you decided to attend?"

Amy watched various expressions cross Mrs. Davis's face. Embarrassment at having committed such a social faux pas was not one of them.

"If you must know, Albert and I had a falling out, and he refused to respond to my efforts to discuss the matter. I knew he would be at the wedding, so it seemed the best time and place to speak with him."

"Even though you knew his wife would also be in attendance?"

"Yes." She flushed, most likely at the memory of accosting her lover at an event to which she'd not been invited and where his wife and other members of his family would be present.

"Since you remain here and live in Bristol, I assume there is no place of employment that is expecting your return?"

Mrs. Davis stood. "I believe I have answered enough questions. If you need any further information from me, I am sure the police can provide it as they spent a great deal of time also asking ridiculous questions."

She moved toward the door, and Amy and William scrambled to gather their things to leave. Amy made one more attempt at appeasement. "I certainly understand how frustrating being questioned all the time can be. I do hope we have not upset you or imposed upon your day very much."

The only response was Mrs. Davis opening the door and waving them out.

Well, then.

They didn't speak until they left the building and walked to the corner where their carriage awaited.

"Not a very pleasant woman," William said as he helped Amy into the carriage.

"I know beauty is a poor measure of a person, but I don't understand Albert. Alice was much prettier than Mrs. Davis. Knowing her all my life, I also believe Alice was much nicer and kinder than Mrs. Davis. At least from what we witnessed just now." She turned to William, grabbing the strap alongside her as they began their trek home. "As a man, what do you imagine he saw in Mrs. Davis? What was it that had him willing to cause Alice embarrassment and no doubt a great deal of hurt in order to dally with a mistress?"

"My dear, remember, she was not the first, nor the only one, to hold the dubious position of adulterous lover. However, as a new husband with a very strong sense of survival, there is no way I intend to comment on another woman's looks or appeal, but I will tell you there is absolutely nothing that attracted me as far as Mrs. Davis is concerned."

Amy gave a curt nod. "Well spoken, husband."

★ ★ ★

Two surprises awaited them when they arrived home. Once Filbert relieved them of their outer garments, he said, "My lord, you have a visitor who insisted that she be allowed to wait for you."

"She?" Amy said.

"Yes, my lady. Miss Munson claimed to be Lady Wethington's cousin and, as I said, was most insistent that she remain to speak with you."

"Where is she?" Amy asked.

"I put her in the front parlor, which I thought was appropriate." He stopped for a minute. "The woman was distraught when she learned you were not at home, and I didn't have the heart to turn her away."

"That's fine, Filbert. Miss Munson is indeed my cousin, and you did the right thing." Amy made her way upstairs, with William right behind her.

"Amy!" Annabelle hopped up from the settee and raced over to her, flinging her arms around her, almost knocking Amy off her feet.

"Annabelle, what a pleasant surprise." Amy disentangled herself from her cousin and led her back to the settee. "William, ring for tea, please."

Once Amy got a good look at her cousin, she realized Filbert was correct. The woman was quite distraught. "Is something amiss, Annabelle?"

"You mean aside from the fact that that horrible man murdered my twin sister?" She patted her swollen, red eyes, her lips trembling.

"I think perhaps Miss Munson might prefer a bit of brandy while we wait for the tea, my love." William walked to the sideboard and poured a small amount of brandy into a snifter and brought it to the woman. "Here, this will calm you a bit."

She took the glass from his hand and shook her head. "I shall never be calm again. Not until that dreadful man is swinging from a rope." Tears dripped down her face as she regarded

Amy. "You have no idea how devastating it is to lose your twin. We had a special connection, you know." She took a sip of the brandy, her hand shaking as she raised the snifter to her lips. "I shall never be the same again."

William looked over at Amy, not knowing how to deal with the woman's pain.

The brandy did seem to calm her, and she placed the glass on the table alongside her and took a deep breath. "I have come to ask a favor."

"What is that?" Amy asked.

"I understand that you are helping to prove Albert did not kill my sister."

Amy glanced up at William, probably at a loss how to respond. "He has asked us, yes."

Annabelle grabbed Amy's hand. "Please. I beg of you. Do not help that man. He deserves to die."

The parlor door opened, and a footman rolled in a tea cart. With the brandy having taken effect, Annabelle appeared more composed as they had tea, along with the biscuits, tarts, and small sandwiches served. In fact, she even commented on the wedding and how sorry she was that her filthy brother-in-law had ruined the day.

Eventually, the woman stood and announced she was sorry for the intrusion and hoped they would forgive her.

"Do not concern yourself. We understand your grief."

As she hadn't again mentioned them not helping Albert, William breathed a sigh of relief as they descended the stairs. Filbert helped Miss Munson into her coat. Amy hugged her and assured her she was welcome to visit at any time.

Once the door was closed, William let out a deep breath. "That was awkward."

"Yes. But my heart breaks for her."

"My lord," Filbert said. "This missive arrived for you while you were entertaining the lady." He handed William a cream-colored envelope.

"Thank you." William opened the note and scanned the words. "What the devil? Oh no. No, no, no."

"What?" Amy said leaning over his arm to look at the paper.

William closed his eyes and groaned. "Mr. Nelson-Graves was able to secure Albert's release contingent on him living here in our custody and under our supervision."

CHAPTER 17

"We need much more information than that," Amy said, attempting to keep the panic from her voice. "What does 'in our custody' even mean? Are we to be gaolers? Can we not leave our house together? Is he to be locked in his room? Can we refuse?"

It was the next morning, and Amy had tossed and turned all night, her list of questions growing as the hours passed. William, on the other hand, had not seemed the least disturbed and slept soundly, even though Amy had nudged him a few times—accidentally, of course—so he could join in her hysteria.

The fool man had slept on. She'd discounted the thought of shoving him off the bed.

William took his seat after filling his breakfast plate from the sideboard. "You need to calm down, sweetheart." He shook out his napkin. "I suggest we make a visit to Mr. Nelson-Graves today and learn exactly what this means. I will be honest. As much as I have sympathy for Albert sitting in Shepton Mallet, I refuse to turn my home into a gaol."

"Thank you." Amy nodded, then gasped when her teacup was halfway to her mouth. "Oh no."

"What?"

"Sometimes going from charges to actual resolution can take months. Many months."

Knowing exactly what Amy referred to—the postponement of their trip indefinitely—his lips tightened, and he shook his head. "No. I have no idea what they have in mind, but I will not be confined for months as if I'm the criminal."

They both felt the need to get out of the house—possibly because they feared that soon their movements might be restricted—so they decided to visit with Mr. Nelson-Graves at his office instead of summoning the man to their home.

Located close to Bath city lockup, Mr. Nelson-Graves's office was well-designed and tasteful. Two rooms—one his office and one his law library—were aligned side by side behind a large, open front room, where sat a desk and a very efficient-looking man, busy on a typing machine.

As they waited to be admitted to Mr. Nelson-Graves's office, Amy watched the secretary with amazement as words spewed forth from the machine, his fingers flying over the keys. She nudged William. "I have one of those," she said, nodding at the efficient young man.

"Do you know how to use it?"

Amy shrugged. "No. Yes. Actually, I do use it, but once you hit the key and it strikes the paper, you can't erase the mark. Well, you can, but it's a bit of a bother. For a writer it can be difficult because many times I write something down and decide that was not what I wanted to say."

"Then you don't use it?"

"I do. I write everything down first, and when I'm certain it's exactly how I want it, I use the machine to make a nice, professional copy for my publisher." She continued to gaze at the young man. "Someday I hope to be able to type as fast as he does. And to make fewer mistakes."

William grinned and patted her hand. "I am sure that machine is something you can easily conquer."

The door to the barrister's office opened then, and an older woman, a bit bent over and making good use of a strong wooden cane, accompanied by another woman who appeared to be her daughter, painstakingly made their way out. The secretary stood, wished them a good day, and turned to Amy and William. "My lord, Mr. Nelson-Graves can see you now."

"Lord Wethington, Lady Wethington, a pleasure." Nelson-Graves stood and offered them a slight bow. "You should have sent for me instead of coming all this way."

William held the chair for Amy to sit and took the one next to her in front of the massive wooden desk. "'Tis not a long way out, and her ladyship and I wanted to take in some fresh air."

The three looked out the window across from them at the rain coming down in torrents.

Nelson-Graves cleared his throat. "How can I be of assistance?"

"My wife and I are concerned about the arrangement you have made to release Mr. Finch into our custody. Can you explain how that came about and what it means for us before we agree?"

"Yes, of course." The barrister thought for a moment, then said, "Mr. Finch will reside at your home awaiting final disposition of the case."

"Yes. That part we understand. However, are we expected to hire someone to guard him?"

"No. Not at all. He will be granted leave to depart gaol on the condition that he remain on your property."

"Then he will be released on his word?" William couldn't hide the surprise in his voice. The man was charged with murder, yet they would simply let him go based on his assurance that he would remain there?

"Yes. The court was reluctant to release Mr. Finch because of the murder charge and what they feel is a strong case against him."

"Yet they are willing to allow *us* to house him? What exactly is their theory on the murder? Have they shared that?" William asked.

"Yes. They believe that since the footmen poured all the champagne, Albert carried the *Atropa belladonna* on his person and slipped it into his own glass and then gave it to his wife, knowing she would accept it because she enjoyed champagne."

"That sounds plausible, I must say. Have they not considered any other suspects? Looked for others who might have a reason to see Mrs. Finch dead?"

"I believe they interviewed her nephew, a Mr. Munson, and a woman who had an illicit association with Albert, a Mrs. Davis, but they are staunch in their belief that Albert did the deed."

William let out a low whistle. "I am, however, curious as to how this arrangement involving me and my wife came about."

"Based on your relationship with Mr. Finch, and your own sense of honor, I appealed to the magistrate assigned to the case since the detectives who are working on the case refused my offer."

"Carson and Marsh?" Amy asked, her annoyance growing.

"Yes. I know you have worked with them before."

"Indeed," William said. "Twice, in fact. But I wouldn't say we worked with them. More like we worked *against* them to prove ourselves innocent of murder."

Amy sighed. If they had to play nanny to a man charged with murder, she doubted they would be permitted to leave Bath.

To use her husband's favorite term, *Shite*.

★　★　★

Another visit to the temporary staffing agency on their way back from Mr. Nelson-Graves's office permitted them to cross Mrs. Caroline Beavers off their very short list of suspects. It seemed the woman had come by for her pay, and the reason she had been late in picking it up was due to her child being sick.

Settled in their library after a light lunch, in front of a cozy fire with a brandy for him and a sherry for Amy, to take the chill from their very wet trek earlier, William sighed with pleasure and placed his snifter on the table alongside him.

Amy took a sip of her sherry and stared into the fire. "This situation with Albert has become quite convoluted. I wish Mr. Nelson-Graves had consulted with us before he made these arrangements. But on the other hand, as a Christian, I should be willing to allow the poor man to leave that horrid place, even if it disrupts our lives."

"I find it telling that the detectives refused Mr. Nelson-Graves request to have him released into our custody. I'm sure they are gritting their teeth knowing we will still be here in Bath, most likely attempting to prove they have the wrong suspect." William shifted and placed his arm along the back of the settee. "I am glad we decided to hire an extra temporary footman from the agency while we were there earlier. I want the man to understand that his job will be to watch Albert, and nothing else. That will give us as much freedom as we want."

After a minute of silence as they stared peacefully into the fire, Amy said, "I went through the papers my aunt Priscilla gave us and found the seating arrangement for the wedding breakfast."

William sat up. "Where is it?"

She smiled and hurried across the room to the desk. Opening the middle drawer, she withdrew the papers. "Right here." She took her place next to him on the settee again. "Actually, I had put these aside when she told us they were lists of flowers, the menu, and other items that didn't seem worth our time. I'm glad I took a second look."

William reached out and removed one paper from her hand, studying it for a minute. "Unfortunately, this doesn't tell us where Mrs. Davis sat, since she would not be on the seating chart, having not received an invitation."

"Yes, you're right." She looked over his shoulder. "According to this, there were no vacant seats."

"Unless someone who was expected didn't arrive and she took that seat."

Amy frowned. "That was somewhat risky. Supposing there had been no extra seats? We must keep our eye on her. What she did almost sounds like desperation."

William folded the paper and handed it back to Amy. "Arriving unexpectedly and uninvited at a wedding breakfast was indeed quite risky. However, given our reception when we visited her before, I don't think she will be willing to speak with us again."

"I'm sure you're right." She yawned; most likely the warmth from the fire and the sherry had made her drowsy. She pointed at a name on the paper she held. "It appears Jared was quite a distance from Alice."

"Yes. It certainly looks like it." He was feeling lethargic himself, as well as other things. "What say you we take a nap this afternoon?" He checked his timepiece. "We have time before dinner and then the Assembly dance."

"A nap? You, a grown man, want to take a nap?"

He stood and took her hand. "Maybe. Maybe not." With a smirk he ushered her out the door and upstairs to their bedchamber.

★　★　★

Later that evening, William helped Amy into the carriage and settled alongside her as the vehicle made its way to the Saturday evening assembly. Amy sighed and stared out the window at the bleak darkness. "This is another event we hadn't planned on attending this week."

William patted her hand. "I know, sweetheart. But one day this will all end, and we will take our trip to Brighton Beach."

"I know I am beginning to sound almost obsessed with the idea, but I had been so looking forward to the trip."

"Indeed," William added with a sigh.

The Bath Assembly Hall had stood in the same place for over a hundred years. It was a huge stone building with several large, airy rooms. The largest room was where the dances were held, with smaller rooms for guests to merely visit or play a game of cards. Oftentimes it was leased out for private balls, mostly come-outs for young ladies with homes not large enough to hold the number of people her parents intended to invite.

He and Amy generally spent their Saturday evenings there, enjoying the music and socializing with friends and other book club members, who usually attended as well.

Once William had helped Amy out of her coat and handed it off to the man at the door who took care of such things, they made their way into the room, where the music had already started. Couples dipped and swayed to the notes of a waltz. Arms linked, they walked the perimeter of the room, nodding at acquaintances, accepting best wishes on their recent marriage.

"William, look there's Michael." Amy gestured to her brother, who was leaning one shoulder against a wall across the room, chatting with a woman, his body blocking their view of his companion.

"I wonder who has garnered his attention," she mused. "It's not easy to tell from here. We must move his way. I know he mentioned he was considering looking for a wife, but I must admit a certain amount of surprise at seeing him here. I've never known him to attend the Assembly."

"He is not in Bath very much either, my dear. I'm sure he does a great deal of socializing in London."

"That's true." She tugged on his arm, apparently anxious to see whom Michael was bantering with. Whoever she was, he certainly seemed to be enjoying himself.

"Amy!" His wife's aunt Margaret hurried up to them, dodging dancers and offering excuses to those whose conversations she was interrupting. 'Twas unusual to see Lady Margaret in such a dither since she was, by nature, a calm, collected woman whose gait could only be described as "gliding," as opposed to barreling through the crowd as she was doing now.

She hugged Amy and nodded over her shoulder at William. "I'm so glad you came tonight."

William smirked. "We didn't have a lot of choices."

"Oh yes. That's right. I'm so sorry about that." She seemed to be attempting to catch her breath from what would have been, for her, a race across the room.

"What has you so agitated, Aunt Margaret?"

"The horrible rain we've had the last two days."

William and Amy looked at each other. Rain in Bath, in fact just about anywhere in Britain, was not so unusual to upset Lady Margaret to this extent.

"Yes, what about it?" Amy asked.

Lady Margaret took a deep breath. "Unbeknownst to us, a heavy branch from the tree outside my bedchamber broke off, possibly in the last bad storm we had."

"And?"

"And it created a huge hole in the roof, of which we were unaware. With all this rain, the top floor of my house is almost flooded."

"Oh no!"

"Yes. We had someone in today to see about repairs, and it looks like it will take at least two weeks to fix the roof, then air out, clear, recarpet, and repaint the rooms."

"All the rooms?"

"Indeed, the water gushed in." She linked her arm into Amy's and walked them over to the refreshment table. "I need a drink. I am quite parched."

"I am very sorry to hear about this—is there anything we can do?" William handed a glass of lemonade to Amy.

"As a matter of fact, there is. It looks like Michael, your father, and I will have to move into your house until the repairs are finished." Lady Margaret slid an apprehensive glance at him.

William went into a spasm of coughing that had the two women pounding him on the back. But, unfortunately, not hard enough to knock him unconscious for the next few weeks.

CHAPTER 18

The next morning, Amy awoke under a cloak of uneasiness. It took her about a minute to remember her disquiet resulted because her entire family would be moving into their house that afternoon. Just for a bit more fun, they were to house a murder suspect as well, most likely arriving tomorrow. She groaned and turned over, placing her pillow over her head.

"I agree," William uttered from the other side of the bed.

Amy shifted and rolled to her side to face him. "I guess it wasn't a nightmare, then? My family is moving in here? And we are to be gaolers for a murder suspect, as well? A man suspected of murdering my own cousin at our wedding breakfast?"

"I'm afraid so." He reached out and played with a strand of hair that had come loose from her nighttime braid. "We will have to make the best of it. Family is family, and Lady Margaret already explained that there were no suitable hotel accommodations available and no furnished houses for such a short duration either."

Amy covered her mouth to stifle a yawn. "Can you imagine trying to get this murder solved with my father looking over my shoulder and reminding me how dangerous it is to get involved in such affairs?"

"I'm still wondering how the dog is going to take to all these people about."

"The dog? Oh, you mean Persephone?" Amy narrowed her eyes. "She has a name, you know."

Hearing her name, the dog began barking and scratching at the bedcovers hanging in front of her face.

"Oh, my poor dear. You are going to be quite distressed for a couple of weeks, I think." She reached down to scoop her warm, furry little body into her arms.

"Not on the bed, Amy."

She sighed, knowing William was right. He didn't want the dog in the room at all and had compromised as long as Persephone didn't sleep in the bed. "You're right." She shifted and stood, her nightgown swirling around her bare feet.

He bent his elbow and propped up his head on his hand. "I didn't mean for *you* to leave the bed." He patted the space alongside him. "Come back."

Amy shook her head. "No, we need to break our fast and get ready for church. I also must speak with Mrs. O'Sullivan and let her know that the demands from the staff will increase for a while."

"No need," he shrugged. "Have her contact that agency and hire a few additional servants while everyone is here."

She bent and kissed his cheek. "Thank you, husband. You are most generous."

He gave her what she imagined he meant to be a seductive smile. "So, are you coming back to bed?"

It almost worked, but remembering what the rest of the day was going to be like, she slowly shook her head. "No. I'm afraid not."

It wasn't as if she didn't want to, but her nerves were a bit stretched, and she wouldn't feel comfortable until she'd spoken to Mrs. O'Sullivan and Cook and made sure they weren't too put out by the crowd about to descend on them.

Placing Persephone on the floor, she made her way to the bathing room attached to their bedchamber to begin her ablutions, anxious to get the day started.

★   ★   ★

"Daughter, while I am most grateful to you and your husband for allowing this inconvenience, I'm afraid I must insist I have access to the library. Michael and I have a lot of work to do, and that is the best place for us to do it."

Amy pinched the bridge of her nose. She'd just told him that William used the library almost daily for whatever it was he did in the library almost daily.

Before she could find the words to say that in a different way without making things worse, William entered the dining room, where Papa had his papers scattered about the table. "Let them have it, my love. There is no reason we can't all share it. I can have one of the footmen bring in a temporary table that I'll use if I have a need."

Church was over, lunch consumed, and two carriages full of clothes, personal items, business papers, and whatnots had been unloaded and stacked in the entrance hall. Aunt Margaret had supervised the placement of the items in the bedchambers while Papa and her brother had proceeded to commandeer the dining room table.

Michael and Papa were to share the bigger of the guest bed-chambers, and Aunt Margaret and Albert would each have their own rooms. With only four bedchambers in the townhouse,

Amy felt they were lucky she and William didn't have someone sharing their room.

Besides Persephone.

Much to her dismay, Persephone had been barking and running in circles for over an hour. Amy had just gotten her calmed down when Aunt Margaret had arrived with her thirty-year-old, Shakespeare-quoting cockatoo, Othello. One look at the bird and Persephone had started up again; the two animals had a mutual dislike for each other. For a while it sounded as though the dog and bird were arguing with each other—if one could consider lines from *A Midsummer Night's Dream* an argument.

Amy rubbed her head and took a deep breath. William walked up to her and took her aside. "Sweetheart, I think we should go for a walk or perhaps a ride. You look a bit overwhelmed."

"Oh yes. I also have a headache, and fresh air would do me well."

Once they were bundled up, William escorted her from the current madness that was their house. "Your gloves don't match."

Amy sighed. "I know. Sophie has Sunday afternoons off, and I couldn't find a matching pair."

William grinned and shook his head. "A walk or shall we ride?"

"I think I prefer a walk." She took in a deep breath as she linked her arm into William's, and immediately felt better. There was no sunshine, but the unusually crisp late September air made for a pleasant walk.

"Where to?" William asked as they reached the end of the pavement and stopped to allow traffic to pass.

"Why not that sweet little tea shop near The Abbey? Even though lunch isn't that far behind us, a cup of tea always settles my nerves."

"Brandy does that for me," William said with a smirk as he clasped her elbow and moved her forward. "But tea it will be."

★   ★   ★

Several hours later, William joined the others in the drawing room, where they all awaited the dinner announcement. The room he'd spent a great deal of time in most of his life had never seemed so small. In fact, the entire townhouse had seemed to shrink.

When his mother had moved in with him the year before, he'd been concerned about losing his privacy. It had all turned out well, however, with her eventually marrying Mr. Colbert. William also thought the time residing with her might have provided him with an easier transition to living with a wife.

But three in-laws, a cockatoo, a dog, and a murder suspect? He scowled at the vision he had of Detectives Carson and Marsh doubled over with laughter when they came to check up on Albert—which he was sure they would do—and found the house overrun with people and animals.

"What's wrong?" Amy asked as she handed him a glass of sherry.

"Nothing, sweetheart. Just a bit hungry perhaps." There was no reason to take a chance on offending her relatives by pointing out the ever-growing argument between her father and Michael in the corner of the room, while Lady Margaret chased Persephone around, the dog having what appeared to be a house slipper in its mouth.

All of that he could probably deal with if it weren't for the blasted bird reciting "To be or not to be" over and over until visions of strangling the annoying animal and hurling it out the window kept him quite entertained.

"I'm sure dinner will be ready soon. Cook was very gracious about the extra visitors we have, and Mrs. O'Sullivan was just as amiable."

"I pay them to be gracious and amiable," he groused.

"No. You pay them to supervise the staff and cook the food, not take on extra duties without advance notice," she snapped.

She stopped and rubbed her forehead. "I apologize. I think I am still a bit frayed."

Feeling a bit remorseful himself, he leaned in close, knowing that with all the noise she probably couldn't hear him. "I suggest once dinner is over, we retire early to our bedchamber."

"Yes. A very good idea."

"With a bottle of wine."

"An even better idea."

"What say you we skip dinner and just retire to our bedchamber with a bottle of wine?"

Just then Filbert walked into the room and announced dinner. Amy placed her hand over her stomach. "I think I would *relax* better if my stomach was full."

Taking her arm to escort her to the dining room, he murmured, "Then eat fast, darling."

Once they were all settled and someone had miraculously separated the animals and placed them far enough from the dining room that peace and quiet reigned, William was finally able to take a deep, calming breath.

For all of a minute.

"William," Amy's father said as he cut his meat with such vigor 'twas almost as if he believed the animal still needed killing, "it has been brought to my attention that there will be a murderer joining us tomorrow."

Bloody hell. For a few minutes William had forgotten about that dilemma soon to arrive at his doorstep.

"Papa, I thought we lived in a society where one was considered innocent until proven guilty?" Amy asked.

Lord Winchester waved his hand. "The man is guilty."

Well, then. So much for a fair trial and a presumption of innocence.

"Why would the criminal justice system allow a murderer to live in a private home? I like to know where my tax money is going if not to pay to keep criminals locked up," Franklin huffed.

William cleared his throat and attempted to convince Amy's father of something of which even he wasn't sure. "Shepton Mallet is a fairly horrible place to be housed. Mr. Nelson-Graves petitioned the magistrate to have a bond posted for Mr. Finch so he could be released from there. They agreed, providing he remains in our custody."

"Why you?" Michael asked.

William hesitated. "The more I think on it, the less I can come up with a feasible answer."

"I am sitting here, attempting to enjoy my dinner and wondering if we will all be murdered in our beds." Lord Winchester turned to William. "Do you have a gun?"

"Yes." He ignored Amy's gasp—they'd had enough conversations in the past about her burning desire to own a gun. Given the trouble his wife seemed to attract like a magnet, he wasn't too fond of her knowing that there was a gun in the house.

After a few minutes of silence, Michael said, "Albert's friend, Mrs. Madeline Davis, approached me yesterday."

That casually tossed-out remark certainly gained everyone's attention.

William would hardly call Mrs. Davis Albert's *friend*, but with ladies present, that was probably the best way to refer to her.

Michael took a sip from his wine glass and wiped his mouth. "It was odd, actually. I have been spending some time visiting the building Father and I are considering purchasing for an office.

"It was when I was leaving there that she stopped me. I know I saw her a few times that morning and almost had the feeling she'd been following me."

"That is odd," Amy said, frowning.

"In any event, when she did speak with me, she knew that Albert was to be released into your custody and asked if I could request she be allowed to visit with him."

"Indeed?" William thought for a minute. "I wonder how she discovered that? We only learned about it recently when we visited with Mr. Nelson-Graves."

Michael shrugged. "She said she'd read in the newspaper about Albert being arrested, and went to the jail to see him. It was there that she found out he was at Shepton-Mallet but was soon to be released into your custody. I was quite surprised, actually, that they provided information to her. I'm sure she gave the impression that they were related in some way."

William looked over at Amy. "I don't even know if Albert will be permitted visitors."

"No matter. I'm sure when the detectives arrive with him, there will be a string of rules and regulations we will have to follow."

The words were barely out of her mouth when Persephone raced into the room, panic causing her short legs to take a flying leap onto the table, then sliding the length, scattering plates, silverware, and glasses, and barking to raise the dead. Right behind her, Othello soared over their heads and took a dive to grab Persephone by the neck.

The dog leapt at William with such force, its four paws slamming into his chest, that his chair flew backward with him ending up on the floor while Persephone at on his chest, calmly licking his face.

"Shite."

CHAPTER 19

Amy wandered into the breakfast room, the back of her hand across her mouth, attempting to stifle a very unladylike yawn. "Good morning," she mumbled to William, the only other person at the table.

He looked up from his newspaper. "Good morning. I had hoped to let you sleep a bit longer. Did I wake you when I left?"

"Possibly." She sat and poured herself tea, taking a deep inhale of the lovely fragrance. "Something woke me up and then you were gone."

He folded the newspaper and placed it alongside his empty breakfast plate. "Your father and brother have already broken their fast and have left to see their solicitor. They are working on completing the purchase of an office building."

Amy added a bit of sugar and a spot of cream to her tea, stirring the liquid as she thought. "I'm assuming we will hear something today about Albert's arrival. 'Twas Friday when Mr. Nelson-Graves told us of the arrangements he'd made. Also, we need to continue with our investigation. I feel as though we haven't done much."

William crossed his arms over his chest and leaned back in his chair. "Frankly, my love, I'm concerned that we have done nothing at all."

She didn't need to question him to know what he meant. "I disagree. We've eliminated the temporary maid, but there is still Mrs. Davis, who won't talk to us, and Albert who insists he is innocent, even though all evidence points to him. And," she continued, "I think it will be worth our while to investigate Jared, who the police have apparently dismissed as unimportant, but we saw his reaction to being cut out of Alice's will."

"Yes, we shall put him on our list. Albert might have some idea about Jared Munson. Maybe Alice threatened to cut him off, and that drove the young man to take a chance that he would end up with part of her fortune upon her death."

"And blame Albert who was sitting right next to her." Amy slumped in her chair. "What I am hoping is that with Albert staying here, we can speak with him at length and also get more information on his relationship with Mrs. Davis that both he and she were reluctant to talk about."

"There must be a reason why Albert refuses to see her, to the extent that she was forced to attend a wedding uninvited." He leaned forward and tapped his finger on the table. "When he arrives, however, Albert must be made to understand that we cannot help him if he is hiding something, or expect us to prove his innocence without his cooperation."

"Good morning, newlyweds." Looking fresh and well put together, as always, Aunt Margaret sailed into the room. "My, aren't we looking glum." She patted Amy on her cheek before taking a chair alongside her. "Still disappointed about your honeymoon trip? Or rather the lack thereof?"

"That and other things." Amy was too polite and owed too much to her aunt to bring up the hordes of people who had descended on them, eliminating the little bit of honeymoon they might have had in their own home.

With the glance William tossed her way, she was quite sure he was thinking the same thing.

"When does the murderer arrive?" Aunt Margaret asked.

"You sound like Papa. It has not yet been proven that Albert killed Alice. That will be up to the justice of the peace to decide."

Her aunt filled her plate with eggs, bacon, sausage, toast and sliced tomatoes. That was another source of irritation for Amy. Not only did Aunt Margaret have all the grace of a princess with the way she dressed, spoke, and glided into a room, but she also possessed a slim frame and could eat tremendous amounts of food and yet never gain any weight.

Amy, on the other hand, was built with a shorter stature and more curves, and with her propensity for treats, had to pass by some of her favorite foods lest she suffer the guilt of having Sophie, her sweet little lady's maid that William had insisted she hire, strain her poor arms trying to tighten her corset enough to fasten her mistress's dresses.

"Don't tell me you both still believe Mr. Albert Finch did not poison his wife?" Aunt Margaret looked surprised as she raised her teacup to her lips. "The poor woman died right at the table, alongside her husband. Dozens of witnesses were all sitting down at the time, listening to Mr. Colbert. How else could she have been poisoned?"

"That's what we intend to find out," Amy said with a sniff.

"And how close are you?" Aunt Margaret's lips didn't smile, but her eyes did.

Before she could answer—and not quite sure what the rejoinder would be—Filbert arrived in the breakfast room. "My lord, the two detectives are here. They request an audience with you and her ladyship."

William threw his napkin down. "It appears our guest—or prisoner—has arrived." He pulled Amy's chair out. "Are you ready?"

"I put them in the front parlor," Filbert said.

"Good luck," Aunt Margaret said. "I think I shall take a stroll into town this morning and look for a sturdy lock and have one of the footmen install it on my bedroom door."

"Yes, you wouldn't want Albert to take exception to Othello's soliloquies and relieve us all of his talents."

"That is not funny, Amyyyy," Aunt Margaret singsonged as they left the room.

Amy looked up at William. "I thought it was quite humorous myself."

The two detectives and Albert stood as Amy and William entered the front parlor.

"Detectives," William said with a nod, "Albert."

Albert looked ill. Only a few days in Shepton Mallet had wreaked havoc on the man's body. He was thinner, his face a gray shade, and the skin around his sunken eyes looked as black as if he'd been punched. Amy shuddered.

William waved at the chairs in the room. "Let's all sit."

Once they were settled, Albert was the first to speak. "I want you both to know how much I appreciate you accepting to house me while we await the court hearing."

William nodded, but given the evidence right before them, Amy couldn't help but consider that Albert was either the best actor this side of Drury Lane, or he was genuinely innocent of the charges against him. But then she recalled Mr. Patrick Whitney from earlier in the year during Mr. Harding's death investigation, when he had fooled them with his acting abilities and stage makeup. Although it was highly unlikely that Albert had had access to stage makeup in prison.

* * *

"Detectives, I have a few questions on how this is going to work with the least amount of disruption for the household." William tried to avoid looking at Albert, who appeared awful. But then with what he'd been through, that was not surprising.

"We unexpectedly have house guests at the present time. Due to some necessary repairs being made at the Winchester Townhouse, my father-in-law, brother-in-law, and aunt by marriage are residing with us for a couple of weeks."

The detectives glanced at each other, and William wondered for a minute if his news would cause them to attempt to rescind the deal they'd been forced to accept.

"I don't expect that to cause trouble," William added quickly, wanting to save Albert from the disappointment of returning to gaol.

The words were barely out of his mouth when Persephone came barreling into the front parlor, barking loud enough to reach London, with Othello flying over her again, screeching and swooping down, appearing to frighten the dog rather than actually harm her.

And seeming to be having a grand time doing it.

Amy jumped up and scooped Persephone into her arms. "Excuse me, gentleman, I must find my aunt and have her return Othello to his cage."

The detectives looked at each other again. "Othello?" Carson said.

The bird left the room with them, still stalking his prey. Within seconds, order had returned to the room. "I apologize for that, but we are all getting adjusted to living together," William said.

Rather than waiting for Amy to return, William began, "I assume my wife and I are not to be gaolers? And am I correct that Mr. Finch will have leave to come and go as he wishes?"

"To some extent," Detective Carson said. "Mr. Finch is in your custody, and while not similar to gaol, because of the charges he faces, we prefer he remain in the residence." Carson looked over at Albert. "If you need to leave Lord Wethington's property, it must be with an attendant and with the knowledge of either Lord or Lady Wethington."

"My housekeeper has arranged to hire additional staff while we are hosting my wife's family," William said. "I have also secured a footman for the sole purpose of seeing to Mr. Finch's needs."

Carson nodded, most likely reading into his words what William had intended to convey: Albert would be guarded.

Amy returned, sans animals, and took her seat alongside him. "Detective Carson, do you have an idea how long Mr. Finch will need to remain here?"

"You can send him back to Shepton Mallet anytime you want, but for the purposes of keeping him out of there, he must remain with you until he appears before the justice of the peace."

"And that will be how long?" Amy was persistent, for which William was grateful because he had the same concerns.

"We don't know, but we will keep you advised."

Apparently, they were not going to get any more information from the detectives, so William was anxious to finish up the interview and get on with their day.

William stood. "If that is all, Detectives, then my wife and I have a busy day, and we need to get Mr. Finch settled."

Carson eyed him suspiciously. "I hope your busy day does not involve what we spoke about before."

"Not at all." He walked toward the door and the detectives jumped up to join him. "Have a good day, and if we have any further questions, we will summon you."

He knew that would annoy the detectives since they always resented having to treat him as a peer, something William had rarely, if ever, used to his advantage.

"I will see you to your room, Albert," William said once the front door had closed.

"Again, I must reiterate how grateful I am for your agreement to this plan, my lord," Albert said.

"You can repay us by not giving any reason for the detectives to return." He was sure his expression clarified exactly what he meant.

Albert bowed his head. "Of course."

"If you will excuse me," Amy said, "I will check with Mrs. O'Sullivan on the expected arrival of our additional staff."

Albert picked up the satchel he'd brought with him and followed William up the stairs to the bedchamber floor. They continued in silence, nodding briefly at Lady Margaret when she left her room. "Ah, Mr. Finch. A pleasure to see you."

"You as well, Lady Margaret." His awkwardness was evident, but then Lady Margaret seemed the same. 'Twas no wonder since she, a temporary resident, was meeting in the corridor of a viscount's home with another temporary resident, a murder suspect. William doubted if there was anything in the etiquette books Lady Margaret had no doubt studied when she was a young lady on how one conducted oneself in such a situation.

He left Albert to settle in and returned to the front parlor where Amy awaited him. "Mrs. O'Sullivan said that she expects the additional staff from the agency to arrive in two days."

"Did she say how many she employed?"

"Yes. Two maids-of-all-work, one scullery maid, and another footman."

"Until the new footman for Albert arrives, which I believe is later today, I think we should ask Filbert to have one of our footmen act as companion to Albert."

Amy smirked. "Companion or gaoler?"

The sound of the knocker signaled the arrival of a visitor. Since Filbert was off somewhere else, William opened the door.

A young man in the uniform of a dispatch service in Bath stood on the front step. "I have a message here for Lord Wethington."

William reached out. "I am Lord Wethington." He took the paper from the young man, offered him a coin, and closed the door. He broke the seal and read the words.

"What is it?" Amy said.

"It's from Mrs. Davis. She is requesting permission to visit with Albert."

CHAPTER 20

Amy took the missive from his hand. "We forgot to cover it with the detectives, but I assume Albert can have callers. This was supposed to make his confinement more pleasant, and even in gaol he was allowed visitors."

"Yes. I'll go talk to him."

"It might be a good idea if we questioned him more extensively once he's settled. He would know more about his wife's friends and possible enemies than we could uncover."

She followed William out of the room and to the bottom of the staircase. "Also, I'm sure Annabelle would be of help. As twins, she and Alice most likely knew everything about each other. I think another meeting with her is appropriate."

Amy tapped her chin with her fingertip, her mind in a whirl. "Perhaps a meeting with Annabelle would go better if I went alone. Since we're cousins and we've known each other our whole lives, I think she would open up to me more." Amy smiled, feeling quite relieved. "I believe we are finally moving forward with this."

With a plan she felt good about, she climbed the stairs behind William and hurried to her small office on the bedchamber floor while he headed to Albert's room. Until she'd married William and moved in, the room had been used as an additional storage space for linens. He had insisted that it be redecorated and had her old, worn, but favorite desk shipped from her home, along with a comfortable chair, proper lighting, and her typing machine that she was still trying to master.

Rather than fool around with the machine now, she penned a note to Annabelle, sealed it, then made a list of questions for which they needed answers as well as any other points about the investigation so far that they may have missed or needed to go over more.

In the confusion of her family moving into the house, they'd gotten sidetracked. She was still not convinced that Albert was guilty. To her it was a lazy deduction on the detectives' part. Or it was quite possible that her brain, which always seemed to be coming up with ways to murder someone followed by a convoluted solution, just couldn't believe that in real life killing someone could be so simple.

★ ★ ★

William knocked on Albert's door, the missive from Madeline in his hand. The door opened and Albert peeked out at him, barely revealing himself. "Yes?"

His breath reeked of alcohol, which was surprising since William had not left any spirits in the room and the man hadn't been in the room more than fifteen or twenty minutes. A bit taken aback by Albert's strange behavior, he asked, "May I come in?"

It looked like Albert was actually considering refusing William entry, but then he opened the door wider and waved him in. Where was the so very grateful man from only fifteen minutes ago? "I'm sorry, I was just about to take a short nap. I didn't get much sleep in the prison."

"No, I'm sure you did not. This won't take long, however. Also, we have a bathing room at the end of the corridor. I believe there are linens stocked in the closet there. You may want to avail yourself of that as well."

Albert merely dipped his head.

"What brings me up here is a missive I just received." He waved the envelope. "It is from Mrs. Madeline Davis."

Albert immediately stiffened. "Indeed."

"Yes. She has asked permission to visit with you."

"No." He walked back to the door and opened it.

William didn't budge from his spot. "From what I understand Mrs. Davis has been staying in a hotel here in Bath, awaiting the opportunity to speak with you."

"It doesn't matter. I have nothing to say to her." Albert ran his hand down his face. "I don't wish to be rude to you in your own home, my lord, but I would like to take a bath and get some sleep."

"Yes, yes. Of course," William said. "Dinner is at seven o'clock."

He left the room and hesitated for a few seconds after the door closed, tapping the letter against his lips. He had to admit he was confused. Considering her connection to Albert, Mrs. Davis was a suspect in Alice's murder. One would think the man would be anxious to speak with her to gain information.

Unless, of course, he knew no information forthcoming from Mrs. Davis would help his case because he was indeed the one who had poisoned his wife.

William returned to the library and wrote a quick note to Mrs. Davis, advising her that Albert did not wish to have visitors. Hopefully that would be the end of it. What he and Amy needed to do was delve further into Mrs. Davis's background.

Perhaps she was only trying to speak with Albert to attempt a reconciliation. A woman scorned and all that. Especially with his wife dead.

After summoning Filbert and asking him to dispatch the note to Mrs. Davis, he strolled to the window in the library and stood with his hands clasped behind his back, staring out at the leaves on the trees, some of them already turning shades of yellow, orange, and red. Autumn was his favorite season. Even though it appeared everything was dying, he found it invigorating with the heat of the summer behind them and the cooler air arriving along with the thought of the holidays in a couple of months.

He never did much for the holidays himself, but every year he had numerous invitations to visit and spend the time at friends' country homes, which he always accepted with pleasure.

This year perhaps he and Amy should host a ball or some sort of party. He liked the idea of decorating his home and planning holiday menus with his wife. He would have Cook prepare some of his favorite breads and treats. It was time to return the hospitality and graciousness of his friends.

With a deep sigh his brain switched to the one subject that continuously hovered over him: Alice Finch's death and their lack of progress with the investigation. The detectives had given up, convinced that they had the right man. William only wished he felt as strongly as Amy that Albert was *not* the right man.

At present, they appeared to be at a dead end.

★　★　★

The following afternoon, Amy kissed William on the cheek, endured him straightening her hat—which always seemed to shift no matter how many hatpins Sophie stuck into it—and left to meet her cousin Annabelle for tea at one of Amy's favorite places in Bath, the Sally Lunn Restaurant.

One of the oldest buildings in Bath, the restaurant still sold hundreds of buns each month from the original recipe of Sally Lunn. The French refugee had lived and worked in the bakery located in the building on what was then called Lilliput Alley for years, beginning in 1680. The building itself had stood in that same spot since 1482.

Wonderful smells assailed her senses as Amy entered the restaurant. Annabelle sat at a corner table, still looking wan and shattered, although she attempted a smile when she spotted Amy.

"How are you doing, Annabelle?" Amy took her seat and leaned across the table to take Annabelle's hand in hers.

"Not well, I'm sorry to say." She sighed and looked out the window. "One week ago yesterday." She turned back to Amy. "My twin sister left me one week ago yesterday."

Amy was surprised when she realized Annabelle was correct. It was a week ago that her wedding had taken place. With all that had happened since that day she'd lost count.

I should be romping on the beach right now, taking moonlight strolls with my husband and enjoying a romantic dinner for two. Instead . . .

"Shall we order?" Annabelle asked, interrupting Amy's bout of self-pity.

"Yes. Of course." Since her intentions had been to learn if Annabelle might shed some light on anyone who might have disliked her sister enough to want her dead, she hoped the conversation would not trouble her too much. They really did need some help with the investigation.

Once the tea things were laid out on the table, Amy poured for them both and decided it was best to jump right in. "Are you aware of anyone who would want to harm your sister?" Stunned by the narrowed eyes and red flush of outrage on Annabelle's face, Amy quickly added, "Besides Albert, that is."

"Everyone loved Alice. No one would do her harm." She blotted her eyes with her napkin and glared across the table at her. "It was her wretched husband. He was the cause of her death." She leaned in close, the look on her face frightening. "She was about to divorce him, you know."

Amy was taken aback. "Truly?

"Yes. She was tired of him running about with other women. No matter how many times he promised to reform, he did not. She had spoken to her solicitor about it."

"I thought divorce was only allowed for adultery by the wife?"

"Yes. That's what Mr. Lawton told her. But she had asked him to research to see if it was possible anyway."

Despite this interesting news, Amy sighed. Annabelle was so fixated on Albert, she would be of no help at all. A change in subject might help. Perhaps this would just turn into a visit and nothing more. "Lord Wethington and I are hosting my family for a couple of weeks."

Annabelle perked up. "Indeed? Why is that?"

At last Amy had hit on something that they could discuss without rancor. "They had some issues with flooding during the last two storms. Apparently, there was an unknown leak in the roof, causing damage that required repairs to the bedchamber floor."

"It is quite nice of your husband to allow them to stay while they have the necessary work done on their townhouse. But I imagine it makes for quite a disruption in the household."

"To some extent that is true, but we have contracted with an agency to send additional temporary help for a couple of weeks. I believe they are expected first thing tomorrow morning."

Annabelle nodded. "That was a good idea. And very generous of his lordship to see that your staff is not overwhelmed." She shook her head. "If only my sister had married someone nice like that."

The silence that ensued was followed by comments on family matters and typical British subjects: the poor roads, the bad weather, and the Queen's birthday.

Once they had consumed their tea and taken care of the bill, Amy placed her palm on Annabelle's hand again. "If there is anything I can do to help you, Annabelle, please let me know."

The woman took a deep breath. "Thank you. I appreciate that. However, I will be leaving on a trip to London for a few days. I have a friend, from school years ago, who has invited me many times, and I feel as though this is the best time to do it."

Amy smiled. "Yes, that's a wonderful idea. It might be just what you need." They stood and made their way out of the restaurant. They hugged and Amy headed to her carriage, feeling quite glum after her visit with Annabelle.

CHAPTER 21

Fortunately, only Amy was in the drawing room awaiting the dinner announcement when William entered the room. "How was tea with Miss Munson?"

"Quite well on a personal level, but nothing gained with regard to our investigation." Amy took the small glass of sherry from William's hand. "Actually, that is not true. There was interesting information. It seems that Alice had discussed divorce with her solicitor, Mr. Lawton."

"Indeed?"

"Yes." Amy sat on the settee and took a sip of her sherry. "Divorce, as far as I know, is only permitted on the grounds of adultery by the wife, but Mr. Lawton was researching it further."

"That puts Albert right back in the spotlight, then, I'm afraid. If he knew of Alice's plans, that gave him incentive to do away with her before she could divorce him or change her will." He took the seat alongside her and stretched his arm along the back of the settee. "Given that information, are you certain I cannot convince you that the current resident upstairs is the culprit, and we are uselessly paddling upstream with no success in sight?"

Amy shook her head, stubborn woman that she was. "There is something odd about this entire matter. With all the opportunities Albert would have had to murder his wife, why pick such a public place to kill her? I'm sorry, but that and other questions keep me from agreeing with you."

"That very fact might be precisely why he *would* pick that opportunity. A public place, with so many people there—why would someone chose that as a location for a murder? An instant alibi."

The others slowly joined them, and they had no time to continue their conversation. The staff had assured him that both Persephone and Othello would be behind separate closed doors.

Dinner was a lively affair. Albert had requested trays in his room ever since he'd arrived the day before, which, given Amy's family's concerns about him being in the house, had been an excellent idea.

They had no sooner sat down then a note was delivered to William from Manor-Whitely confirming that the expected temporary staff would arrive early the next morning. He asked Filbert to pass the note along to Mrs. O'Sullivan.

Perhaps, with the footman who'd already arrived dedicated only to Albert, and another footman as well as extra maids to lighten the workload for his staff, things would settle down. At times William felt as though he were riding on a high-speed railway car that was close to losing control. This was certainly not how he'd expected the first couple of weeks of his marriage to go.

"How is the contract on your building proceeding?" Amy asked her father as she took a piece of fish from the platter the footman presented.

"Very well. I anticipate finalizing the contract in another week or so," her father said in between bites. "We are also working on another project that will increase our business presence here in Bath."

They continued their meal, with innocuous subjects and no one mentioning the suspected murderer residing one floor above them.

★   ★   ★

The next morning, more chaos ensued as the temporary employees arrived en masse. William tried his best to concentrate on the reports his man of business had sent over, but it was impossible. He stumbled over strange maids, answered numerous questions about Albert that the temporary footman asked, and found his brother-in-law and father-in-law locked in a verbal battle in the library. And to his dismay, Persephone had decided she was in love with him and followed him everywhere.

He discovered Amy hiding in her office. She appeared to be working, but with the blank paper in front of her, he assumed she was merely using that excuse to avoid the pandemonium that had become their home.

"Are you hiding?" he asked with a smirk.

"Perhaps," she agreed. "I just spoke with Mrs. O'Sullivan, who told me she'd been busy with another crisis when the temporary staff arrived, so Cook kept one of them there to help with breakfast and sent the others to the employee dining room to await her instructions. I'm sure it will all be under control shortly."

"I must get out of the house," he said—with desperation.

She jumped up so quickly he stepped back in alarm. "Yes. That is just the thing. We can go for a walk in the park or for tea—no forget tea, I feel as though I've drunk enough to sink a ship. Maybe a carriage ride, then, or a bit of shopping or the new bookstore that opened recently."

She hurried past him, and he grabbed her hand and pulled her back. "Be at ease, sweetheart. I believe you have picked up the turmoil surrounding us."

Amy took a deep breath and wrapped her arms around him, leaning her cheek against his chest, calming at the sound of his steady heartbeat. "Yes. Most definitely. I am at sixes and sevens all the time." She tilted her head and looked up at him. "I am sure you regret ever suggesting marriage to me."

He smiled back. "Not at all. This is all temporary—I hope—so we do not need to embrace it as forever. Go fetch one of your silly hats and meet me downstairs. I'll send for the carriage." He stopped and smirked. "The very quiet carriage."

Once they settled in the vehicle, Amy said, "I have an idea. Why don't we visit with your solicitor and ask him how we can see a copy of Alice's will?"

He frowned. "Why would we need that? We have already attended the reading."

"Mr. Lawton read the list of those receiving bequests of personal items and set amounts of money quite quickly. I would like to see that list."

"We can try." He stepped out and gave the driver instructions to take them to Mr. Joseph Melrose's office on Broad Street. The carriage moved forward, and William relaxed in the silence, feeling as though a huge boulder had been lifted from his back. He really hadn't wanted to complain to Amy because he didn't want her feeling bad about the turmoil, which was the result of her family. And pets. And the extra staff to help. Of course, Albert's stay in their house could be attributed to them both.

Taking a deep breath, William closed his eyes and leaned against the squab, enjoying the peace. "I think perhaps we should attend the book club meeting tomorrow evening."

"Another way to get out of the house, my lord?"

"Yes."

They both laughed and enjoyed the silence with no inane conversation for the rest of the ride.

Mr. Melrose's office on Broad Street was in an older building, but well maintained. They climbed the stairs to the first floor and stopped at the third door. "Mr. Joseph Melrose, Solicitor" was painted on the glass portion in gold lettering. William turned the doorknob and stepped aside to allow Amy to enter.

They were greeted by Melrose's secretary, a young man with spectacles and an alarming loss of hair for his age. "Good afternoon, Lord Wethington." He glanced at Amy. "I understand you recently married. Is this your charming wife?"

"Yes, Mr. Morris." He looked over at Amy. "May I present to you Mr. David Morris, Mr. Melrose's secretary?"

"It is a pleasure to meet you, Mr. Morris."

"Oh indeed, the pleasure is all mine, Lady Wethington."

The preliminaries finished, he directed his comment to William. "Do you have an appointment, my lord?"

"No." William shook his head. "If Mr. Melrose is too busy to see us, that is fine. I just took a chance on seeing if he could speak with us for a few minutes."

"I am never too busy to see you, my lord." A large man emerged from behind the closed door and extended his hand to William. "And best wishes on your marriage." He glanced at Amy. "You are truly a lucky man."

"Amy, may I make known to you Mr. Joseph Melrose. Joseph, my wife, Lady Amy Wethington."

"It is truly my pleasure, my lady." He bowed toward her and turned to William. "Come in. Tell me what I can do for you."

As usual, his solicitor had to move files and stacks of papers from the chairs in front of his desk to a table on the far wall. William and Amy then sat, and William leaned forward. "We are in need of seeing a will for the woman who was murdered at our wedding breakfast last week."

Joseph's brows rose. "I did see something about that in the newspaper, but I had no idea it was *your* wedding breakfast."

"Unfortunately, yes. Lady Wethington and I find ourselves in the middle of an investigation—"

"—Again," Joseph cut in.

William nodded. "And we need to see a copy of the woman's will. Since my wife is a relative of the victim, we attended the reading the day of the funeral. However, there are parts of it we would like to examine further."

Joseph thought for a minute, then said. "A will does not become public until it has been probated, and sometimes that can take up to twelve months." He picked up a pen and dipped it into an inkwell. Pulling a pad of paper toward him, he said, "What is the victim's name? I don't recall from the newspaper article I read."

Amy said, "Mrs. Alice Finch. Her maiden name was Munson."

Joseph wrote down the name, then looked up at him. "Who drew up the will?"

"Mr. Stanford Lawton from Melrose and Lawton."

The solicitor nodded. "I am familiar with the firm and attend the same club as Lawton. I should be able to wrangle a copy of the will from him." He laid the pen down and folded his hands on his desk. "I can send a missive when I have a copy of it. Knowing you and your lovely wife as I do, I assume you are conducting your own investigation?"

"Yes, and as strange as it sounds, the one who stands accused of the woman's murder—her husband—is currently residing in our home, in our custody."

Joseph's brows rose almost to his hairline. "Indeed? What a strange arrangement that is."

"Just so." William rose and helped Amy up. "I don't want to take up more of your time."

Joseph stood and nodded. "As soon as I receive information on the will, I shall send a missive."

William and Amy said their goodbyes and returned to the carriage. After a stop at the new bookstore, Once Upon a Book, they returned home with five new books to add to their library.

They strolled up the steps, hand in hand, and smiled as Filbert opened the door. Unfortunately, the butler did not look as cheerful as he generally did.

"Is something amiss, Filbert?" William asked.

The man opened his mouth to speak, but before he uttered a word, Lady Margaret came barreling down the corridor—very odd for that very graceful lady—and stopped in front of Amy, her hands on her hips.

"What have you done with Othello?"

William looked over at Amy. "The bird?"

"I have no idea what you are talking about," Amy said as she shrugged out of her coat. She removed her hat and gloves.

"Othello is missing." Lady Margaret's eyes narrowed. "I have a feeling you did something with him because of how he's been chasing Persephone. Which, I might add, is quite strange since they've lived together for years."

William cleared his throat, hoping to avoid an escalating argument between the ladies. "Perhaps the change of environment and the extra people have the animals a bit unsettled."

Lady Margaret's expression softened, and she dropped her arms to her side. "Did you take him, Amy?"

"No, Aunt. You know I would never do that."

"Then he is missing. Kidnapped."

William decided to take charge. "Shall we move into the drawing room, ladies? I think standing here in the entrance hall is not a good idea."

The three of them continued up the stairs to the drawing room, where Michael and Franklin hovered in the corner over what looked like a contract.

William poured a brandy for himself and a sherry for each of the ladies. They all sat, Lady Margaret still visibly upset.

"Are you sure your bird is not in the house?" William asked.

"I've been searching for two hours. Plus we have this special whistle I use to call him, and he did not respond." The poor woman looked lost.

"Did you search the garden?"

"Yes. And I called him from there too. But he never goes outside. He hates outside." Lady Margaret shook her head, and her eyes rimmed with tears. "He has been kidnapped!"

CHAPTER 22

The next evening, when there had been no more information on the bird, and Lady Margaret had taken to her bed with a megrim, William and Amy prepared for the book club meeting.

Earlier in the day, Joseph had sent over a note that he would be able to provide a copy of Alice's will in a day or two. The extra staff had been taken in under Mrs. O'Sullivan's wing. It still jarred William a bit when he passed one of the temporary maids in the corridor, since all his staff had been with him for years. But things were truly running smoother.

However, nothing new had been uncovered in their search for another suspect, and William's new wife was frustrated.

"I feel as though we are slogging around in thick mud with this investigation," Amy said as the carriage rolled over bumps on their way to the book club meeting.

It was a misty night, quite common in England, and the dampness seeped into the carriage. William pulled the woolen blanket from under the seat and covered them both with its warmth. "We should have Alice's will soon, and it is my intention for us to visit with Mrs. Davis once again at her hotel. Also, I have started a search to locate Mr. Jared Munson."

"Thank you, that feels good," Amy said, snuggling next to him. "I believe we should speak with Albert again too. Force him to give you more information. At least let you know why he will not speak with Mrs. Davis."

"I will state it clearly to the man that we will not continue to assist him in his hopes to acquit himself if he won't answer more questions than he has so far. Jared was a favorite of Albert's wife, so he should certainly know where to find the lad."

Amy shrugged. "That is what I find confusing. If Albert truly wants us to help him, why is he being so secretive?"

The bookstore came into view, the lights inside providing a mellow glow outside. William opened the carriage door and turned to help Amy down. He placed his arm around her shoulders, and they hurried into the building.

At least it was warm inside, with the pot belly stove in the middle of the front room giving off a nice amount of heat. They browsed the shelves as they normally did for about ten minutes, then headed to the back room where the meetings were held.

A few members had already gathered. William's parents stood near the front of the room, conversing with Lord Temple, Mr. Davidson, Mr. Rawlings, the O'Neill sisters, and Michael.

William and Amy looked at each other. "Michael?"

Amy made her way to the group. She nodded at everyone. "Good evening." Once she accepted their return greetings, she looked at Michael. "What are you doing here?"

"Good evening to you too, sister. As father and I are moving to Bath permanently, I thought I would see what your book club is all about. I understand they sometimes read your novels."

"Yes, they do on occasion." She continued to study him. He grinned at her confusion. "What?"

Amy shook her head. "I'm just surprised to see you. That's all."

Mr. Colbert called the meeting to order. They all took their seats and Mr. Colbert cleared his throat. "I am pleased to see all of you tonight. I am looking forward to finishing up our discussion on *The Mystery of Edwin Drood*. If I remember correctly, I suggested you all come up with an ending to the book since Mr. Dickens—"

The door opened and Eloise, late—as usual, hurried through the door. "I'm so sorry, everyone. I really thought I would be on time."

Amy nudged William to move over and waved at Eloise, who then proceeded to shake her head and walk determinedly over to where Michael sat on a settee, and take the seat next to him.

They smiled at each other.

★   ★   ★

A dark and gloomy morning greeted William and Amy as they entered the breakfast room together. They were alone, Franklin and Michael having already broken their fast and left for parts unknown to do whatever it was they did each day. Lady Margaret, as always, had a tray in her room.

"I've been thinking about what you said yesterday, and agree we should investigate Mrs. Davis further," Amy said. "There must be a reason that Albert ended their relationship. Especially since he's been so vague about it. Then to refuse to see the woman when she requested an audience is quite telling. One would think if he were genuinely interested in finding the true culprit to clear his name that he would be happy to question her since she won't talk to us. And, as Albert's mistress, she certainly had a motive to kill Alice."

He stirred a bit more cream into his coffee and thought about her words.

She continued, "Another thing I've learned is that Albert has refused to leave his room except to use the bathing room and water closet. One of the temporary maids Mrs. O'Sullivan had assigned to clean Albert's room and take care of anything he needed told Mrs. O'Sullivan that he has repudiated her multiple requests to clean his room. The poor girl is forced to watch his door in the morning, and when he leaves to use the facilities, she rushes in and does what she needs to do before he returns."

His brows rose. "Indeed? How very strange. I wonder what he's doing in there all that time?"

"I can't imagine," Amy said. "As a side note of interest, though, Persephone seems to have developed a fancy for the man."

"Really? How can that be when he rarely leaves the room?"

Amy shrugged and laid her fork down, her brows drawn together. "I'm not sure, but I found her sniffing around his door last night and then this morning I had to practically drag her away from the doorway."

"Most likely she smells someone different."

"Perhaps."

They both looked up as Filbert entered the room. "My lord, Mrs. O'Sullivan would like a word with you or her ladyship when you have a moment."

Having finished breakfast, William pushed his plate away and leaned back in his chair. "Very well. Send her in—we can see her now."

William stood as his housekeeper arrived. His gentlemanly manners had been bred into him. To him the relationship of servant and employer made no difference. She was a woman, and he stood when a woman entered a room.

"Please, have a seat, Mrs. O'Sullivan. I believe the teapot is still warm, if you would like a cup." Amy offered her a warm smile.

Truth be known, William had had a bit of concern that Amy and Mrs. O'Sullivan might not get on, but he needn't have worried. As when his mother had joined his household earlier in the year, charming Mrs. O'Sullivan from her very first day, Amy had wormed her way into every one of his staff member's hearts. It made for a pleasant household when the mistress and housekeeper weren't vying for top-dog dominance.

As much as he cared for his wife, he shuddered to think of how things might be if she were in charge. Lady Margaret had run the Winchester household, and Amy had been more than happy to leave it to her.

"How can we assist you, Mrs. O'Sullivan?" Since she'd turned down the offer of tea, he got right to the point.

The woman took a deep breath, then lowered her voice. "I am a bit concerned about Mr. Finch."

William slid at glance in Amy's direction. They both leaned forward. "Oh, why is that?"

"I believe I've already spoken to her ladyship about the temporary maid I assigned to his room. She tells me he won't allow her in the room to clean or change the linens. But now it appears he is not eating either."

"Why do you think that?" Amy asked.

"Because his instructions were to leave his tray outside his room and give a slight tap on the door, and he would retrieve it and place it back outside when he was finished."

William gave a curt nod for her to continue.

"Yesterday's lunch and dinner were all brought back by his footman to the kitchen. He hadn't eaten either of the meals. This morning I checked, and his breakfast tray still sits in front of his door."

Amy and William both hopped up as if shot from a cannon. "Thank you, Mrs. O'Sullivan, we will take care of it. You may resume your duties."

It was practically a race up the stairs to the bedchamber level. "Are you thinking what I'm thinking?" William said.

"That he climbed out the window?" Amy answered.

"Yes."

"I would not be surprised. Having a murder charge hanging over one's head could make one do dangerous things. There is at least a thirty-foot drop from that window." Amy barely got the words out as they reached the bedchamber floor.

They hurried down the corridor and stopped in front of Albert's door. As Mrs. O'Sullivan reported, the breakfast tray sat on the floor, untouched.

William nodded to the footman assigned to Albert, who lounged against the wall across from Albert's room. "Have you seen Mr. Finch today? Or yesterday?"

"Only when he left his room early yesterday morning to use the water closet." He shrugged. "Not since then, but that's not unusual."

"And you've been bringing his meals up here and returning the full trays back again?"

"Yes, my lord. Except his breakfast yesterday. He never placed the empty tray outside. I assumed the maid would pick it up when she cleans later this morning."

"I think we should give him the benefit of the doubt before we barge our way inside," William said, returning his attention to Amy. "Perhaps he is ill, and we need to summon a physician."

He gave a sharp knock on the door. "Albert? Will you open the door, please?"

No response.

"Albert, are you ill?" William turned to Amy. "He could have caught a disease in Shepton Mallet."

Amy shivered. "Yes. I hope if he did, it's not contagious. We'll have to air out that room quite well."

Just then Persephone joined them, pawing at the door, barking and whining.

Amy scooped the dog into her arms and then knocked. "Albert, it's Amy. Can you at least tell us if you are ill?"

Nothing.

William sighed and ran his fingers through his hair. "I'll have to see Mrs. O'Sullivan and get the key to the room." He looked at Persephone, who was still wiggling and barking in Amy's arms. "You have your hands full with that one." He then smiled at her over his shoulder as he left to find the house-keeper. "No pun intended."

It didn't take long to find Mrs. O'Sullivan in her small office next to the kitchen. She was taken up with food cost ledgers and looked up when he entered the room. "How may I help you, my lord?"

"I'll need the key to Albert's room. You were right—there is something amiss. We knocked a few times, but he is not responding. I'm just hoping he hasn't done something as foolish as climbing out the window."

Mrs. O'Sullivan pressed her hand to her chest. "Oh my lord, I do hope he hasn't done anything like that. The man could kill himself."

Shaking her head, she took the ring of keys attached to her dress and removed one key, holding it out to him. He was amazed with all the keys on the ring that she knew which one to give him.

"Yes, 'tis true. Or he could have contracted an illness from the gaol. In any event, we do need to check on him."

"Of course. Do let me know if you need my assistance."

William made his way upstairs to the sound of Persephone barking and whining. "Can't you put her somewhere so we can have quiet? Perhaps Albert hasn't answered because he can't hear us above the din."

For the first time William had ever noticed, Amy looked annoyed at her precious dog. "Of course. Let me put her in our bedchamber. It's far enough away that she won't be such a disturbance."

William nodded as Amy scurried down the corridor. He knocked on the door once more. "Albert, will you please open the door?"

Amy was back in a flash, obviously not wishing to miss anything. Her spirit of adventure, even when it involved gruesome things, was one of many reasons why he loved this new wife of his. Theirs would never be a normal life, one that he had always assumed would be his when he married.

Thank goodness for that.

He inserted the key into the lock and unlatched the door. The room was dim, the window drapes drawn. William whispered. "Perhaps he is still sleeping, and we have invaded his privacy for no reason."

Amy shook her head. "I don't believe so." She took a deep breath. "Do you smell that?"

He sniffed. "Yes. Something odd."

Amy took his hand. "William, I have a bad feeling about this. I think for the first time in my life I'm a teeny bit frightened."

He had picked up on her mood and had his own feeling of unease. Without either of them saying it outright, he began to consider that their cousin was no longer with them. Hands clasped together, they moved toward the bed and William yanked back the bed hangings.

Amy gasped and he had to swallow a few times. Mr. Albert E. Finch lay in the bed, on his side, facing them. He appeared to be peacefully sleeping.

Except he was not.

He was dead.

Amy turned to William and grabbed his shoulder right before her legs crumpled.

CHAPTER 23

When Amy opened her eyes, she was lying on the settee in the front parlor. Confused at first, she attempted to sit up when William gently touched her cheek. "Don't try to get up too soon. Just lie there for a minute."

She frowned. "What happened? I never faint."

William grinned. "Yes, I know."

Amy gasped and, despite his advice, sat up, then held her head as the dizziness threatened to overcome her.

"Whoa, careful there, sweetheart." William wrapped his arm around her shoulders.

She blinked a few times and looked up at her husband. "Am I correct? Albert is dead?"

"Yes." He handed her a glass of water. "Here—drink this."

"Why does everyone give you a glass of water when you faint?" She smirked at him, then frowned. "Not that I faint."

"Probably because no one knows what else to do. But drink it anyway."

She took the glass from his hand and gulped the water down, admitting—at least to herself—that it had restored her. "What do we do now?"

"I think you know the answer to that. I've already notified the police."

"Should we go back upstairs and take a look around before they come?"

William studied her. "Do you feel up to it?"

She swung her legs around and stood. "Yes. I feel fine. You know they will seal the room off when they get here. Surely you find it quite strange that now both husband and wife have been murdered."

"Just a minute before you jump to that conclusion. We have no evidence that Albert was murdered. As I said before, he could have contacted an illness at the gaol that killed him. We have to wait for the coroner to make known his findings."

"I agree, you are correct." She raised her eyebrows. "Don't get too used to hearing those words, husband dear. However, in case he was murdered, we need to look in that room before the police get here. That might also answer the question we've had for a few days: Why wouldn't he allow anyone into the room?"

He nodded and took her by the hand, and they made their way upstairs. Amy hesitated a bit before they entered and then chastised herself. She'd been through this before—sadly—and had handled it quite well. This was not the time to become squeamish.

It only took about ten minutes to examine the room. Albert had arrived with only his satchel, which they went through now. Besides an empty whiskey bottle, clothing, and grooming products, there was nothing important inside. His last breakfast tray sat, partially empty, on the table next to his bed.

Amy held up the whiskey bottle. "I wonder how he got this, coming directly from Shepton Mallet." She stood in the center of the room and turned in a circle, her eyes searching everywhere. "Why would he refuse entry to the room? There isn't anything out of the ordinary here."

A knocker sounded at the front door. William strode to the bedchamber doorway and waved at her. "We better close this up and wait downstairs. I am sure that's the police."

They settled in the drawing room after Amy had requested tea be sent in. "I know we just had breakfast, but tea will calm my nerves," she said once she returned to William's side after speaking with the footman.

"The police have arrived," Filbert's announcement drew their attention to the doorway. The butler stepped aside, and in walked Detectives Marsh and Carson.

Carson studied the two of them with a speculative look. "Another dead body?"

Amy was not at all surprised to see their nemeses. She had reconciled herself to the fact that, despite the growing population in Bath, the police department employed only two detectives who handled suspicious deaths. Either that or she and William were the unluckiest people in the kingdom.

"Good morning, Detectives." She looked them square in the eye, refusing to be intimidated, even though Albert's demise was the fourth time she and William had been involved in a murder.

However, she consoled herself with the thought William had offered: that murder, while not being ruled out, was not necessarily the cause of Albert's death. Since the man was already dead, she felt no compunction in asking the good Lord to have it be from an illness.

Detective Carson inhaled deeply and took a seat across from William and Amy. Detective Marsh opened his notebook and began flipping pages. Did the man have a special notebook only for them? If he did, it would be full by now. She had to stifle a giggle at that thought.

Detective Carson got right down to business. "What happened this time?"

Amy felt William stiffen at her side, but he responded cordially. "'Tis quite simple, really. As you are well aware, Lady Wethington and I were designated as Mr. Finch's keepers. He has been here since Monday, when you left him. Aside from greeting him upon his arrival and seeing him settled, we had not laid eyes on the man since."

Carson narrowed his eyes. "I don't understand. He is living in this house. Why haven't you seen him?"

Amy jumped in. "He never left his room except for trips to the water closet and bathing room. A maid cleaned his room while he was busy taking care of his needs. Meal trays were brought to his room by his footman and left outside his door, then picked up when they were emptied."

"Was that his idea or yours?"

"His," they both said.

Carson thought for a moment. "Tell me how you came to discover his body. This morning I assume?"

"Yes," Amy said. "Our housekeeper brought to our attention at breakfast that Mr. Finch had not eaten his lunch or dinner from yesterday, nor his breakfast this morning. Concerned that he might be ill"—there didn't seem to be any reason to let the detectives know that they had suspected he had climbed out the window—"we went to his room to check on him."

William took up the story. "We ascertained that the footman he'd been assigned hadn't seen Mr. Finch since yesterday morning. When we knocked, he did not answer, despite numerous requests from us to open the door. Finally, I secured the key to the room from my housekeeper, and Lady Wethington and I entered the room and found the body."

"You are sure he is dead?"

Amy nodded. "There was an odor."

"Ah," Carson said. He slapped his thighs and stood. "Let's take a trip to Mr. Finch's room."

The four of them trooped upstairs, down the corridor to Albert's room. William opened the door and ushered the two detectives inside. The footman was nowhere to be seen.

"I think it's best if we wait outside," William murmured to Amy.

With the smell growing stronger, or perhaps they were just more aware of it now, Amy nodded. "I agree. In fact, downstairs in the front parlor or drawing room would be best."

"Detectives, my wife and I will be downstairs. I will send a footman up to direct you when you are finished."

Instead of answering, Carson merely waved at them.

Just as they reached the entrance hall, the knocker sounded again. Filbert opened the door and a man stepped through. It unnerved Amy that she recognized the man as the coroner. He nodded at them. "My lord, my lady, good day to you."

"Mr. Terrill," Amy said as William nodded in the man's direction.

"You are well, I hope?" Mr. Terrill asked. The man's demeanor was quite suited to his line of work. He was of undetermined years, small, thin, and partially bald. He wore wire-rimmed spectacles and looked as pale as the cadavers he worked with.

"As well as can be expected," William returned. "Filbert, will you please escort Mr. Terrill upstairs, where the detectives are examining Mr. Finch's room."

They watched the two men ascend the stairs. Amy and William returned to the drawing room just as a footman entered with a tea cart. As she fixed tea for them, she pondered on the fact that her life had become so bizarre that she knew the name of the Bath coroner and they had exchanged pleasantries as if they were meeting at the Assembly.

They drank tea, Amy nibbled on a biscuit that tasted like sawdust, and William gave in and poured himself a small sherry. "Would you care for one, my dear?"

"No. 'Tis a bit early for me, even with this being, dare I say, an unusual day."

She stood and swept away the few crumbs that had landed on her dress. The tea had calmed her a bit, but she still felt restless. "Now that I have had time to process this, I find my mind is clearing, and I'm beginning to think in terms of our investigation."

William held up his palm. "Before you begin to consider this another investigation, let us make sure Albert's death was not merely due to an illness."

He had barely gotten the words out when the two detectives and the coroner entered the room on the heels of one of the footmen.

"Murder." Carson shook his head. "Another murder. I am pondering locking the two of you up for the safety of the citizens of Bath."

★ ★ ★

"Hopefully, Detective, you won't immediately jump to the conclusion that my wife or I was involved in Mr. Finch's death." William felt the need to get that out there, posthaste. The last thing they needed while still trying to salvage some sort of honeymoon was to be again suspected of a murder.

"Until someone is charged, everyone is a suspect," Detective Carson returned.

Wishing to get the interrogation over with, William waved his hand. "Can we move on with the questions?"

Carson leaned back in the chair he occupied and said, "Who resides in the house?"

Amy said, "As we mentioned to you before, my father, brother, and aunt have been residing here since right before Albert arrived. The repairs from water damage on their townhouse have not yet been completed."

Carson offered something between a laugh and a snort. Marsh scribbled.

"Detective, can you tell us the manner of death?" Amy asked.

The man assumed his usual demeanor of viewing them as if they were schoolchildren to whom he needed to patiently explain something they should already know. "We must wait for the coroner's full report, but it appears he died from the same substance that killed Mrs. Finch."

"Belladonna?" they both asked.

"Poison, at least. The exact type, what time, and how it was administered will be determined by the coroner, although we have reason to suspect the breakfast he'd been served yesterday morning was poisoned. It's our job to begin the investigation."

They continued with their questions, some making sense and some not at all. William grew restless and allowed his thoughts to wander since Amy was doing a good job of responding to the detectives' queries.

Both Alice and Albert had been poisoned. He and Amy now had to redirect their findings and thoughts. But they had been at a dead end anyway, with Albert their only solid suspect and Mrs. Davis and Jared Munson on the list as possibilities. It was possible, of course, that Albert had done away with himself rather than face a swinging rope, but William didn't feel it likely to have been suicide. It had seemed more likely that Albert would climb out the window as they had first thought, and then run for his life.

Did that mean he had killed his wife? Or was he just not confident that William and Amy could find the culprit before he paid the ultimate price for the crime?

Some questions continued to plague him. Why all the secrecy since Albert had arrived at the house? Why break up with Madeline and then refuse to even speak with her? If he had killed Alice, why use something that was so easily traceable to him?

And most of all, who disliked Alice and Albert enough to kill them both?

Amy nudged him in the side. "My lord?"

So deep in thought he was that he actually jumped. "What?"

"The detective asked you a question." She gestured toward Detective Carson, who viewed him with raised brows.

"I apologize, Detective—can you please repeat your question?"

"I asked, my lord, if your housekeeper has a list of the temporary staff members you have employed?"

They had apparently been discussing the addition of maids and the footmen while his mind had wandered. "Yes. I'm sure she does. If you will excuse me, I will request it of her." He left the room and asked Filbert to summon Mrs. O'Sullivan.

Amy was in the middle of describing the routine the household followed regarding serving meals and cleaning bedchambers, when he returned. Within minutes, Mrs. O'Sullivan entered the room. "My lord? How may I help?"

He just then realized that word of Albert's demise had most likely not reached the staff yet. He cleared his throat. "Mrs. O'Sullivan, it seems the reason Mr. Finch was not eating his meals was because he has passed away."

Mrs. O'Sullivan's eyes grew wide, and she paled. Her hand rose to her throat, and she seemed to struggle for words. "Oh my goodness. How terrible. The poor man. Here he was, out of that horrible prison and in a much more comfortable place, and he lasts mere days." She shook her head.

William took her by the arm and led her to the settee where Amy sat. "Please have a seat, Mrs. O'Sullivan. Would you like a cup of tea?"

Her lips were as pale as her face, and she seemed to have a hard time breathing. "Yes. That would help. Thank you so much, my lord." A testimony to the woman's shock was that she remained in her seat while Amy hopped up to prepare the tea for her. Mrs. O'Sullivan would never have allowed that to happen had she been in her normal state of mind.

Since the housekeeper had not been present at Lady Granville's home when Alice collapsed into her breakfast, this was most likely the poor woman's first experience with a guest dying in a home she was in charge of.

"When you are feeling up to it, Mrs. O'Sullivan, the detectives would like a copy of the list of temporary employees that have been here these past couple of days."

She appeared to have recovered a bit, her color a lot better. "I will get that for you right off, my lord."

"Why don't you finish your tea first. I'm sure the detectives won't mind waiting for a minute."

Detective Carson glared at him, but William chose to ignore him. After a few minutes, however, Mrs. O'Sullivan returned to her office and was back in no time with the list of employees.

"This is the list of employees the agency sent—four as I requested, the three maids and the second extra footman—but Cook seemed to think there were five when they all arrived. I'm afraid in all the confusion"—she stared in horror at her employers at her remark, hoping they did not consider her words a complaint—"she miscounted."

Before the detective could take the paper, Amy reached out and removed it from Mrs. O'Sullivan's hand. She scanned the list, her eyes grew wide, and she handed the paper to the detectives.

"Considering you two have been through this before"— Carson glowered at them as if they purposely put themselves into situations where people were murdered—"you know what comes next. Once Mr. Terrill is finished with his initial examination, we will have the body removed and then seal the man's bedchamber and begin to question everyone in the house."

"At present, my father and brother are not at home. My aunt Margaret is in her bedchamber, and we don't generally see her much before noontime. And perhaps will not see her at all today since she is suffering from the effects of having her bird kidnapped."

Carson raised his eyebrows at that one. "Kidnapped?"

"Yes," Amy said. "Her bird has gone missing. I think she might have notified the police."

"Nobility. This is a hell of a house you run here." Carson shook his head, then apologized for his language.

Passing on the slight to Amy's aunt—in fact, to everyone of the aristocracy—William said, "Sir, we can provide you with the use of our drawing room and begin to send in our staff so you may question them."

'Twas best to get this moving along since he knew without a doubt Amy would be quite anxious to begin their own investigation. Truth be known, he was just as impatient since this would cause another delay to their honeymoon.

Bloody hell.

CHAPTER 24

Amy made her way downstairs to Mrs. O'Sullivan's office. The poor woman had still not recovered from hearing about Mr. Finch's death. She sat at her desk, mumbling to herself.

"Are you all right, Mrs. O'Sullivan?"

"Yes, yes, my lady. I will be fine in a trice." She placed her hand against her chest. "'Twas quite a shock."

"I agree, unexpected deaths are always disconcerting."

Mrs. O'Sullivan looked up at her. "I assume, with the detectives here and looking for names of those who were hired temporarily, that they suspect poor Mr. Finch met an unfortunate end?"

Amy nodded. "Yes, I am sorry to say that's true."

Mrs. O'Sullivan fanned herself. "So disturbing to know someone was murdered right here in our house while we were all going about our business."

Amy nodded. "I agree." Noting the poor woman's pallor, Amy sat in the chair next to her and took her hand. "I would normally never suggest such a thing, Mrs. O'Sullivan, but I feel as though you might do well with a bit of spirits."

Despite Amy expecting the woman to refuse, Mrs. O'Sullivan nodded. "I believe you are correct, my lady. If it is acceptable to you and his lordship, I shall prepare some tea for myself and add a touch of the brandy I keep on hand." She straightened and looked Amy in the eyes. "For medicinal purposes only, I assure you."

Amy hid her grin. "Yes, that is perfectly acceptable, Mrs. O'Sullivan. I have never had any reason to assume you would have brandy for any other reason. I know a housekeeper's responsibility is to look after the staff, and oftentimes a touch of spirits is just the thing to calm a young maid."

"Indeed."

"May I trouble you to begin to send the staff members, one at a time, into the drawing room? The detectives want to start their questioning, and we are all anxious to have this completed as quickly as possible."

Mrs. O'Sullivan nodded. "Yes. Does it matter in what order I send them?"

After thinking for a minute, Amy said, "Yes. If it does not disrupt the running of the household, can you send in the temporary staff members first? I do not wish to appear to be casting aspersions on them, but since they are unknown to us, it might be better to have them speak with the detectives first."

Mrs. O'Sullivan stood, then seemed to sway for a moment.

Amy grabbed her elbow and looked at her with concern. "Are you sure you do not need a lie-down for a bit, Mrs. O'Sullivan?"

The housekeeper drew herself up and patted the sides of her hair. "Not at all. I shall send one of the temporary maids in and then make myself tea with a bit of brandy, and all will be fine."

Still a bit concerned about the older woman, but knowing she would not be gainsaid, Amy left her to begin the somber process of alerting the staff of Albert's death and informing each member of the household that he or she would be questioned by the detectives.

Upon her return, she found William and the detectives still in the drawing room, Detective Marsh continuing to scribble in his notepad and Detective Carson staring out the window, his hands behind his back.

William stood as she entered, and Detective Carson turned toward her.

"Mrs. O'Sullivan will begin to send in the employees. She will direct the temporary staff members in first."

"Good," Detective Carson said. "Furthermore, it will not be necessary for the two of you to be here while we question the suspects."

Amy sucked in a breath. "I beg your pardon, Detective, but these employees are certainly not suspects. They are hardworking people who will be treated with respect by you, or I will refuse you access to them and take the matter up with your superiors."

Carson waved his arm around, unconcerned with her tirade. "There is no reason to get into a tizzy, Lady Wethington. I've told you and your husband before that until a murder is solved *everyone* is a suspect."

Amy smirked. "Including yourself, Detective?"

William leaned in close. "Don't antagonize him, love. He can make things uncomfortable for us, as you well know."

Taking in a deep breath, Amy gave him a curt nod. William took her by the elbow and escorted her from the room. "If you have need of us, Detective, you may ask one of the footmen to summon us," he said over his shoulder. "I suggest we retire to the library, where we can discuss this further," he said to her.

Amy rubbed her palms up and down her arms and walked in circles around the room. There was a distinct chill in the air. Or perhaps it was simply her as it had not been a pleasant morning by any means.

William moved to the sideboard and poured two sherries. He returned and handed her one.

"I must say, my lord, if dead bodies keep popping up, you and I will soon develop an unwelcome dependence on spirits. I have barely digested my breakfast."

"If dead bodies keep popping up, my dear, we will soon have to provide a bedchamber for the two detectives in the other room. I believe we have seen more of them in the past year and a half than we have some of my closest friends."

Amy shuddered. "Please don't say that. I really prefer to write stories about pretend murders than spend my time solving real ones."

William took a sip of his sherry and turned to her. "I noticed you were a bit taken aback by the list Mrs. O'Sullivan provided."

"Yes, I was, in fact." She paused, then added, "One of the maids who has been assigned here is Mrs. Caroline Beaver. In case you don't remember, she is the maid who worked at Aunt Priscilla's house during our wedding breakfast."

William's brows rose. "Oh yes. She hadn't picked up her pay. But I believe it turned out that she had been caring for a sick child. How very interesting that she is here now."

"I am quite sure it is only a coincidence, but it did strike me as notable." More than odd if truth be told. Were she writing this as a murder mystery, she would certainly have something sinister in the maid's background. But this was real life, not fiction.

"I agree. However, if she had nothing to do with either death, and I have no reason to believe she did, it certainly must rattle the poor woman. I am sure she will never work for us again."

★   ★   ★

The detectives occupied the drawing room for the rest of the day and would have continued into the night had William not firmly evicted them.

"I must ask you to continue your investigation tomorrow, Detectives." William entered the drawing room, dressed for dinner and not too pleased that the men were still there.

Trays of empty plates and cups were stacked on a low table. Apparently Mrs. O'Sullivan did not permit men to starve in her house.

Detective Carson stood. "We are finished here for now, my lord." He took Detective Marsh's notepad from him, and the man almost looked as if he'd lost his best friend. Flipping through the pages, Carson said, "The only members of the household we have not spoken with are your brother-in-law, the Earl of Davenport, and your father-in-law, the Marquess of Winchester." He looked up with a slight smirk. "I believe I got their titles right—I know that is important to peers of the realm."

Before William could respond, the detective continued, "Do you know their whereabouts?"

"I do not. They do not apprise me each day of what their plans are. I know they are in the process of setting up a business here in Bath, as well as procuring an office building for their use. It keeps them quite busy."

William was anxious to bring the day to an end. Albert's body had been removed hours before, and the detectives had been busy searching the room once again and speaking with the staff members.

He and Amy had considered conducting their own question-and-answer session, but not with the detectives in the house. William had no faith in these men coming up with the killer. Especially now that the suspect they had been so focused on for the first murder was now dead. And by the same means.

Had it been suicide? Had Albert's grief over his wife's death driven the man to end his own life?

'Twas doubtful. If he had been conducting an affair with other women for most, if not all, of his marriage, it did not seem likely his grief would move him to do such a thing.

"Very well," Detective Carson said, "we would appreciate it if you would send word when the two men become available. Again, I reiterate that the bedchamber upstairs is to remain untouched."

"I do not appreciate that, Detective. You have done a thorough search of the room, and my housekeeper is quite anxious—as you can well imagine—to strip the linens and air out the room."

Carson thought for a minute. "Very well. I do believe we have seen enough, and despite your opinion of us, we do understand the necessity to clean out the room."

"Our opinion of you?" William asked.

"Lord Wethington, we are fully aware that Detective Marsh and I are not on your and your lovely wife's list of favorite people. Police do not strive to be on *anyone's* favored list. We have a job to do, and most times it annoys people to have to deal with us. Especially those of your status. But murders must be solved, regardless of where they occur."

William was successful, after a bit of chastising himself, in not pointing out that it was he and Amy who had uncovered the true murderers the last two times the detectives had dealt with homicides. Mentioning that could very well encourage the men to make things difficult for them. William wanted them out of his house and some semblance of normalcy returned to his life.

Although that didn't seem likely with a new dead body showing up here.

He escorted the men out the door—more so to be sure they left—and returned to the front parlor, where the family was gathering, awaiting the call to dinner.

"Are they gone?" Amy asked as he handed her a glass of sherry.

"Yes. I only wish we didn't have to see them again."

Lady Margaret took the other glass of sherry from William. "This is becoming a bit trite, my dears. One can't help but wonder if it is safe to be around the two of you."

"Please don't joke, Auntie." Amy took a seat near the fireplace. "I still can't seem to warm up."

"The sherry will help," William said as he joined her on the settee.

"The two of you seem to be quite adept at solving these mysteries," Lady Margaret said, "Have you done anything to uncover Othello's kidnapping?"

"We must wait to hear from whoever took him. If it is truly a kidnapping—and I can't imagine why anyone would take him otherwise—we should receive a note of some sort," William said.

Lady Margaret gasped. "That was not well said, my lord."

He bowed his apology. "Frankly, we haven't had much time to dwell on it or Alice's murder. I had to spend time with my man of business for several hours today, and I believe Amy had to assist Mrs. O'Sullivan with hunting down the employees and sending them to the detectives."

"Poor Mrs. O'Sullivan is quite distressed," Amy added.

Lady Margaret took a sip of her sherry. "No doubt because she doesn't have your history of stumbling over dead bodies all the time."

Amy sniffed. "That is an exaggeration."

The only answer Lady Margaret gave her niece was a pair of raised eyebrows.

Like a whirlwind, Amy's brother and father entered the room, their cheeks still red from the outside cold. Franklin rubbed his hands together and headed for the brandy bottle. "We just saw the detectives and the coroner leaving as our carriage pulled up."

He poured two brandies and handed one to Michael. He took a sip and focused his attention on his daughter. "Truthfully, I am quite relieved to see the three of you, hale and hardy. But tell me, my dear. Who was murdered this time?"

CHAPTER 25

"I don't know why you would assume there was a murder," Amy replied to her papa's statement. Then she took in a deep breath, slumped in her chair, and mumbled into her drink, "Albert. We found him earlier today in his bed."

"Not merely dozing, I assume?" Leaning against the fireplace mantle, Michael swirled the liquid in his snifter.

"Poisoned," William added. "Our favorite detectives are thinking the same drug that killed Alice."

"What the devil is going on?" His face flushed as waved his glass around, drops of brandy splashing on the carpet, Papa shouted, "A married couple! Murdered. Right under our noses!"

"And my bird kidnapped," Lady Margaret added with a curt nod.

Papa threw his sister an exasperated look. "I don't like this, not one bit. I am going to contact these detectives tomorrow and tell them we are all retiring to my estate in the country, where it is safe."

Amy glanced over at William and gave a slight shake of her head. William cleared this throat. "Franklin, I don't believe the detectives will permit us to leave Bath. The man died of poisoning in our house while under our protection."

"Nonsense. I don't care what those two bumbling idiots want. While they are fumbling around, more people are dying. I will demand they allow us to leave. They cannot deny a peer." He walked over to the sideboard and poured another brandy.

Amy regarded William with bemusement. The last thing that would impress the detectives was hearing that their family must be treated differently because they were members of the nobility.

Aunt Margaret shook her head. "No, Franklin. I am not leaving until Othello is returned to me."

There was a distinct growl from Papa's direction.

"Um, I don't care to leave Bath right now myself either," Michael said, which Amy took particular notice of.

Her father snorted. "Then I guess we will all remain here until we are one by one murdered in our beds."

Filbert entered the drawing room then, his eyes wide at all the shouting. "Dinner is served, my lord, my ladies."

They all moved into the dining room, Franklin still bloviating about what he considered a serious situation that no one else would admit.

"We know it's a serious situation, Papa, but I don't think we are in any danger." Amy sat as William held her chair for her. She shook out her napkin and placed it on her lap.

"Certainly my bird was in danger," Aunt Margaret said between sips of wine.

"Forget the bloody bird, Margaret," Franklin growled.

"How dare you!" Aunt Margaret jumped up from her seat, knocking her wine glass into Amy's lap. "I loved that bird—I mean *love, love, love* that bird." She grabbed her napkin and patted the corners of her eyes.

Amy bolted from her seat, the wine running down the front of her gown. William stood and pulled her chair out so she could move back.

Michael grinned at the lot of them. "I suggest everyone settle down. We are all a bit overwrought, but there is no need to swear or toss wine at each other."

"I need to change my gown." Amy headed for the door, holding the wet fabric away from her legs. She considered asking for a tray in her room.

"I will help," William added and followed her out.

"William!" she said as they left the room. "Whatever will they think? I have a lady's maid, you know."

"Yes. I know. However, I feel the need for a tray in our room right now."

She smiled to herself. "Good idea. I wish I had thought of it."

Once they had changed into their night clothes and two trays of baked salmon, new potatoes, roast pork, turnips, warm bread, and truffle for dessert had arrived, they sat in comfortable chairs in front of the fireplace, relaxed and happy, with a bottle of wine to share. And far away from the rumbling crowd in the dining room.

"This looks wonderful. I hadn't realized how hungry I was until I smelled this," Amy said as she forked the flaky fish into her mouth.

"While everyone is downstairs sniping at each other, I suggest we take time after eating to examine Albert's room once again. I don't trust that the detectives did a thorough job."

"That is an excellent idea, my lord."

★ ★ ★

The room smelled better since the last time they'd been there. Mrs. O'Sullivan had sent two maids in to clean the room and air it out. The bed coverings and drapes had been stripped. In all, the room seemed eerie, as if it held secrets that she and William needed to uncover.

They both carried lanterns but still lit the two paraffin lamps in the room. William turned in a circle, holding his lantern up. "Since I don't give our detective friends much credit for diligence, I suggest we search every corner of the room, including the wardrobe and dressers."

They began their examination, Amy going in one direction, William in the other. It took them only about fifteen minutes to search every nook and cranny in the room. "Look at this," William said, standing next to the window.

Amy joined him and eyed where he pointed. The window casing had scratches on it. "Is this new?" she asked.

"I can't say for sure as I never examined the window casings in my house before now. But it could fit into our original theory that Albert was coming and going via the window, which was why he didn't allow anyone in here to notice his absence."

"I can see him leaving by the window, but how would he get back inside? And furthermore, if he was out and about, *why* would he come back? I would think he'd want to escape."

William continued to study the window casing, and then opened the window to look outside. He motioned to Amy, "Look here."

He pointed to the ground. In the dim light from the moon, they viewed the ground, where lovely flowers used to grow in a small bed against the building. The flowers were still there, but crushed beyond recognition. Sitting next to it, leaning against the house, was a ladder. "I guess that clears up that question."

The night air being a bit chilly, William closed the window. Amy moved to the center of the room, rubbing her hands up and down her arms. An idea occurred to her, and she waved William over. "Help me pick up the mattress."

With the two of them working together, they picked it up and threw it to the side.

"Oh. My. Goodness." Amy's hand covered her mouth as they stared at the pile.

Heaped together was a timepiece and fob that appeared to be William's, two silver candlesticks, Amy's pearl necklace—that she hadn't known was missing—and several pieces of silverware. She reached into the pile and removed three pieces of paper and handed them to William. "What are these?"

He took them from her hand and looked them over. "Pawn tickets. It appears Albert was stealing items from us and selling them to pawnbrokers."

"Well, that wasn't very nice after we offered him hospitality," she huffed. "I guess he intended to escape once he had enough money." Amy took the tickets back and looked at them, never having seen a pawn ticket before.

"Yes. But the question remains: Where is the money he got for those items?" William gestured toward the small gray papers in her hand.

★ ★ ★

The next night, trying their best to force death and murder to the back of their minds, William and Amy decided to attend the Assembly. Lady Margaret begged off, still mourning her lost bird. Michael indicated he would be at the Assembly also, and Franklin sulked and waved them off, settling in the drawing room with a large brandy and a book that he was apparently enjoying while reading it upside down.

Earlier in the day, William and Amy had made the trip back to the hotel where Mrs. Davis had been staying. The same majordomo greeted them, bowing and scraping as if they were entering the Queen's palace.

"She's not here." The man at the desk, whom they'd also encountered before, spoke before William could even open his mouth.

"Mrs. Davis?" Amy asked.

"Is that not the woman you came to see before? The one who you said was a family member? And who later chastised me for letting you up to her room since you are not a family member? That one? Yes. She is not here."

William leaned his elbow on the counter, attempting a friendly demeanor. "Did she leave the area, do you know?"

"The last time I saw her, she was being carried out on a stretcher."

"What?" Amy gasped.

"She took ill. A maid found her moaning in her bed, and we sent for a physician. He arranged for her to go to hospital." He pulled out a newspaper from under the counter and began to flip the pages. "I wish you both a good day."

"When was this?" William refused to leave with no further information. Not with Albert only dead a day and Mrs. Davis on their list of suspects for Alice's death. This was becoming grim.

"Yesterday." The man shook his newspaper. "Again, I wish you a good day."

They were not going to get any more information from the man, and since William preferred not to be subjected to the

ignominious consequence of being thrown out of the establish-
ment, he took Amy's elbow and escorted her from the hotel.
He looked at his newly recovered timepiece and said, "We
don't have time now, but I suggest tomorrow we visit the hospital and see if we can get more information."

"If she is still alive, that is," Amy said and shivered.

Now, as they entered the Assembly, looking for their group
of friends, William could almost pretend this was any other
Saturday night. But then, since childhood, he'd always had a
wonderful imagination.

"William, how lovely to see you. Is all well?" His mother
glided over and offered a kiss on his cheek.

"I am well, Mother." He nodded at Mr. Colbert, not more
than twelve inches from his wife. For goodness sake, couldn't
the man keep a decent amount of space between them? Did he
expect her to disappear?

Mr. Colbert stuck out his hand. "Good evening, William.
A pleasure to see you."

Mr. Colbert was an extremely nice man, and William was a
little bit ashamed of himself for his feelings, and probably actions,
toward the man ever since he'd shown an interest in William's
mother. Resolving right then and there to change, he stuck his
hand out too. "A pleasure to see you as well, Mr. Colbert."

The man slapped him on the back. "Ah, I think it's time we
ended the formality. I ask that you call me Charles."

When he hesitated, Amy gave him an elbow to his middle.
He winced. "Very well. Charles." He glowered at his wife and
rubbed his side.

"I wonder if my papa is aware of Michael's attraction to
Eloise." Amy nodded toward the dance area, where Michael
and Eloise were in the middle of a waltz.

"I must say I find that attachment to be quite . . . interesting."

"Why? Eloise is a nice woman. We've been friends forever."

"I know. It's just that she is a bit flighty, and while I can't say I know your brother very well, he always seemed to be quite a serious sort of man."

"Frankly, since we've lived apart most of my life, I don't know Michael that well myself either. He might not be so serious."

"Opposites attract," his mother said.

"Yes, but if the attraction becomes permanent, they need to live together," William replied.

Mother latched onto her husband's arm, turning them from the doorway. "What do you say we join the book club group? I believe they are still debating the ending of *The Mystery of Edwin Drood*."

William leaned close to Amy as they made their way across the floor. "Right now I am more concerned about the ending of the mystery of Albert Finch."

"And Mrs. Alice Finch and Mrs. Madeline Davis."

"Indeed. The list grows." He shook his head. "And the honeymoon moves further away."

Chapter 26

No matter how chaotic or stressful the week was, Amy always drew a great deal of peace and strength from church every Sunday morning. Generally, it was just her and William, and most times Aunt Margaret and Eloise. Today, with all the house guests and unusual attachments—Michael and Eloise came to mind—the family pew was overflowing.

Even though she, Papa, Michael, Eloise, William, and Aunt Margaret barely had enough room to open their hymnals, Annabelle arrived and squeezed into the pew alongside Eloise.

Amy was surprised since her cousin's family had their own pew, and Annabelle had said she was going to be visiting a friend in London. Perhaps that hadn't lasted too long. The poor woman still looked dreadful. She had obviously lost weight, and from the dark circles under her eyes, it was apparent she wasn't sleeping well either. Amy prayed that her cousin would find some peace.

Mr. Palmer, the vicar for St. Swithin's Church gave his usual uplifting sermon. The singing, as always, was a bit off-key, because the elderly, half-blind Mrs. Edith Newton played the organ.

Amy took a deep breath as they exited the church, smiling and trading greetings with the Misses O'Neill, Pastor Palmer, and other church members whom she saw on a regular basis.

"I thought you and Lord Wethington were on your honeymoon?" Mrs. Frances Coxcomb greeted Amy as she stepped away from the vicar.

Although it hadn't seemed possible, perhaps the woman had not heard of the murder at their wedding breakfast. "We were unable to leave town just yet."

The woman's face turned bright red, obviously acknowledging that she had heard about the murder. "Oh, Lady Wethington, I am so sorry." She used her gloved hand to fan her face. "I forgot about the horrible occurrence at your wedding breakfast."

Amy patted the disturbed woman's arm. "'Tis all right, Mrs. Coxcomb. Hopefully, it will all be cleared up soon, and we will be able to travel to Brighton Beach."

"Yes, I do hope so." Apparently eager to be away from the matter, she waved at someone over Amy's shoulder. "If you will excuse me."

"Are you ready?" William asked as he walked up to her. "I have invited my parents to join us for luncheon, along with everyone else."

"Eloise?"

"Of course. Doesn't she usually join us?"

"Yes, but now I wonder if it's for our company or my brother's." She gestured toward Michael and Eloise, chatting away and laughing. Luckily, Papa was involved in a conversation with Mr. Elroy and didn't notice his son flirting with the woman.

Amy had no doubt that when Papa came to realize what was going on, it would not go well for Michael. She looked around at those who were drifting toward their carriages. "I wonder where Annabelle went. I had thought to invite her for luncheon also."

William took her elbow. "I saw her walk away from the church several minutes ago."

"She is in such a state, the poor woman."

The group divided into two carriages, the one Papa had rented while he and Michael were staying in Bath, and William's. Amy, William, and Aunt Margaret climbed into William's carriage, and Papa, Michael, and Eloise into the rented one. If Papa saw anything unusual in Eloise joining them instead of her and William, he didn't show it.

Back at the house, they gathered in the drawing room, with small glasses of sherry all around.

"I think a visit to hospital to see Mrs. Davis is a good way to spend the afternoon," William said.

"Yes, and I also believe we should see when Mrs. Beavers is working again and have a talk with her. I know coincidences happen, but my mystery writer brain says to be skeptical of them. Readers don't like them, you know."

She placed her almost full glass of sherry on the table. 'Twas just too early for her. "I thought of another thing. I wonder who claimed Albert's body? We haven't heard anything about him since he was carried out two days ago."

William's brows rose. "Very true, my dear. In fact, I assume funeral arrangements need to be made as well. Annabelle took care of her sister, but I doubt very much if she is feeling kindly enough toward Albert to arrange anything for him."

"Hardly."

Luncheon was announced, and the group moved into the dining room. Hopefully this meal would be a tad calmer than the last. Eloise sat as Michael held out her chair. It was the first time Papa seemed to notice their interaction. He frowned at Michael, who ignored him.

Oh please. Let us not have another row at the table. Attempting to avoid that, Amy said, "I understand Cook has prepared a lovely cod fish soup for luncheon, as well as beef with roasted potatoes."

No one commented.

They all took their seats, with Papa throwing questioning glances at Michael, who was busy chatting again with Eloise, totally oblivious of his father's notice.

"Papa, how is your business deal coming along?" Amy nodded her thanks at the footman who poured wine into her glass.

"Very well, daughter, very well." He began to eat his soup, and Amy relaxed, hoping the delightful luncheon would keep her father happy and not so concerned with Michael.

Amy leaned close to William and lowered her voice. "You know if no one has claimed Albert, we must do it. We cannot leave him lying in the morgue or relegated to a pauper's grave."

"Yes." He nodded. "Do you know if anyone is familiar with his family?"

"I have no idea." Amy looked over at Aunt Margaret sitting across from her. "Aunt Margaret, do you know anything about Albert? I mean, aside from the fact that he was married to Alice?"

Her aunt shook her head. "Not really. Alice never talked much about him. I just know they met at the Assembly—here in Bath, I believe." She paused for a moment. "I wonder if Annabelle knows his family?"

"I don't think we will get much help from her."

"Daughter, I don't believe nattering on about the recently deceased is proper conversation at the dining table."

"Yes, Papa." She lowered her eyes and continued her meal. It rankled that she was a grown, married woman and her papa could still make her feel like a girl of ten years.

★   ★   ★

After visiting the morgue to learn that Albert's body was still unclaimed and then arranging with an undertaker for a quick funeral, they decided to visit the hospital, hoping that Mrs. Davis was still there—or even alive, since they had no idea why she had ended up being taken out of the hotel on a stretcher. William offered a quick prayer that Mrs. Davis had not succumbed to poisoning as well.

A nurse greeted them as they entered the Royal United Hospital, looking quite efficient in her dress. "May I help you, my lord?"

"We are here to see a Mrs. Madeline Davis, who, I believe, was brought here from the Francis Hotel in Queen Square. It would have been within the past few days."

"And you are?"

"I apologize. I am Lord Wethington, and this is my wife, Lady Wethington. My wife is related to a close friend of Mrs. Davis."

No need to mention the close friend was dead and they suspected Mrs. Davis might have something to do with that as well as his wife's death. He smiled at her, offering his best, charming grin.

He held his breath, waiting for the "I'm sorry, she has passed" statement. However, the nurse said, "If you will wait over there." She waved to a grouping of chairs along the wall, "I will check for you."

The chairs were wooden and worn. William imagined numerous people sitting in them over the years, blotting tears from their eyes at bad news or wringing their hands in anxiety.

They waited about ten minutes for the nurse to return. "Mrs. Davis is about to leave. You've caught her just in time. I will show you to her bed where she is dressed and ready to go."

William nodded, and he and Amy followed the nurse to a large room with about twenty beds lined up on both sides. Some of the patients looked as though they would only leave the place to be delivered to the undertaker, others were sitting up, eating from trays. One woman's leg was contained in some sort of a contraption that held it up in the air.

They spotted Mrs. Davis as she sat on a well-made bed, a small satchel on her lap. She looked up as they approached, and she drew in a deep breath.

"I understand you are about to leave hospital?" Amy said.

"Yes."

William glanced at Amy, then back at the woman. "May we speak with you for a few minutes?" When it appeared Mrs. Davis was about to refuse, he added, "We will be happy to escort you to a restaurant for tea or a meal and then put you on a train or whatever means of transportation you would like to return home."

Her shoulders slumped and she nodded. "Yes. That would be very kind of you. I find myself a bit short on funds. It took the last of my money to pay my hospital bill, so I was not provided lunch."

The three of them left the building and climbed into William's carriage. He instructed the driver to proceed to Sally Lunn's Restaurant.

Silence reigned in the carriage as they made their way through Bath traffic. Mrs. Davis tapped her finger on her satchel as she looked out the window the entire ride.

William had decided it would be much better to wait until the woman ate before they began their interrogation. Luckily, the restaurant was not too crowded, and they were seated immediately.

"Please, Mrs. Davis, order what you want," William said as he saw her checking over the prices of the items on the menu. She smiled and closed the menu. "I am not very hungry. A bowl of soup will do."

When the waiter arrived, William ordered the soup for Mrs. Davis, along with a roast beef sandwich, tea for all of them, and a tray of biscuits and tarts.

"I am unable to pay for more than soup, my lord."

William waved his hand. "I am a gentleman, Mrs. Davis. A gentleman does not invite a woman to dine with him in a restaurant and expect her to pay. 'Tis just not done."

He had no idea what Mrs. Davis's involvement with Albert's death might be, but he found it hard to imagine this poor woman killing Alice and then Albert. In fact, from what the man in the hotel had told them, it was quite possible that Mrs. Davis had been in hospital when Albert drank or ate the poison.

Once they had finished their food, with he and Amy merely taking tea and a biscuit since they'd only recently finished lunch, William wiped his mouth on his napkin and placed it alongside his plate. "Mrs. Davis, I would like to ask you a few questions about Mr. Finch."

She frowned and practically snarled. "That man is the devil's own spawn. If he hangs for Mrs. Finch's murder, it is what he deserves."

It occurred to him that Mrs. Davis was unaware that Albert was dead. Or she was a fine actress. He cleared his throat. "Mr. Finch is dead."

Her eyes widened and she paused for a moment. "When?"

"Friday, last. Lady Wethington and I found him in his bed, he had been poisoned."

Mrs. Davis blew out a lungful of air and slumped against the back of her seat. "How terrible."

He gave her a moment to recover, then pressed on. "I assume you attended our wedding breakfast to speak with Albert?"

Mrs. Davis nodded. "I apologize for that. I did not mean to disrupt your wedding and was quite nervous about doing it, but he refused to speak with me, and it was imperative that I relay some information to him." She offered a sad smile. "Not that it matters. Not anymore."

He had begun to think that perhaps Mrs. Davis had attempted to kill herself and that was why she was in hospital. "Mrs. Davis, my wife and I are attempting to unravel the murder of Mrs. Finch as well as that of Mr. Finch. I am hoping you might help us in our investigation by answering a few questions."

She limply waved her hand around. "Go ahead. As I said, it doesn't matter anymore."

Amy learned forward, perhaps thinking she might get more from her as a woman. "Why were you in hospital, Mrs. Davis?"

She hesitated, drawing circles on the tablecloth with her fingernail. Just when William thought she was not going to answer, she said softly, "I suffered a miscarriage."

Amy reached over and took her hand. "Albert's child?"

"Yes." She wiped away the lone tear that slid down her cheek and took a deep shuddering breath.

CHAPTER 27

Hers was a sad tale, albeit not a rare one. Mrs. Davis said she'd met Albert when he came into the shop where she worked.

"I didn't know he was married at first. I am a vicar's daughter and should have stopped his attentions once I learned this, but he told me his wife didn't understand him and they were going to get a divorce, even though that was difficult and scandalous. Then we would be together."

Amy was able to control the roll of her eyes—but just barely.

"He was so handsome and friendly. He gave me the attention I'd never had before." She shook her head and gazed out the window alongside them. "My deceased husband, Mr. Davis, was not a nice man." Taking a deep breath, she looked back at them. "When he entered our shop that first day, Albert said he was buying handkerchiefs for his mother and wanted my help in selecting the perfect ones."

Another squelched eyeroll.

"He came in a few times after that, then invited me to dinner. As a widow, I had few opportunities to dine out as my wages scarcely covered my food and rent, with only a few shillings left over to save."

Not sure she could tolerate hearing anymore of this sad and infuriating tale, Amy jumped in. "How did you know he would be at our wedding?"

Mrs. Davis sighed. "He told me weeks before, when I asked him to escort me to a play I was anxious to see, but it was the same day as your wedding.

"Some time ago, I had reason to believe that I was . . . in trouble." Her bright blush told them what she meant. "I hadn't seen him in a while and I was very panicked. I did not have the means to raise a child by myself. My parents are dead, and even if they weren't, I would never have expected them to help me out since my fall from grace was my own."

"Have you no other family, then?"

"Just some distant cousins in America." She took a sip of her tea, then sniffed and patted her eyes with her napkin. Amy and William both looked in different directions, giving the poor woman time to gain control. Thankfully, the restaurant was almost empty.

"I found the announcement in the newspaper of your wedding, so I dressed in the best outfit I owned and hired a hackney to the church. Albert was not there, so I followed the guests to your house." She gestured toward William. "I simply had to speak with him."

"Just a slight correction, Mrs. Davis. That was my great-aunt's home." Amy nodded for her to continue.

"I was quite nervous when I entered, because I hadn't been invited and didn't know what to expect, but I was desperate. Albert was very upset to find me there, but I could no longer continue without telling him about my problem."

Amy found herself patting the woman's hand, hating what Albert had done to her. Also hating that, by community standards, it was *Mrs. Davis's* problem, not Albert's, though he had certainly participated in the event that led to her circumstances.

She didn't have the heart to tell Mrs. Davis that she was one of several women he'd dallied with over the few years he'd been married to Alice. 'Twas best if she didn't know that. The poor woman was miserable enough.

Had Mrs. Davis been upset enough at her situation that she poisoned Albert's wife's champagne, believing he would marry her if Alice were dead? But then, she would have had to bring the poison with her, hoping to do away with her rival—and know that she suffered from asthma and used belladonna.

While that didn't seem likely, one thing she'd learned in her research was that life was often stranger than fiction, and people in desperate situations did strange things.

However, it would do them well to keep in contact with the woman. "What will you do now?"

"I don't know. I am sure I've lost my position because I haven't been to work for more than a week. I still owe the hotel where I stayed." She covered her eyes with her hands. "I wish they had left me to die rather than calling a physician."

Amy had had enough. She straightened in her chair. "Mrs. Davis, I am prepared to offer you a position in our household. My cook could use help in the kitchen, and you will have a room to sleep in and food to eat." She threw William an "I dare you to object" look.

"Yes, yes, of course. I agree, Mrs. Davis," William said, picking up on Amy's determination. "There is always plenty to do at our house. I will take care of your hotel bill—"

"No!" Mrs. Davis's head snapped up and she glared at him. "My papa would not be proud of me for what I've gotten myself into, but he would never allow me to accept charity."

After a pause, William nodded. "Very well, then. I will pay the bill and deduct it from your wages."

She looked at them with amazement as she wiped the tears from her cheeks with her hands. "Why would you do this? I haven't been exactly nice to you."

"That matters not, Mrs. Davis. You were obviously quite distressed and are in dire straits now, and we have the ability to help you."

Mrs. Davis shook her head and closed her eyes, two small teardrops sliding down her cheek. "God bless you both."

They went to the hotel, where William paid Mrs. Davis's bill and collected her belongings. They then traveled to her single room in her village, where she gathered the rest of her things.

If Mrs. O'Sullivan or Cook thought it odd that Amy and William returned to the house right before dinner to present them with a new employee, as well-mannered servants they did not comment.

"I had an ulterior motive in offering Mrs. Davis a position here," Amy said as they settled on chairs while waiting for the rest of the family to join them in the drawing room before dinner.

"Indeed? How so?"

"Although it might sound strange to think that Mrs. Davis traveled to our wedding carrying poison to use on Alice, the possibility remains that she knew about the woman's affliction and what medication she used. Mrs. Davis did sound as though she'd been quite desperate when she told us her story. I think she should remain on our suspect list, and I can't think of a better way to investigate her than to have her right here under our nose."

William raised his glass of sherry in a salute. "Well done, murder mystery writer."

Amy bowed her head. "Thank you. However, you are a nice man, my lord, to offer employment to her."

"'Twas your idea, wife."

"But it is your home and your staff. It was quite generous."

William bent and kissed her on the cheek. "No, my love. This is *our* house and *our* staff. And you are the nice and kind one."

"Oh for goodness sake, must we put up with this sort of conversation before dinner?" Lady Margaret groused as she entered the room.

"Good heavens, Aunt, you get grouchier by the day."

Aunt Margaret took the glass of sherry from William's hand and sighed. "I know. I can't believe how much I miss Othello."

Deciding silence was the better part of valor, Amy said nothing. Then she felt a bit uncomfortable at her unkind thoughts. Of course Aunt Margaret would miss her bird. Amy would certainly miss her little dog if she disappeared one day.

She nearly choked on her drink. "Has anyone seen Persephone today?"

★   ★   ★

William fought the smile that tempted to erupt at the thought of the annoying little dog disappearing. Seeing the look of distress on Amy's face, however, soon dimmed his joy, thinking how upsetting it would be for her. "I'm sure she's around here, Amy."

"But I haven't seen her all day."

"We have been gone almost all day."

She placed her sherry glass on a table and headed to the doorway.

"Wait," William said, catching up to her. "I will search with you."

"Do you think there is an animal kidnapper in the neighborhood?" Amy lifted her skirts and hurried up the stairs, William right behind her.

"I doubt it." What else could he say? *Yes, hopefully there is, and thank goodness they've taken the annoying bird and irritating dog. Bad form, William.*

"Persephone!" Amy began chanting the dog's name over and over as they searched the bedchamber floor.

No dog.

They checked all the rooms on that floor; then the servant's quarters floor above; the main floor, including the kitchen; then the basement. Amy grew more agitated as time went by.

"I'm sure she's fallen asleep somewhere in the house and is quite comfortable right now," William said. However, that didn't seem to appease his wife, and frankly, he was becoming concerned himself. How the devil could animals simply disappear?

Well, more importantly, how could a man be murdered in his bed right under their noses?

What the devil was happening to his once happy home?

After a futile search, he grabbed Amy's hand. "My dear, it's time for dinner. After we eat, we shall do a thorough search again and check the gardens as well."

"I can't eat with my dog missing," she said, wringing her hands.

"I insist. In fact, I will set a couple of the footman to check the house again, as well as the garden and the general neighborhood."

Amy took a deep breath. "Thank you."

Franklin, Michael, and Lady Margaret awaited them in the drawing room. "Did you find her?" Lady Margaret asked.

"No." Amy retrieved her sherry glass and downed the liquid. William finished his brandy off just as Filbert entered the room to announce dinner.

Once they were all settled and service began, Franklin looked over at Michael. "Why don't you tell me about you and Miss Spencer?"

William threw a quick glance at Amy, who shook her head slightly.

Michael offered no reaction that William could see. "What would you like to know, Father?"

Franklin stiffened in his chair. "I would like to know, firstly, why there even is *a you and Miss Spencer.*"

Michael shrugged. "Who said there was?"

"I just did," Franklin groused. "I'm sure you heard me."

"Papa, I don't think it is a good idea to bring this up at the dinner table," Amy said.

"Daughter, this is between your brother and me." Franklin turned to Michael. "You know I don't care for Miss Spencer. In fact, if memory serves, I told you to have nothing to do with her.."

"Careful, Father," Michael said softly, raising his wine glass to his mouth, his eyes boring into Franklin.

"I have been after you for years to select a fine, proper young woman, make her your wife, and produce some heirs. Why you are wasting your time on this woman, who—"

"Franklin," Lady Margaret interrupted, "perhaps you can discuss this some other time?"

Franklin straightened in his seat. "Very well. In the interest of good digestion, I shall refrain from offering my opinion."

"An opinion that was not solicited." Michael glared at his father.

"Now see here, Michael—"

Lady Margaret threw her napkin down and stood. "I have a kidnapped bird, and now it appears Amy's dog has suffered the same fate. Add to that two people murdered in the past week, one of them at my dear niece's wedding and another right under this roof. I am distraught, as I am sure Amy is. We do not need this." She pushed her chair back and left the room.

William dropped his head into his hands. Dinner had become a battlefield, and life had become surreal. He looked over at Amy, who sat with her hands in her lap, her chin quivering and tears in her eyes. That was enough for him. He touched her on the shoulder. "Come, sweetheart."

He pulled her chair out, and they left the room after he instructed one of the footmen to bring them both trays to their bedchamber. And a bottle of wine.

After checking with the footmen who had searched the house and grounds thoroughly with no luck, he and Amy changed into their nightclothes and once again sat in front of the fireplace, eating their meal. "Amy, we will find Persephone. I promise."

She nodded dully, pushing the food around her plate. Very much unlike his wife, who enjoyed a hardy appetite.

William looked up as a knock sounded on their door. He rose and padded across the room, a familiar sound bringing a smile to his face. He opened the door to see the cursed dog in Filbert's arms. "She has returned, my lord."

Amy raced over and took Persephone into her arms, nuzzling her. "Oh, my sweetie. I'm so glad to see you." She looked up at Filbert, a bright smile on her face. "Was she found in the garden?"

"No, my lady," Filbert said. "When one of the maids went out the back door to remove trash, Persephone stood at the back steps, staring up at her."

"How very odd. Well, I'm sure my wife is happy to see her." William was truly glad for Amy. Truly.

"Yes, my lord. Quite odd indeed, because standing right alongside her on the back steps was that bird."

"Othello?" They both said at once.

"Yes."

Chapter 28

No one discovered where Othello had been during his absence, nor how Persephone had ended up on the back steps with the bird. Had Persephone actually searched for Othello and led him back to Wethington Townhouse?

At breakfast the next morning, those questions were tossed about, with no answers because neither Persephone nor Othello were talking. Actually, Othello was talking but would only recite the "Now is the winter of our discontent" monologue from *Richard III*, over and over. Papa threatened to remove the bird from the house permanently.

Aunt Margaret warned that if he did so, she would set his bed on fire.

Amy promised herself she would personally visit her old home to see how the repairs were coming. She oftentimes wondered if poor William regretted his marriage. She glanced over at him, but he seemed engrossed in his newspaper and ignored the bickering going on around him. Perhaps the man had luckily gone deaf.

The household currently had *three* subscriptions to the *London Times*. None of the men at the breakfast table was willing to give up his right to read it first; hence three newspapers arrived each day.

"It is my hope to interview Mrs. Caroline Beavers today, William." Amy took her last sip of tea, her voice lowered so as not to alert Papa to the fact that she and William were still trying to unravel the murder of Alice and her husband.

Her frustration with their current living arrangements was only surpassed by the stalemate with their investigation. That did not sit well with the murder mystery writer in her.

"With Albert's funeral tomorrow, I imagine the entire day will be taken up with that event. I checked with Mrs. O'Sullivan, and Mrs. Beavers is still employed here as a temporary maid."

"It makes me wonder if she should be considered a suspect merely because she happened to be in the wrong place at the wrong time—twice."

"And she arrived the day the poison was administered to Albert. 'Tis quite disturbing to my methodical, murder-solving mind that I can't come up with anyone who could have poisoned both husband and wife." Amy shook her head. "We are not even certain if it was the same person or two people who had death wishes for the couple."

William glanced over at Michael and Papa, who were glaring at each other, pointing at something in the newspaper. He sighed. "I have a meeting this morning with my man of business. Due to the current . . . situation here at home, I arranged to go to his office. I doubt it would be interesting for you, but would you care to accompany me?"

"Would you mind if I used that time to interview Mrs. Beavers? I had hoped to visit my former home this afternoon to see how the repairs are coming."

William grinned. "Yes, that seems like the best of ideas. I shall go with you this afternoon and offer to pay the workers double if they finish by the end of the week."

★ ★ ★

Amy found Mrs. Beavers busy changing the linen in Aunt Margaret's room. She startled when Amy knocked lightly on the open door and turned. "Oh, my lady, you gave me a fright."

"I apologize, Mrs. Beavers. I didn't mean to scare you."

The woman took a deep breath and bundled up a pile of dirty linens. "Can I help you with something, Lady Wethington?"

"Yes. I would like to ask you a few questions."

"Is something amiss?" Mrs. Beavers blanched and gripped her throat. "Please don't tell me you've found another dead body."

The poor woman must have been in desperate straits to continue to work in a house that apparently caused her such distress.

"No, not at all, Mrs. Beavers. Everything is fine."

Well, as fine as it could be with dead bodies, leaking roofs, disappearing animals, and family members threatening to burn beds.

"I know you have spoken with the police twice, but there are a few things I would like to ask you. Will you please finish up what you are doing here, as I don't wish you to get into trouble with Mrs. O'Sullivan, and then meet me in the drawing room?"

Still looking uneasy, the maid nodded. "Of course, my lady. I should be finished in about another fifteen minutes."

"Excellent. I shall await your visit."

Amy made a list while she waited for the maid. She would ask pertinent questions to eliminate Mrs. Beavers—or add her to their very short suspect list—and then attempt to ascertain if the woman had any information they had not learned from other sources.

A slight knock on the door alerted Amy to Mrs. Beavers's arrival. "Please enter."

The woman looked nervous, but then considering how her temporary jobs had gone with this family, it was no wonder she was a bit uneasy. "Please have a seat, Mrs. Beavers."

She took a seat but glanced uneasily toward the door, almost as if she were assuring herself of a way to escape.

"Please do not be anxious," Amy said softly with a smile.

Mrs. Beavers licked her lips and nodded.

"I understand you have a small child who was ill when it was time for you to pick up your wages from the agency."

The maid nodded.

"Is there no Mr. Beavers?"

"No, my lady. Mr. Beavers went to his eternal reward five years ago. My mother lives with me to care for my son."

"May I ask you why you only take temporary assignments? According to Mrs. O'Sullivan, you are an excellent worker, and she is quite pleased with your performance."

Mrs. Beavers blushed slightly. "Thank you, my lady. I do try my best."

Amy waited to see if the woman was going to answer her initial question. She blushed once again and cleared her throat. "In my last position, it became necessary for me to leave, and I was not given a reference."

Although she was quite certain what the answer would be, she asked the maid anyway, "And why was that?"

Mrs. Beavers glanced away. "My employer's son returned from university and decided I would make a fine bed partner."

She glared at Amy. "I did not agree. I am not that sort of woman." She paused for a moment. "He informed his father that I had attempted to seduce him, so I was dismissed."

Life was so very difficult for women, it made Amy want to rail against the injustice. She studied Mrs. Beavers and determined she was telling the truth. "Mrs. Beavers, I am happy to offer you a permanent job with my household."

Mrs. Beavers's jaw dropped, and her eyes grew wide. "Truly, my lady?"

"Yes. We can certainly use more help on a steady basis. However, since you have your mother and child to think of, I assume you would wish to be a day maid?"

"If I could, my lady. That would be perfect."

"Very well, then. I will inform the agency and Mrs. O'Sullivan that you are to be permanent as of today."

Much to Amy's dismay the woman burst into tears. "I apologize, my lady. I am not usually a watering pot, but I am so concerned for my little boy. He requires medicine that is quite expensive, and I am always fretful about not being able to secure an assignment."

Amy stood and the maid rose also. "Well, you are permanently employed now, Mrs. Beavers. I will inform our man of business that you are to be paid what our other employees receive, which I am quite certain is more than the agency was paying you. Now you may return to your duties."

"Thank you again, my lady. You will not be disappointed, I assure you." She offered a bow, wiped her wet cheeks, and glowing like a lantern, hurried from the room.

Amy put a check next to Mrs. Beavers's name. Because her arrival coincided with Albert's poisoning, she remained on their list of suspects. And permanent employment assured her she could also be watched.

★ ★ ★

"You hired Mrs. Beavers?" William stopped as he raised his cup of tea to his mouth and gaped at his wife. They were peacefully alone and enjoying tea. Franklin and Michael had left the house to visit the owner of the building they were purchasing, as there was a hold-up of some sort. Lady Margaret was out for the afternoon, making social calls. He had no idea where the Shakespeare-spouting bird was, and Persephone was lying peacefully in the corner of the room, asleep.

"It was so sad, William," Amy said. "The poor woman was let go from her last position because the son of the household decided she would make a better courtesan than maid. When she refused, she was turned out with no reference."

He rubbed his eyes with his thumb and index finger. "My love, was it not your intention to question Mrs. Beavers about the two murders we are attempting to solve?"

"Yes. I did question her, and I believe she should remain on the list since she arrived the day Albert was poisoned. That might be a coincidence, but having her present when both Alice and Albert were killed warrants an investigation into her background."

William thought for a moment. "Let me see if I have this correct. We now employ two superfluous women who we suspect were involved in murders?"

"Yes." Amy pointed her finger at him. "They are not superfluous. This is a very busy household. And I am convinced their backgrounds need to be investigated. And let me add, my lord, that both these women were left in dire straits because of men."

"Or so they say." William grinned but quickly grew more somber at Amy's glare. "I understand. Yes, that seems to be true. I guess it is my duty to recompense them for the injustices my gender has thrust upon them."

He refused to drop his head into his hands and moan, which is precisely what he wanted to do. Only a few weeks ago, he had lived in this house with just himself and a staff of five.

Now he had a wife, a brother-in-law, a father-in-law, an aunt, a bird, a dog, and an ever-growing staff of temporary and permanent employees. This was certainly not what he had intended when he'd proposed to Amy.

However, looking at her uneasy expression as she studied him, he decided it had been well worth it.

Mostly.

Once tea was finished, they made their way to Winchester Townhouse, where they found the workers busy, but not far along enough to please William.

"There was much more damage to the walls than we first thought," the head laborer said as he wiped the sweat from his forehead on the sleeve of his dirty shirt. "It will most likely be another week, or possibly more, before we finish everything."

I am an adult man. I will not groan. I will not curse. I will not cry.

Amy must have picked up on his mood, because she took his hand and looked into his eyes. "I am so sorry, William."

"'Tis fine. Even if the detectives allow us to leave town to commence our trip to Brighton Beach, we cannot leave while they are going in circles over these two murders."

"That makes me wonder why they haven't been back in three days. I would love to know their opinion on Albert's murder—he was their definite culprit in Alice's murder."

"Whatever easy way out they can convince themselves of, I'm sure."

The ride home was quiet as they were both consumed with their own thoughts. It was near dinner time when they drew up in front of their house and William helped Amy out of the carriage.

He opened the door and escorted Amy inside. Lady Margaret came hurrying down the corridor. "Othello is gone again. I am going to set Franklin's bed on fire."

CHAPTER 29

Dear God, the poor woman had gone mad. Aunt Margaret actually barreled past them, intending to race up the stairs to burn Papa's bed.

William reached out and took her arm as she passed. "Lady Margaret. A word, please?"

"What?" she snapped.

He glanced down at the flint in her hand. "I believe we should retire to the drawing room and have a chat." Although his words were soft-spoken, the steel behind them brought Aunt Margaret to a halt.

She took in a deep breath. "Yes, of course, William."

They all trooped upstairs to the drawing room. William poured a sherry for Amy and Aunt Margaret and began to pour one for himself, but quickly switched to pick up the brandy.

She'd been correct. Before this was all over, they would be searching for a cure for alcohol addiction.

After the contractors told them it would still be a couple more weeks before their work was finished, Amy was afraid William was ready to toss her family out on the street, with this latest hysteria. Possibly her along with them, she feared.

"Lady Margaret. You may not burn Franklin's bed. I am sure you would like to—you seem most vexed—but I cannot permit you to burn his bed."

Aunt Margaret narrowed her eyes. "I know he had something to do with Othello's disappearance."

Amy reached out and laid her hand on her aunt's. "I don't believe Papa would do anything to the bird. He has been gone all day."

"He could have hired someone to do it."

For heaven's sake, Aunt Margaret needed to develop a hobby or find a beau—or something. She was beginning to sound like a candidate for Bedlam.

"Hired someone to do what?" Papa entered the drawing room, Michael on his heels. "Are you speaking of our townhouse? I would hope we can move back soon. I cannot abide Michael's snoring another night."

Aunt Margaret stood and raised her chin. "Where is my bird?"

Papa looked at her as if she had just grown another head. "Sister, dear, do you honestly believe that I have so little on my mind that I am concerned about your blasted bird?"

Michael moved past Papa and poured a brandy. "Missing again, Margaret?"

"Yes." She turned to Michael, her eyes narrowed. "Why do you ask? Did you take him?"

Her brother had the nerve to laugh. "Surely you don't think I care at all about that bird? What I care about is why we are even concerning ourselves with it again."

Aunt Margaret fisted her hands at her sides. "Because he's gone again."

"Ah, a peaceful dinner." Papa turned to Amy. "Is that blasted dog gone too?"

Amy jumped up and immediately left the room. She hurried up the stairs to their bedchamber and opened the door with such fervor that it crashed against the wall. She released a breath when she saw Persephone sound asleep on the small bed on the floor.

When she returned to the drawing room, Aunt Margaret, Michael, and Papa were in a heated debate, voices raised, arms waving about. She looked over at William and mouthed, "A tray in our room?"

He nodded and she followed him over the threshold and back up to their bedchamber.

★ ★ ★

The next afternoon, William adjusted Amy's hat and rebuttoned her coat as they prepared to leave the house. It was the day of Albert's funeral, and as far as she surmised, it would be a scant showing. Papa and Michael had deferred attending, but Aunt Margaret agreed to go with them.

There had been a notice in the newspaper about the funeral, but while they were planning his service, it occurred to Amy that no one knew very much about the man except that he had married Miss Alice Munson. When they checked, they found no source of employment for Albert, which meant he had been living on Alice's largesse. No surprise there.

They'd spent some time speaking with Mrs. Davis—who had deferred attending the funeral also—and came up with no friends of Albert's that she knew either. It appeared that when the two of them had spent time together, it had been quite clandestine, with them attending virtually no events where he would be seen.

Although a valuable addition to the household according to Mrs. O'Sullivan, when it came to Albert Finch, Mrs. Davis was tight-lipped and caustic. She certainly had reason to be so, considering the mess he'd left her in, with no regard for her distressing situation.

Amy had considered speaking with Annabelle about the man, but she was certain the poor woman would not wish to help with planning Albert's funeral or notifying friends or relations.

The three of them left the house together and rode silently to the funeral home. After a short visit there to pay respects to Albert, they would proceed to the same church where Alice's service had taken place not that long ago.

William had been kind enough to purchase a plot for Albert, as well as pay the funeral costs and the vicar's fee. Amy noted that in the short time since their wedding, her family had created more expense and trouble for William than a normal wife would cause in years of marriage.

She patted him on the arm, and he looked at her with raised brows. No point in telling him how uncomfortable she was with all the difficulties and troubles that had descended on him with their marriage. He would merely wave it off, making her feel even worse.

She had been correct in her assessment. When they entered the funeral home, they were the only people in the room. Surprisingly—or perhaps not so—after about five minutes, Jared Munson passed through the door and sat across from them. He nodded in their direction and faced forward, staring at the body of Albert Finch.

Now that Albert was dead, Amy was quite sure that Jared expected to receive all of Alice's money. She gave the man a second look. Now there was a man with a good motive to murder Albert. It was perhaps time to move him to the top of the list.

Just as they were about to notify the undertaker to close the coffin and prepare to leave for the church, the door opened, and a woman with two boys entered. The older child appeared to be nearing fourteen or fifteen years. The younger lad was no more than five. The woman and the two youngsters took a seat behind her and William.

★   ★   ★

William leaned toward Amy. "Who is that?"

"I have no idea," Amy whispered. "I've never seen her before."

William looked past Amy, at Lady Margaret, and gestured with his head toward the woman and children sitting behind them. She shrugged her answer.

Whispers behind them went on for a few minutes, and then the woman stood and walked to the front of the room. She gazed down at Albert's body and pursed her lips. Then she returned to the two boys.

That appeared to be all the woman had been interested in; so, not expecting any other mourners, William notified the undertaker to proceed to the church.

"I wonder who that woman is?" Lady Margaret said as soon as they were seated in the carriage.

"I don't know. But then we don't know very much about Albert anyway. I'm thinking she might be a sister—or perhaps a cousin?" Amy said.

"Or another scorned paramour. She seemed a bit resigned about his death. Did you see the tight lips when she viewed his body?"

William nodded. "Yes. I'm hoping she introduces herself after the service."

The small church hid the lack of attendees. The unknown woman and the two boys were there, along with William, Amy, Lady Margaret, and Jared. William was surprised to see a few of the people who had been present at the reading of Alice's will in attendance also, even though they hadn't made it to the funeral home.

Once they were all settled, the vicar cleared his throat, and the scant gathering looked to him.

The eulogy was short, but considering no one, including the mourners present, knew anything about Albert, there really was not much to say. The vicar relied heavily on Bible quotes and promises of eternal reward.

Given what they knew of Albert's dalliances, and with a murder charge hanging over his head when he died, William had his doubts as to what sort of an eternal "reward" Albert would receive.

The small group left the pews, to file behind the vicar to the plot of dirt, at the back of the church, that had been opened for Albert's casket. To William's amazement, Amy's cousin Annabelle stood at the gravesite. This funeral was turning into quite a surprise.

The vicar waited for them all to gather around and then he began. "Dear Lord, into your hands we deliver the soul of Mr. Albert E. Finch—"

"Stop!" The woman with the two boys stepped forward. She pointed to the casket awaiting burial. "The man in that casket is not Mr. Albert E. Finch."

All heads turned in her direction. Stunned silence ensued.

"Pardon me, madam?" The vicar looked around at the rest of them, his eyes settling on William, who had made all the arrangements for the funeral. "My lord?"

William moved next to the woman and lowered her voice. "Excuse me. Let us continue with the service, and we can discuss this afterward."

"What is there to discuss? He is not Albert Finch—or whoever it is he was calling himself this time."

Her voice carried to the rest of the group. Mumbling and shocked whispers followed her announcement.

"Mrs.—" William said, hoping the woman would fill in the missing name.

"Lawrence, Mrs. David Lawrence."

"Well, Mrs. Lawrence may I ask you to please allow the service to continue, and I assure you that your concerns will be dealt with. We will be retiring to my home when the vicar has finished. You, and your children, are welcome to join us for a meal."

William had had no intention of hosting an after-funeral event as he'd only expected Amy, Lady Margaret, and himself to be at the gravesite. However, with the turn of events, it seemed the proper thing to do.

Fortunately, he had full confidence that Mrs. O'Sullivan and Cook would be able to provide the necessary food on such short notice.

The woman stepped back to where the boys stood, a stoic expression on her face. The vicar said a quick prayer and swiftly closed his Bible. He nodded at the group, turned on his heel, and headed for the vicarage. Probably to his brandy bottle.

William cleared his throat and addressed those still standing there, shocked expressions on their faces. "If you will all follow our carriage, Lady Wethington and I would be pleased to have you join us for dinner."

He took Amy's arm, and before they had moved even one step, Annabelle walked up to the casket and spit on it.

Bloody hell, could things get any worse?

Apparently, they could. When they arrived back at the house, Franklin and Michael were already there. Pleased to see her favorite person, Persephone began to run in circles, barking, jumping up on Amy's knees, begging to be picked up.

Lady Margaret stepped up to Franklin, who was pouring a brandy. "Has Othello returned?"

"I have no idea, Sister."

William held up his hands. "Excuse me. Behind us are a few carriages. They are guests. *My* guests. I ask you all to please refrain from bickering about the bird, burning beds, and unfinished work at your townhouse. It appears we have enough on our hands to manage right now."

Franklin looked at Lady Margaret. "What is he talking about?"

"The people arriving are from Albert's funeral. There is a woman with us who is making some confusing statements."

The guests began to arrive in the drawing room, led by Filbert. Jared had elected to attend; Annabelle had not. Along with Jared were Mrs. Lawrence and the two youngsters, who William assumed were her children. Fortunately for Cook, the few extras who had shown up at the church had not elected to join them for dinner.

Amy had gone to the kitchen when they arrived to instruct Mrs. O'Sullivan and Cook to count on additional guests for dinner, and to make dinner a tad earlier so this dreadful day could end.

Franklin took it upon himself to offer drinks to all those in attendance, which William was grateful for. At least it kept his father-in-law from sniping at his sister. Once Amy had returned and they were all settled with a drink, William looked to Mrs.

Lawrence. "Mrs. Lawrence, would you care to enlighten us on your claim that Mr. Finch is not who he purported to be?"

The woman looked William in the eye. "I certainly can, my lord. The man who was buried today is not Mr. Albert E. Finch as stated in the obituary in the newspaper. His name is Mr. David Lawrence, and he is my husband."

Jared began to choke on his brandy, and William stared with shock at the woman. "Your former husband?"

"No. My current husband. We were never divorced."

CHAPTER 30

Jared jumped up and shouted. "Then the money is all mine!"

Amy glared at him. "I don't think this is the best time to speak about inheritances, Jared."

"Why not? I've said from the time the old solicitor read my aunt's will that Albert didn't deserve the money because he killed her."

"No one has proved that," William added.

The young man shrugged. "It looks like he was a bigamist, which provides an even stronger case."

From the little bit of law that Amy knew from research on her various books, if Albert had truly been still married to Mrs. Lawrence, he was, indeed a bigamist, which would invalidate his marriage to Alice. The question in her mind was the wording of the will. It said, *"To my husband, Albert . . ."* If he was not her legal husband, and Albert E. Finch was not his true name, then there was indeed a legal mess to be cleared up.

Wishing to pull the conversation back to where it should be, Amy looked at Mrs. Lawrence and then the two boys. "Are these boys his sons?"

"Yes." She raised her chin. "David has been supporting us all these years. Whenever he goes off to assume a different name, he manages to marry someone with money and sends enough to support us."

William's eyes glazed over. "Marry someone else? You mean, you allow this? Have allowed it for years?"

Mrs. Lawrence shrugged. "That's the way David was. As long as he sent money, I didn't care." She narrowed her eyes. "However, now that he is dead, I will claim my right to the money he inherited from his dead wife." She looked over at Jared. "David was perhaps not the most honorable man, but he would never kill someone. Especially the woman who was giving him money."

Amy kept it to herself that Alice had been planning a divorce. There was no reason to make this unbelievable story any worse than it already was. "Mrs. Lawrence, you may have forgotten the fact that since Albert was not Mrs. Finch's legal husband, and that was not his real name, he most likely would not have inherited her money."

Mrs. Lawrence waved her hand around and took a sip of sherry. "No matter. I will speak with a barrister." She glared at Jared. "I assure all of you, the money will be *mine*."

Jared glared back and opened his mouth to speak.

"Dinner is served, my lord, my lady." Filbert made that very normal announcement in the middle of the most bizarre conversation Amy had ever witnessed.

Ever.

William stood and nodded to the guests, cutting off whatever it was Jared had intended to say. "If you will follow me, my wife and I will lead you to the dining room."

Papa, Michael, Aunt Margaret, Mrs. Lawrence, her two sons—who had not as yet been introduced—and Jared, all trooped behind them.

Once they were settled and the dinner service had begun, William said to their guests. "Since good digestion depends on pleasant talk, I prefer if we continue the conversation from the drawing room after our meal."

Neither Jared nor Mrs. Lawrence looked pleased, but they both nodded, and the dinner continued.

Usually quite adept at light conversation—part of her training in social niceties as a young girl—for the first time in her life, Amy could think of nothing to say to ease the tension.

Papa and Michael managed to speak softly between themselves, but everyone else ate in silence.

"What are your boys' names, Mrs. Lawrence?" At least she could raise that question without any rancor from the woman.

Mrs. Lawrence beamed, obviously a devoted mother, if not a very strange wife. "My oldest is John. He is fourteen years, and my little one is Peter, five years."

"My, quite a number of years between them," Aunt Margaret said, obviously also trying to bring some normalcy to the meal.

"Yes. Well, in between his roaming, David would stop in for a few months at a time. But there were quite a few years between John and Peter when David was in France, I believe. He sent our money to a bank in London."

Amy glanced over at William, who looked as stunned as she felt. Albert's—rather David's—lifestyle had been so unusual that every time Mrs. Lawrence opened her mouth, the story grew more outlandish. Further proof that true life was stranger than fiction.

William cleared his throat and looked across the table at Mrs. Lawrence. "I assume you have a valid marriage license?"

Although they had decided not to speak of the strange situation during dinner, it seemed no one's mind was on anything else, as all eyes turned to Mrs. Lawrence with anticipation.

"Yes. Of course I have it. We were married in St. Bride's Church on Fleet Street." She glanced over at Amy with a beaming smile. "Isn't that the perfect church name for a wedding?"

For one of the few times in her life, Amy was truly speechless. She gulped some of her wine, then nodded at Mrs. Lawrence.

There were simply no words.

The dinner crept along in mostly silence. Even Papa and Michael had stopped speaking with each other. Everyone's focus remained on the food.

Filbert stepped into the room. "Excuse the interruption, my lord. Detectives Marsh and Carson have arrived and have requested your and her ladyship's presence."

★   ★   ★

William managed to swallow the fish in his mouth without choking to death. Yes, this day could truly get worse. He glanced at Amy, who looked as discombobulated as he felt. He turned to Filbert. "Please inform the detectives that Lady Wethington and I are in the middle of entertaining guests. Please ask them to return at another time. And to send a note before they do."

Filbert was back in less than a minute. "My lord, the detectives said they can wait, and it will only take a few minutes of your time."

Bloody hell. He stood and tossed his napkin at his place. He looked over at Amy, who also rose. They might as well get this over with. Besides, the unease at the table was so strong it couldn't be cut with the sharpest knife from Cook's collection.

William strode into the room. *Vexed* didn't even begin to cover his current disposition. "Detectives, from now on, I would appreciate a note ahead of your arrival. We are currently in the middle of dinner, where we are entertaining guests. 'Tis quite rude of us to leave the table."

Detective Marsh flipped open his notebook, and Carson settled himself in a chair and said, "We did not ask you to leave your guests. We said we would wait."

"Perhaps you are able to enjoy your meal while awaiting an interrogation, but I find myself—and, I am sure, my wife—are not so inclined."

Carson waved him off. "Not an interrogation, my lord. Merely a few simple questions."

Steeling himself for another round of *simple* questions, William nodded.

"I understand you arranged and paid for Mr. Albert Finch's funeral." Carson spoke as Marsh scribbled. Their usual procedure.

William considered playing with the annoying detective and denying his statement since they'd learned that Albert Finch was not in fact Albert Finch and had lived a number of different lives.

"That is correct. When we contacted the morgue, they told us no one had claimed his body. Not wanting to have the man buried in a pauper's graveyard, I made the proper arrangements."

"Very nice of you, considering he killed your cousin."

Amy straightened in her seat. "Mrs. Finch was *my* cousin, Detective, and even though Mr. Finch had been charged with his wife's murder, it had yet to be proven in a court of law."

Carson leaned back and rested his foot on his other knee. "Yes. I understand that."

"How is the investigation going into Albert's death?" Amy asked.

"The matter is all resolved."

William gaped at the detective. "How so?"

"Simple, really. Mr. Finch killed Mrs. Finch to be with his lover Mrs. Davis and then killed himself while suffering from grief and guilt."

Amy gaped at the man. "You are serious."

"Yes. So whatever investigation you two think you have—and don't believe for one minute I didn't know you were doing so against our warning—you can end. We intend to close both matters."

William stood, his blood pounding in his head at the detective's smug stupidity. They didn't even know Albert was not Albert, nor about the compilation of additional people and situations that had emerged this very day. "Very well. You may leave now, Detectives."

Carson lumbered to his feet, and Marsh flipped his notebook closed. "The reason for our visit was to close the last piece of the story by confirming you paid for the funeral, my lord. Also, to tell you that you and your wife may leave Bath at any time and take your long-awaited honeymoon."

The man had the gall to smile. To act as though he and his partner were not incompetent and lazy. To take the easy way out; look for the simplest solution to the problem and make the facts fit their conclusion. Although he knew withholding information in a murder investigation was a chargeable offense, he felt no remorse in escorting these men, ignorant of the latest information and complication in Albert's death, out of the house.

"Well, Detectives, this is the end of our relationship, then." William waved toward the door.

"William?" Amy glanced back and forth between him and the detectives. Then she gestured with her head toward the dining room with a puzzled expression.

William shook his head and walked the detectives down the stairs to the front entrance. "Have a good day, Detectives."

Carson had the nerve to grin and bow. "Until the next murder, my lord."

"Indeed." William left the men shrugging into their coats and returned to the drawing room. Amy paced the area.

"William, they closed the case, and they don't even know about Mrs. Lawrence. Or Albert's lifestyle or Jared's claim to the money that Mrs. Lawrence insists is hers, which it probably isn't since Albert—rather David—was not legally married to Alice." She collapsed onto the settee. "What a mess."

"However, we now have two more people to add to our suspect list. Mrs. Lawrence and Jared. Although I believe we'd already added Jared before now. But Mrs. Lawrence, with her acceptance of Albert's—David's—lack of compunction in treating his marriage vows so cavalierly, and her assumption that she now has a claim to Alice's money, now jumps to the top of our list, I believe."

"And what about her son?" Amy asked. "The oldest one. She says he is fourteen years, but he looks much older and bigger and has not spoken a word since we set eyes on him. Yet, he glowers at everyone in turn around the table."

"True. But one major glitch in our theory of either Mrs. Lawrence or her son being involved is that if either was responsible for Alice's murder, then how did he or she get the poison into Alice's glass?"

They both sat in silence, considering William's words. Amy stood and shook out her skirts. "We really should return to the dining room. I don't like the fact that things are so quiet."

"No one knows what to say. This situation is truly one of the most awkward states of affairs I've ever dealt with at my dinner table."

Amy reached out and took his hand. It was a testament to his befuddlement that his wife had stood up and he remained in his seat. Gentlemen never did that. He took her hand and moved alongside her, placing his hand on her lower back. "I believe that first thing tomorrow morning, we should go over all our notes and add our new information to them. As much as I would love to finally take our trip to Brighton Beach, I cannot in good conscience let the detectives' theory stand. There is at least one, and possibly two, murderers out there."

CHAPTER 31

The dinner continued with as much social pain after the detectives' visit as it had before. Amy noticed Mrs. Lawrence's older son, John, remained slumped in his chair, scowling at everyone when he wasn't glowering at his plate of food.

She and William would do well to examine the lad's background, as well as the mother's. Her boy was certainly old enough to know that what his father had done most of the child's life was unusual as well as illegal.

With a flash of brilliance, Amy excused herself from the table once the fruit, cheese, sweets, and tea had been served. She ignored William's raised brows and made her way to Mrs. O'Sullivan's room, connected to her office right outside the kitchen.

The woman was sitting in a very cozy-looking chair, her feet up, a warm blanket spread over her lap, and a small glass of brandy by her side. She was reading a book and appeared to be the perfect image of a hard-working woman at rest.

She startled when Amy knocked and entered. "Oh, my lady." She went to stand, but Amy shook her head and said, "Do not get up, Mrs. O'Sullivan. You look very comfortable, and I apologize for interrupting your well-earned rest."

The woman was obviously ill at ease with her mistress's presence, so Amy sat and tried her best not to appear threatening. "I just wish to ask you a few quick questions."

"Of course," Mrs. Sullivan said, closing her book and laying it aside.

"First, is there any chance that the temporary maids are still here, or have they been sent home for the night?"

"They have all gone, my lady. An excellent job they are doing too," she added.

Amy nodded. "That is good to hear. And I assume our newest permanent employees, Mrs. Davis and Mrs. Beaver, are working out well?"

"Yes. They are also hard workers and seem to be settling in. Well, Mrs. Beavers has been here a while, but Mrs. Davis is proving to be quite industrious."

Amy nodded. She had hoped if the temporary maids were still about, she could have them visit the dining room on the pretense of removing dishes or cleaning up and take a look at Mrs. Lawrence. There was a chance that she was the extra employee who Cook seemed to think had briefly appeared with the other temporary employees.

Truth be known, Mrs. Lawrence would have had more reason to kill Alice than Albert/David. She seemed quite accepting of her husband's peculiar life, but the money had come from Alice. Perhaps Alice had told her husband of her plans to divorce him, and he in turn had passed that information along to Mrs. Lawrence.

In light of her skill with charcoals, perhaps asking Aunt Margaret to sketch Mrs. Lawrence from memory and taking that to the temporary agency to see if she resembled those who had worked the day of her wedding might be worth their time also.

"Mrs. O'Sullivan, I will need to speak with the temporary maids sometime in the morning. I will let you know what time as it depends on my aunt Margaret. She will be needed to help with what I am hoping to accomplish."

The housekeeper frowned at her, looking decidedly confused. "I am sorry, my lady—are you sure there isn't something I can do for you?"

"No." Amy stood and smoothed out her skirts. "This is a minor issue that does not reflect on the temporary maids." She moved toward the door, wishing she and William were currently ensconced in *their* room with brandy, warm blankets, and books instead of dealing with the tension and unease at the dinner table.

"I wish you a good evening, Mrs. O'Sullivan, and again I apologize for intruding on your personal time."

"It was my pleasure, my lady. Good night."

Amy made her way back to the dining room, where strained silence reigned. No more than ten minutes after her return, Mrs. Lawrence stood. "I believe it is time for us to depart." She looked at her younger son, whose head was drooping, his eyes closed. "I must get my little one to bed."

William jumped up. "Of course. I will have your carriage brought around." He left the room. Mrs. Lawrence said her goodbyes, and the three of them started down the stairs, Amy following behind.

There was a great deal of shuffling around as Filbert presented their outer garments to the three of them, assisting Mrs. Lawrence while she helped her younger son with his coat.

William smiled at Mrs. Lawrence. "It has been a pleasure, Mrs. Lawrence. May I ask your driver to give your direction to my man? My wife and I would like to speak with you further."

She looked suspiciously at him, then over at Amy, who also offered her a smile. "We just want to ask you a few questions. I think it might help with your claim to Mrs. Finch's money." Amy tried not to grimace at the blatant lie that had just spouted from her lips, but it seemed the best way to get the woman to cooperate was to wave money under her nose.

It appeared to work, and Mrs. Lawrence smiled broadly. "Of course, my lady. I imagine I could use all the help I can to gain my rightful claim."

There was no rightful claim, and Amy was quite certain that once Annabelle heard about all of this, she would see that her sister's money did not go to this woman. In fact, Amy had no doubt that Alice's twin had already contacted her solicitor to dispute the will's content based on her belief that Albert/David had killed her beloved twin sister.

This had indeed become quite complicated.

★   ★   ★

The next afternoon, William assisted Amy into the carriage that would take them to the offices of Mr. Stanford Lawton of Melrose and Lawton, Solicitors. He had sent a note around that morning requesting a two o'clock appointment. The man had sent back an agreement, and now they were on their way.

After the awkward dinner the night before, and once Jared had taken his leave shortly after Mrs. Lawrence and her sons, William and Amy had retired to their bedchamber, where Amy had insisted they wrap themselves in blankets and sit in their comfortable chairs with a brandy and a book.

Not questioning her request, he enjoyed the time they spent with the books they never did read, but they sipped their brandy while they conversed about the peculiarities of the murder investigations of Mr. and Mrs. Finch. Or, more rightly, Mrs. Finch and Mr. Lawrence. Or maybe it was Miss Alice Munson and Mr. Lawrence.

Now that it had been revealed that Mr. Albert E. Finch was actually Mr. David Lawrence, Amy had pointed out, and that there already was a Mrs. Lawrence, perhaps Mrs. Finch was now back to Miss Munson. But since she was deceased, she continued, the woman could not go back to anything anyway.

It was at that point that William's left eye began to twitch and a headache arrived, so he suggested they finish their brandies and retire for the night, where they found other ways to ease their tension and forget about the murder investigations.

William tapped on the ceiling of the vehicle to alert the driver that they were ready to proceed. It was a typical damp dreary British day, with a bit of chill in the air not uncommon in early October.

"I think it's time I called on Annabelle again. I am concerned for her health. She looked terrible and was distraught enough at Albert's funeral—sorry, *David's* funeral—to spit on the man's grave."

William nodded. "I'm quite sure she was close enough to hear Mrs. Lawrence declare to the vicar that Mr. Albert E. Finch was actually Mr. David Lawrence and married to her."

"Yet, she left so quickly I never got to speak to her. I wasn't surprised that she didn't want to join us for dinner, but she certainly scurried away."

Mr. Lawton's offices were in a newer building on Milsom Street. The area was home to a great number of shops and stores, making the traffic extensive. William signaled for the driver to stop. 'Twas better to walk the short distance from where they were stuck in traffic so they would make their two o'clock appointment.

"If you cannot find a place to wait for a while, return home, and Lady Wethington and I will secure a hackney," he shouted to the driver and then took Amy's arm as they hurried against the cold wind down the street to the building.

A small sign in the lobby of the building indicated the offices of Melrose and Lawton, Solicitors was on the second floor. They made their way up the stairs and down the dark corridor to a wooden and glass door with the names of the solicitors painted in black and gold.

A young man behind a large wooden desk stood as they entered. He was painfully thin and tall, with black spectacles and red hair. His bright smile brought one in return to William's lips. "Good afternoon. I assume you are Lord and Lady Wethington?"

"Yes. We are here to see Mr. Lawton."

The young man waved to two wooden chairs lining the wall. "If you will kindly take a seat, I shall notify Mr. Lawton of your arrival."

They had barely settled when the young man returned and escorted them down a short corridor to a large office. Because the space was located on the corner of the building, with windows on both the south and east sides, even the gloom of the day hadn't dimmed the room.

Mr. Lawton stood as they entered. "Good afternoon, my lord, my lady. It is a pleasure to see you again." He waved at the two much more comfortable chairs in front of his massive desk. "Please have a seat. Would you care for tea?"

William looked at Amy, who shook her head. "No, thank you, Mr. Lawton."

The man settled behind his desk. "What can I do for you, my lord?"

"Mr. Albert Finch was buried yesterday. The service was short and poorly attended, which was no surprise to my wife and me since we were unable to locate any friends or relatives when we arranged for the funeral."

Mr. Lawton dipped his head. "I understand. I always had a curiosity about the man. In the years I've been working for Mrs. Finch, both before and after she married Mr. Finch, the man never accompanied her to visits here, nor was he at home when I called at their residence."

"Did you ever know if that was his wish or Mrs. Finch's?"

"No, I did not. She never said, and I never asked. But I must say I had always found their relationship a trifle—shall we say—unusual?"

William shifted in his seat and said, "It appears their relationship was even more unusual than you might have guessed."

Mr. Lawton's brows rose. "Indeed?"

"It appears Mr. Albert Finch was using a pseudonym. He was Mr. David Lawrence and was married to another woman."

"Divorced? Or widowed?"

"Neither."

The silence was deafening. Mr. Lawton merely stared at them, his eyes moving back and forth as he processed the information William had just relayed. He opened and closed his mouth a few times, his face pale. He began to tap his fingertip on his desk. "Are you saying this Mr. Lawrence illegally married Miss Munson? That he was a bigamist?"

"Yes. With two sons."

"Excuse me." The solicitor stood and moved to the side of the room, where he looked out the window, his hands behind his back. "Are you sure I cannot offer you tea?"

"No thank you, Mr. Lawton. Take your time. We've already had some time to process this information," Amy said.

Lawton nodded. "Just so."

Once Mr. Lawton returned to his seat, he didn't look quite as pale. "This is a problem."

"That is precisely what we thought." William leaned forward. "My first question is, if Mr. Lawrence was using a false name and was not legally married to Mrs. Finch, would he have inherited her fortune?"

"Of course I would have to do some research in the matter, as this is not a question that arises every day, but my inclination is to say no, he was not able to inherit."

"Then what is the position of Mrs. Finch's nephew, Mr. Jared Munson?"

Mr. Lawton stiffened in his chair, and his lips tightened. "I am still researching that situation as well, in conjunction with the will as written."

William glanced over at Amy, who raised her brows.

"Is there a difficulty with that, Mr. Lawton?"

The man folded his hands and looked directly at William. "A bit of a problem legally, of course, but the young man has visited my office several times since Mrs. Finch's death."

William sensed something Mr. Lawton did not say. "And?"

"On his last visit he brought a rather large and rough-looking sort of man with him. A bruiser, one might label him. When I told Mr. Munson that I had no answer for him as to his possible inheritance, and it would do him well to have some patience, the man with him threatened me.

"He threatened you?" Amy and William said at the same time.

"Indeed. Mr. Munson's companion said I had two more weeks to clear it all up or it was quite possible something unpleasant might happen to me."

CHAPTER 32

"Othello has returned." Amy was greeted the next morning with those words from Aunt Margaret as she and William descended the stairs from their bedchamber. "When?"

"She showed up on the doorstep about an hour ago. With Persephone again."

They all proceeded to the breakfast room. Amy settled in the seat William held out for her. "However are they getting out of the house?"

"I have no idea. But, this is the second time Othello has disappeared, so I am keeping him in his cage until we move back to our townhouse. I'm thinking the reason he is escaping is to return home."

"That could very well be, but that doesn't explain how Persephone goes after him and finds him. At least, that's how it appears." Amy shook her head. Just another in a long string of odd events lately.

"Aunt Margaret, I do have a favor to ask of you. I would like to have you sketch what you remember of Mrs. Lawrence from the dinner last night."

Her aunt raised her brows, looking back and forth between her and William. "What have I missed?"

"I am suspicious of the woman."

"She seems like a woman with very few morals, but in what capacity do you suspect her?"

Amy took a sip of her tea. "For Alice's murder. And possibly Albert's as well. We would like to bring a likeness of her to the agency that provided the temporary staff to Aunt Priscilla's house for the wedding breakfast. I would be interested in seeing if the owner of the agency recognizes her as one of the maids he sent. Also, I am having our temporary staff working here take a look, to see if she resembles the so-called 'extra' person who Cook seemed to think arrived with the other temporary help."

Aunt Margaret shook her head in confusion. "Yes, I heard mention of that, but I was under the impression Mrs. O'Sullivan said Cook miscounted during all the frenzy of that morning. In fact, has she even said if it was an extra man or a woman?"

"No. She was that confused." Amy stopped and thought for a moment. "Perhaps you are correct. If you can do the sketch for us, we'll check with the agency about the temporary wedding breakfast staff. That might be a better use of our time and your talent to clear up that question."

"Another mystery, Daughter? Haven't you had enough?" Papa entered the breakfast room, Michael right behind him.

"Nothing new, Papa." It would be best to deviate from this conversation because Papa would not be happy to know they were still investigating two murders.

"Our book club meeting is tonight, Michael. Will you be attending again?" Amy asked.

Papa placed his full plate on the table and drew out the chair to sit. "Since when are you interested in book clubs?"

Michael shrugged. "I like to read."

Amy watched as Papa studied Michael for a minute, his eyes moving back and forth, telling her his brain was busy. "Why?" Papa finally asked.

Michael set his plate in front of him. "Why what?"

"Why the book club?" Papa took a bite of his toast and looked over at Amy. "That hoyden belongs to that club, doesn't she?"

For as annoyed as Amy was at her father's continued dislike and disrespect for Eloise, it was apparently nothing compared to Michael's reaction. He held his knife and fork in his fisted hands and glared at Papa; his jaw tightened, and a slight flush rose on his cheeks. "I will not have you insult Miss Spencer."

Papa wiped his mouth with this napkin. "Do not dare to go where I think you are headed, my boy. I have badgered you for years to settle down and select a wife. In case you did not understand, I meant a *proper* wife. Not some ill-mannered chit who talks too loudly and comes from the lower class—not to mention that every time I have seen her, she is rushing here and rushing there, like no lady every would."

To Amy's surprise, Michael did not erupt, but merely said, "I will not discuss this now. In fact, I will not discuss it with you at all. I am my own man, and I will make my own decisions. And unless they relate to business, they will not involve your opinion."

Her brother's calm apparently affected Papa. He took in a deep breath and said, "Just remember who you are, Michael. You are an earl, in line for a marquessate. That is no small matter, and you must present yourself to the world you were born into as an intelligent man who knows what is proper and what is not."

"Did you know Othello returned?" Aunt Margaret jumped in, no doubt anxious to have the discussion come to an end. After last night's tense dinner, they certainly did not need drama at the breakfast table.

Papa snorted and Michael grinned. Amy looked over at William, who appeared disinterested in the current fuss, busy turning the pages of his newspaper. She might have been fooled had she not known her husband so well. Given the way he was gripping the newspaper and turning the pages, he was not reading anything.

Today she would go to her old home and see how the workers fared. If it took all her quarterly allowance and a withdrawal from her royalty bank account, she would offer it to the man in charge to speed up the repairs to the townhouse.

After she and William had married, Michael had placed her royalty account in William's name, the proper procedure for a married woman. However, her new husband had turned right around and had the bank change the account back to her name. When she'd thanked him, he'd shrugged and said she'd worked for the money, so it should be hers.

Very revolutionary. Suffragette Emmeline Pankhurst would be impressed.

"To be, or not to be, that is the question: Whether 'tis nobler in the mind to suffer the slings and arrows of outrageous fortune, or to take arms against a sea of troubles," Othello's scratchy voice sounded in the silence.

★   ★   ★

After a mostly indigestible breakfast, William took the sketch of Mrs. Lawrence to the temporary employment agency while Amy visited her former home to check on the progress. His poor wife was most likely just as frustrated with the goings-on with her family members as he was.

Unfortunately, the visit to the agency was futile as the sketch did not resemble any of the man's employees. Discouraged with that attempt to move forward, William secured the directions to Mrs. Lawrence's residence from Filbert, who had escorted the woman and her two sons to their carriage the night before, when she gave the information to his driver. He joined Amy at the front door for their trip to seek out Mrs. Lawrence.

William examined the paper with the directions as the carriage rolled away from the house and joined the congested traffic. The neighborhood where they were headed was neither the best nor the worse in Bath. "'Tis surprising to me that Mrs. Lawrence lives right here in Bath, where her husband lived with another wife. One would think she would prefer another town."

Amy shook her head and grabbed the strap as the vehicle bounced over ruts in the road. "I believe if we try to understand Albert or his wife or their relationship, or anything else about them or this entire situation, we will go slowly—or perhaps not so slowly—mad."

"That is definitely true, my love. This whole matter from the time Alice collapsed into her plate of eggs until Mrs. Lawrence showed up at Albert's gravesite claiming to be his wife, leaves one with a sense of just stepping off the carousel at Aylsham Fair."

"Indeed."

They remained silent for the rest of the journey, William taken up with the most recent squabble at his breakfast table. From what he'd seen, it was truly amazing that Michael and his father got on so well with regard to business matters. They certainly butted heads over Eloise.

The woman Franklin was so set against would never have been William's choice of a wife. Or a wife for one of his sons either.

That brought his meandering thoughts to an abrupt halt.

Sons.

And daughters.

When he'd contemplated marriage, he had been so taken up with Amy and how well she would fit into his world, as well as how much he'd grown to care for her, that he hadn't spent much time considering the natural outcome of marriage.

Children.

That, despite knowing from a young age that providing an heir to his title was a must.

What sort of father would he be? Would he also be appalled if his daughter wanted to write gory, murderous books? Would he care if his son decided he wanted to marry an unacceptable woman?

Those thoughts never came to a resolution because the carriage came to a stop in front of a small townhouse in a neighborhood that used to be fashionable but had fallen into neglect over the past ten years or so.

William exited the carriage and turned to help Amy down. He double-checked the directions on the paper in his hand, and they moved up the steps and dropped the rather ugly monkey-faced knocker.

No answer.

He dropped it again.

No answer.

A third time.

No answer.

"Perhaps we should have sent a note first," Amy said.

William stepped back, then looked up at the building. He leaned over the railing to peer into a window in order to see a vacant room. "I'm not certain, but it looks to me as though this house is empty."

"Is this the correct number?"

He glanced again at the paper. "Yes, it is."

Just then a woman, obviously a maid, came down the small alley between the two townhouses. She carried an empty market bag in her hand.

"Pardon me, ma'am," Amy said.

The woman looked up at her. "Yes, my lady?" She was a rosy-cheeked woman, one who wore a perpetual smile, which warmed an individual to immediately like her.

"We are looking for Mrs. Lawrence. We were told this is her address, but it appears to be empty. Do you know her?"

The woman stiffened and the automatic smile disappeared. "Yes. She did live there but moved last week." She nodded her head. "And good riddance I say."

Amy glanced over at William, and they both made their way down the steps to where the woman stood. "Was there trouble with Mrs. Lawrence?"

The woman's eyes narrowed. "Are you her family?"

Not knowing which would be the best answer to encourage the maid's continued cooperation, William decided on a third option. "No. We just returned from a trip to Brighton Beach and spent time with someone there who asked us to stop by and offer Mrs. Lawrence her best wishes." Before she had time to digest that, he added, "May I ask your name?"

"Mrs. Blanchard. I am the housekeeper to Mr. Ronald Deems." She gestured with her thumb to the townhouse next to them.

"We would like to fulfill our promise and convey the message to Mrs. Lawrence. Do you know where she has moved?"

"No. I do not. And I would advise you to stay away from that family. The son is trouble."

"Do you refer to her oldest boy—John, I believe his name is?"

"Yes. A bad sort, that one. I caught him hitting and punching his little brother more than once. Another time he yelled at his mother with language that would have gotten me a week cleaning out the barn with nothing but bread and water to eat, and with a great deal of difficulty sitting down." Mrs. Blanchard shook her head. "She had no control over that demon child."

"What of Mr. Lawrence?"

She huffed. "Oh, he was another one. He showed up maybe every few months. He and the boy didn't get on either. I often thought if he spent more time with his family, he might have been able to make something of the child."

It seemed odd to William that this housekeeper, as a servant, knew so much about the family. She must have had a source for her information. "Did they employ a housekeeper also?"

"Yes. Mrs. Krampton was their housekeeper. She and I were friends of a sort."

That explained the woman's knowledge.

"Do you know if Mrs. Krampton moved with the family?" If they could locate her, they might get a great deal of material to help their investigation.

"No. They turned her out when they moved. We've lost touch, but the last I heard she was still looking for a position. The poor dear was having problems since her health is not what it should be."

When Amy opened her mouth to speak, William said, "No. We already have a housekeeper."

"What?" She attempted to look innocent, but he knew if he hadn't mentioned it, he would be adding yet another member to his staff. His new wife picked up stray people like others did stray kittens.

"I must hurry, my lord. The best vegetables are gone by late afternoon. I wish you a good day." The housekeeper began to move forward.

Before she passed them by, William said, "Can I give you a message to deliver to Mrs. Krampton? She might have some information on where the family has gone."

The woman shrugged. "I'm not sure when I will see her again; my employer keeps me quite busy."

William slid out of his pocket a notepad he generally carried, along with a pencil. He scribbled a quick missive asking the woman if they could call on her to discuss her former employer.

Mrs. Blanchard reluctantly took the paper from his hand.

"Thank you for your help, Mrs. Blanchard."

"As I said, I don't know when I'll see her again." She turned to walk away, then looked back and took the few steps to return to where they stood. "One thing about the son that troubled me."

"What is that?" William asked.

"He seemed to truly hate his father. They always fought when Mr. Lawrence was about. I know men and their sons oftentimes clash, but I remember feeling particularly concerned one time when the boy shouted at his father as he hurried down the steps, *"I will kill you one day."*

She paused and shivered. "It wasn't his words as much as the look on the lad's face that I will never forget."

CHAPTER 33

As Amy and William entered Atkinson & Tucker for the weekly book club meeting, they were greeted by the Misses O'Neill, dressed, as always, in identical outfits. They rushed toward them with excitement in their eyes.

"Oh, my dear, I understand that nasty man who killed his wife at your wedding breakfast is now himself dead?" Miss Gertrude O'Neill, her eyes wide as an owl's, gripped Amy's hand with her cold fingers.

"Yes. Although it was never proven that Mr. F-Finch," she said, thinking of the man with two names and two identities who'd had her stumbling over the appellation, "killed his wife. However, you are correct that he was found deceased in his bed."

"In your house, I understand!" The women tsked and shook their heads.

"Nasty business," Miss Penelope O'Neill added. "Why was he not in gaol?"

William took the time to explain to the ladies how Albert's release into their custody had come about.

"So strange," Miss Gertrude said as she nodded to her sister, who echoed her words.

They chatted for a few minutes, both Amy and William trying to get the women away from talk of murders. Amy glanced at the doorway and spotted Eloise entering the room. That itself was unusual since she always scurried in late for the meeting. And late for mostly everything else as well.

"If you will excuse me, I need to speak with Miss Spencer." She hurried off, feeling only slightly guilty about leaving William to manage the O'Neill sisters.

Amy hugged her friend, then leaned back, her hands on Eloise's shoulders. "Have you been keeping something from me?"

Eloise's attempt at an innocent look did not quite succeed. "What?"

Amy narrowed her eyes. "Michael?"

When Eloise flushed but didn't answer, Amy added, "My brother?"

Eloise sighed. "I know who Michael is."

"Apparently better than I had realized." Amy smirked and linked arms with Eloise, walking her toward the rear of the room. "I didn't know you even knew Michael that well."

"Well . . ."

"Yes?" Amy grinned at Eloise's discomfort, something she rarely saw in her friend, who normally oozed confidence.

Eloise took in a deep breath and turned toward Amy, releasing her arm. "Do you remember all those trips I took to London to see my cousin?"

It was true that Eloise had seemed quite devoted to her cousin. At least four or five times a year she would make a visit to London for a couple of weeks. Amy never questioned it, but now she had a feeling there was more to her holidays than she had supposed. "Yesss. I remember quite well."

"I met Michael at an event my cousin, Louise, invited me to. I knew him of course, through you, but had never really spent much time with him."

"And?" Amy had to work very hard to hide her grin.

"Well, we, sort of, became, you know, friends."

"Friends?" She loved dragging this out, since she'd received a few well-chosen hints and teasing remarks from Eloise when she and William had first begun to spend time together.

"All right. We courted. I like Michael. He is charming, funny, honorable, and handsome."

"Why did you never tell me? We are best friends. Or so I thought."

"We are." She reached out and took Amy's hand. "Until Michael moved to Bath, we kept our relationship quiet because I knew your father would never approve. However, Michael has assured me it makes no difference to him, and since he now plans to stay in Bath . . ."

Amy pulled her friend close. "I can't think of a better match for you—or Michael. You will do very well together."

Eloise drew back. "Now wait a minute, dear friend. Nothing along those lines has been mentioned or settled. We just enjoy each other's company."

"Uh-huh. Sort of like me and William?"

"Yes."

"Um, we enjoyed each other's company so much we got married."

Eloise swatted Amy's arm. "Stop." She turned serious. "How is it anyway? Marriage, I mean. I've always been rather leery about it."

Amy could not control her grin. "Just fine." She was abashed to find herself blushing. "Yes. Quite remarkable, in fact."

Just then Michael entered the room and strolled up to the two of them. He gave a slight bow. "Good evening, sister, Miss Spencer." Amy took note of the definite gleam in his eyes as he spoke with Eloise. In fact, he'd barely looked at her once he saw Eloise.

"Good evening, Brother." She wiggled her fingers in his face to get his attention.

William joined their small group and greeted Eloise and Michael right before Mr. Colbert called the meeting to order. Once again, William's mother sat in the very front, where her husband could gaze upon her. Amy realized she'd been so caught up in Eloise and Michael that she hadn't even greeted William's parents. She must redress that lack of manners when the meeting ended.

Michael, Eloise, William, and Amy settled on a comfortable settee together. Eloise leaned over and spoke into Amy's ear. "I assume you are still investigating the murders?"

"Yes. You and I must have tea soon so I can let you know what we've discovered."

Amy sighed as Mr. Colbert began to speak. *Or more precisely, what we have* not *discovered.*

★　★　★

"We must move ahead with this, William." Amy's frustrated words echoed his own helpless feelings. They had two murders and a few suspects, and despite the police closing the cases, he was not convinced that Albert/David had killed Alice and then himself.

"There is every evidence that Albert had planned to escape," he said. "Since we know he had another wife, there is a good possibility that he planned to turn his thievery into cash and move his family away from Bath before he could be sentenced in Alice's death."

"Or he planned to use the ill-gotten gains to disappear from the murder charges and his family both. He was not the most honorable of men. Plus we must review our list of suspects and see if there is anyone on the list who wanted both of them dead."

"That is where I am stumped. Was this a matter of one person killing Alice and another Albert? Or one person killing both? Of course, I don't know them as well as you do since they were your family members. Can you think of someone who could want them both dead?"

Amy shook her head. "No. Even though I knew them for a long time, Alice in particular, I didn't know them well. I suggest we go over our list carefully and go through each suspect."

It was the morning after the book club meeting, and they were seated in the drawing room, in a blessedly quiet house. Michael and Franklin had gone off to do their normal daily routine. Lady Margaret had departed about fifteen minutes earlier to visit friends, her bird locked up securely in its cage, behind a closed door, so they didn't hear the animal's latest attempt at auditioning for Drury Lane.

Persephone lay peacefully on the rug in front of the fireplace, sound asleep. At last they could speak to each other openly without having to retire to their bedchamber, where they never got too much done in way of the investigation, with much more pleasant activities taking up their time.

Amy returned to the seat next to William, a piece of paper and pencil in her hand. "We shall start with Alice's murder. Who would benefit from her death?"

"Obviously, Mrs. Davis."

Amy wrote the name as she shook her head. "I'll add her name, but"—she waved her finger at William—"she is our employee now, and according to Mrs. O'Sullivan, doing an excellent job."

"Amy, dear, even criminals can do outstanding work."

Choosing to ignore his comment, she held the pencil over the paper. "Next?"

"I overheard the maids speaking this morning and was quite surprised to hear Mrs. Beavers say that her son is four years old."

"And why is that a surprise?"

"Because Mr. Beavers died five years ago, she told me."

"At one time we suspected Mrs. Beavers, since she was present at the wedding breakfast—"

"And was here in the house when Albert was poisoned," Amy added.

"—but we did eliminate her," William finished.

Amy nodded. "Until we can find out more information about her, I don't believe we should eliminate her. However, Mrs. O'Sullivan says she is doing an excellent job as well."

William sighed. "Amy, we need to make a list regardless of how well these women clean the house."

"Speaking of cleaning the house, I asked Mrs. O'Sullivan, and it was Mrs. Beavers who was assigned to clean Albert's room."

"So she had access."

"Yes." She put a check next to Mrs. Beavers's name. "All things considered, we must put her down. I will do more investigation into the circumstances surrounding her son."

They both stared off into space. "Again we're back to the question: Did the same person kill both of them?" William said.

"Let's finish a list of suspects for each murder and then see if one name appears on both."

William pointed to the paper. "We should add Jared, Alice's nephew. He was at the wedding breakfast, and once Alice died, he had every reason to kill Albert."

"But did he have a reason to kill Alice?" Amy tapped her pencil against her lips. "She was supporting him."

"Possibly she threatened to cut him off, and the only way to get the money was to kill her."

"Except it would be normal for her husband to inherit," Amy said.

"But she was planning a divorce, which meant Albert would not inherit anything. Also, if Jared killed her in a way that made it appear as though her husband had given Alice the fatal glass of champagne, Albert would not inherit, and it would all go to Jared."

Amy nodded and wrote his name in two columns. "Do we have anyone else for Alice's list?"

"I guess we should put Albert down as a suspect too. We're limited with suspects for her murder because whoever put the belladonna in her glass had to have been at the wedding breakfast."

"Which is Albert, Mrs. Davis, and Mrs. Beavers." Amy sighed as she studied the paper in her hand. "We can certainly add John Lawrence to suspects for Albert's death."

William nodded. "Definitely, especially after our conversation with the neighbor's housekeeper, Mrs. Blanchard. Hatred and death threats make for good motives, but Albert's death cut off the money he'd been sending to the boy's mother."

"Yes, there is that." She paused and studied her hands as she thought for a minute. "I have found young men tend to be a bit on the reckless side by nature. They don't always think of the consequences of their actions. If he was ruled by passion and hatred, he could very well have justified his actions as 'saving' his mother."

"How would he get into the house to kill Albert?"

Amy shrugged. "The ladder Albert left leaning against the house for his own trips out and about?"

William rubbed his eyes with his index finger and thumb. "I'm getting a headache. This one is far too complicated for my brain. Was it two killers? One killer? Lastly, did whoever kill Alice not have a motive to kill Albert until Alice's murder became known?"

Amy closed her eyes and shook her head. "You're giving *me* a headache."

William slapped his hands on his thighs and stood. "I suggest we get some air. We can take a stroll in the park and clear our heads. Maybe stop at Sally Lunn's and have lunch."

Just as they were shrugging into their coats, the knocker sounded. Filbert opened the door as William adjusted Amy's hat.

"Good afternoon, we would like to speak with Lord and Lady Wethington." Detective Carson grinned broadly. "Well, how fortunate for us. They are standing right here."

"I don't believe my headache is going away anytime soon," William mumbled.

CHAPTER 34

"What a surprise, Detectives," Amy said as they all stood in the entrance hall, staring at each other, Filbert still standing straight and stiff, holding the front door open.

"We need only a few minutes of your time," Detective Carson said.

Amy glanced at William, whose expression mirrored her thoughts. With a deep sigh, William said, "Very well." He waved them up the stairs, where they all entered the drawing room.

Neither Amy nor William removed their coats. Amy hoped the detectives would take that as a signal for them to make the visit as short as possible.

Once settled in chairs, Detective Carson said, "We have reopened the murder cases of both Mrs. Finch and Mr. Finch."

Those words from Detective Carson surprised her more than just about anything the man had said in all the time they knew him.

"Why is that?" William asked.

Carson's face flushed, and he looked down at his hands, which dangled between his spread knees. "Our chief investigator felt there was more to the cases than we originally thought."

Neither Amy nor William said anything, waiting for the detective to continue. Apparently, his remorse had ended because he looked up at them with the same supercilious sneer he usually delivered.

So much for penitence.

"Why are you here, Detective?" William had clearly lost patience with the man.

"There are a few things we need to clear up, and we have reason to believe you and your wife have the answers we need."

Silence.

Carson cleared his throat. "It has come to our attention that Albert Finch was an assumed name, the victim's real name being Mr. David Lawrence."

Silence.

"We have also learned that Mrs. Finch's nephew, Mr. Jared Munson, was being supported by his aunt and had been disruptive at the reading of the will."

Silence.

"It seems Mr. Finch also had a family hidden away, including a wife and two sons. One of whom threatened his life."

Silence.

"Do you have nothing to say?" Carson's frustrated voice was loud enough to be heard in the entrance hall.

Amy straightened in her chair. "Detective, you have not asked one single question of us. All you've done is recite some facts that you have discovered. What is it you expect me or Lord Wethington to say?"

Detective Carson pounded his fist on the arm of the chair. "I want to know if you are aware of these things, and since I am positive you are, what you have made of it."

Amy's jaw dropped and she swung her head toward William.

William said, very slowly, "Are you asking us for help, Detective?"

"No. Yes. Perhaps."

William grinned. "Well. That cleared the mystery up quite well."

Carson narrowed his eyes. "Don't think for one minute we were not aware of your continued work on these murders despite repeated warnings from me to stay out of police business."

William stood. "You are correct, Detective. We should stay out of police business, so if you are finished, my wife and I were about to take a stroll to the park."

Carson gritted his teeth, his jaw so tight Amy was amazed his teeth didn't crack. "Sit down, *my lord.*"

"Is that an order?" William asked, looking down his nose at the detective.

"No. A request. Please, have a seat, my lord." The detective's face was so flushed Amy was afraid he might suffer an apoplexy right there in the room. Hopefully not, as she didn't want to deal with another dead body.

Detective Marsh merely sat the entire time, his faithful notepad and pen at the ready. He'd spent the time they were speaking looking back and forth between William and Detective Carson as if he were viewing a tennis match.

Carson ran his finger around the inside of his neckcloth. "It has been noted that you and your wife have helped to solve other murder cases."

"Helped?" Amy asked, with a smile. "Detective, we solved them for you."

"I wouldn't say 'solved.'" He waved his hand. "But I think if we put our heads together, we might be able to clear this whole thing up."

William took his seat again. "I will say that everything you mentioned, Lady Wethington and I have also found to be true."

Detective Marsh began to scribble.

"I ask you"—he looked at William—"not order you, but *ask* you, to advise us of any other people you have on a suspect list that I am certain you have compiled."

Amy looked at William, who gave her a curt nod. She picked up the paper they had been working on that sat on the table next to her. "As far as both Mrs. Finch's and Mr. Finch's unfortunate deaths, we have reason to suspect Mrs. Caroline Beavers, a maid who worked at the wedding breakfast and arrived here as a temporary maid on the day Albert was poisoned. There are things in her background that warrant further examination.

"We also have not eliminated Mrs. Davis, as her situation was desperate the day she attended the wedding breakfast."

Detective Carson darted a quick look at William before he said, "What about the nephew, Mr. Jared Munson? How close to Mrs. Finch was he seated at the wedding breakfast?"

Amy shook her head. "I honestly don't remember."

"What are your thoughts on him?"

William took over. "He was being supported by Mrs. Finch, and we keep him on our list for both murders since he did not receive what he expected from Mrs. Finch's will. We suspect, but have no proof, that Mrs. Finch might have threatened to cut him off."

They had nothing more on young John Lawrence except his threat, so they kept that to themselves. However, the questions went on for some time. Amy and William both shared information the police hadn't discovered, including the fact that Albert had been stealing and pawning things from their house.

"Why did you not tell us that?" Carson groused.

"Because you closed the case with the theory that Albert killed himself in grief and guilt for killing his wife, and there didn't seem to be any reason to let you know that. Your mind had been made up."

"And," Amy couldn't help but add, "we were told to stay out of police business."

At a signal from Detective Carson, Detective Marsh flipped his notepad closed and tucked it into his pocket. The two detectives stood. "That is all for now."

The four of them trooped down the stairs and, as they all still wore their outer garments, they made their way out the front door and down the steps together.

Detective Carson hesitated for a moment, then blurted out, "Thank you for your help. We would appreciate any further assistance you can provide." With those hurried words, he and Detective Marsh strode away.

Amy and William looked at each other and burst into laughter. Amy wiped the tears from her eyes. "I would never have guessed."

"They must have been subjected to quite the dressing down from their superior to come here and admit they were wrong."

"And ask for our help!"

William took her arm, and they strolled down the pavement toward the park. A perfect day for a stroll. Not a cloud in the sky.

★ ★ ★

"He's gone again." Lady Margaret met William and Amy at the door to the drawing room, where they gathered awaiting the dinner announcement.

"Othello?" Amy asked.

"Yes." Lady Margaret did not look distressed over this disappearance, but more frustrated and angry.

"I thought you had the door to your room closed and the bird ensconced in his cage?" Amy accepted the glass of sherry William handed her.

"I might have forgotten to close my door. And maybe the cage door was open since I let him fly around my room last night." Lady Margaret swirled the brandy in her snifter. Apparently sherry was not strong enough for her tonight.

"I'm afraid things are not looking good, son." Franklin entered the room right behind Michael.

"I told you not to trust that man," Michael said as he poured a brandy. "Thieves, the lot of them."

"I worked with that company for years. I've never had a problem before." Franklin poured himself a hefty snifter of brandy.

Michael shook his head. "The entire management of the organization changed last year. I heard enough rumors to warn you we should back out."

"Is something wrong, Papa?" Amy asked.

"Not much, my dear daughter. Just that the project Michael and I have been working on, the one that should have closed last week, has fallen through."

"Oh, I'm sorry," Amy said. She looked from her brother to her father. "Will this affect your move to Bath?"

"No," Michael said and shook his head.

"Yes," Franklin snapped right behind him.

Filbert entered the drawing room. "Dinner is ready, my lords, my ladies."

Once they were settled at the table, Franklin turned to Michael. "I don't see why we would need to continue in Bath. There is no reason to stay here."

Michael's eyes narrowed. "There is a very good reason for *me* to stay here.

Amy jumped in, evidently attempting to smooth things over between father and son. "Papa, I thought you said you would prefer to leave London and live here?"

Franklin glared at Michael. "That was before I became aware of things that I had not previously known."

"Franklin, please, do not do to your son what you did to me years ago," Lady Margaret said.

William remembered earlier in the year, when they had been dealing with the murder of his man of business, Mr. James Harding. They'd been surprised to learn that Lady Margaret had hoped to marry James back in their youth, but her brother had forbidden her to see the man and sent her to their country home to "come to her senses."

Of course, considering the way James had turned out in the end, blackmailing and cheating his clients, Lady Margaret had been better off without him, but it hadn't stopped her from suffering a broken heart at the time.

Franklin waved his hand. "That silliness in your youth was nothing compared to my son, and heir, courting a woman who is totally unacceptable."

"Not to me," Michael said as he placed a piece of salmon on his plate from the serving platter one of the footmen held.

William had to give his brother-in-law credit. He wasn't so sure he would remain that calm if someone were insulting Amy. On the other hand, given Franklin's propensity to allow his temper free rein when things did not go his way, Michael probably knew the best way to handle his father.

"May we please dispense with uncomfortable subjects at the dinner table?" Lady Margaret said. "I am quite sure William is weary of all the arguments. In fact, I am quite tired of them myself."

The meal continued in silence, which made William wonder if it was impossible for Amy's family to share a meal without contention. This might very well be why her mother had brought Amy to live in Bath with Lady Margaret all those years ago. Franklin might not have been the most pleasant husband to handle on a daily basis.

"Othello is gone again," Lady Margaret repeated. Franklin scowled.

More silence as the meal continued.

They were just about to begin tea, sweets, cheese, and fruit when Filbert entered the room. "My lord, there is a guest awaiting you in the drawing room. She said it would only take a few minutes of your time."

"Who is it?"

Filbert looked down at the small card in his hand. "A Mrs. David Lawrence, my lord."

William wiped his mouth with his napkin and placed it alongside his plate. He looked over at Amy. "Are you coming?"

"Yes." She took a sip of her tea and stood.

"Who is that? And why would a woman appear uninvited at the dinner hour?" Franklin asked.

William stood and moved around the table to pull Amy's seat back. "No need to concern yourself, Franklin. This won't take long."

With that nebulous answer, he and Amy left the room and walked down the corridor to the drawing room.

Mrs. Lawrence paced the area, wringing her hands. She turned when they entered. "Oh, thank you so much for allowing me to interrupt you, my lord. I would never have presumed to impose upon you and your wife were this not a dire emergency."

William waved at the settee. "Please, Mrs. Lawrence, have a seat. May I get you a drink or send for tea?"

She sat on the very edge of the chair closest to the fireplace, her back ramrod straight. "No, nothing for me, thank you."

"How can I help you?"

She took a deep breath and said, "I have come to ask your assistance. My son, John, has just been arrested by the police."

Amy leaned forward. "Whatever for, Mrs. Lawrence?"

"I'm afraid he broke into a house not far from ours and stole some things."

William studied her for a minute. "I don't understand. Why did you come to us? Why not hire a barrister or solicitor?"

She patted the corner of her eyes with the nearly shredded handkerchief in her hands. "Because I didn't know who else to turn to. The police have charged him with the theft, but they told me they were preparing charges against him for the murder of my husband."

CHAPTER 35

"Perhaps you should take a seat, and I will send for tea." Amy waved Mrs. Lawrence toward the comfortable red and black velvet settee.

"Yes, perhaps tea would help calm me." Mrs. Lawrence sat and continued to shred her handkerchief while Amy rang for a footman and ordered a tea tray.

William studied the woman once Amy returned to sit beside him. "Mrs. Lawrence, perhaps you can tell us how this all came about with your son. I must add, before we begin, that we visited your residence based on the direction you gave my man, but found it empty."

She flushed and looked down at her lap. "I apologize for that, my lord. Because the money David was sending me has stopped, we were forced to leave that townhouse. We moved to another place only two blocks from where we were living, but certainly not as nice. I didn't tell your driver the correct direction since I was embarrassed to have you visit me there."

"You have no means of support?" Amy asked.

"I have asked at several shops in our area, but so far I haven't been able to secure employment." She looked up at William with tightened lips. "That is why John stole those things. He knew we needed money."

Amy opened her mouth to speak, and William stopped her with a raised hand. "No, Amy. Just no."

She slumped in the chair. The poor woman had two children to feed. How was she to keep a roof over her head and food on her table, with no means of support?

But William was correct. If she kept hiring these poor women who found themselves mixed up in two murders, they would soon be unable to keep a roof over their own heads. Perhaps she could ask around and find a place for Mrs. Lawrence to work.

"I assume you do not expect to receive anything from Mr. Lawrence's estate?"

Mrs. Lawrence shook her head. "No. I visited the solicitor, and he made it quite clear that because David married Mrs. Finch illegally, he was not entitled to anything from her estate, and therefore, I get nothing either."

The woman had permitted her husband to dally with other ladies for years while she turned a blind eye. Perhaps Amy's sympathy should rest elsewhere.

"I still do not understand what you expect from me," William said.

"I had hoped you could at least recommend a barrister who could help me get my son out of gaol. If I could make payments to the man, that would help a great deal. I do have a bit of money put aside, but I have to save that for food and rent."

Amy squeaked and William cast her a dark look. "No."

She sighed and said, "Mrs. Lawrence, you said the police were intending to bring charges against your son for your husband's murder. Do you have any idea why?"

"Mr. Lawrence and John never got on very well. I think as he got older, my son disapproved of my husband's life. I had learned years ago to look the other way, as he always took care of our needs and did come by on a somewhat regular basis."

Stopped by long enough at least to get her with child twice. Amy was still stunned at the woman's acceptance of this strange life.

"The last time Mr. Lawrence visited, John became quite enraged when he began to take his leave. When he confronted Mr. Lawrence on his behavior, it turned into quite the squabble, and my son might have threatened my husband."

"Might have? Or did?"

Mrs. Lawrence sighed. "He did."

"And apparently someone must have overheard the conversation for the police to be pursuing murder charges against him," Amy said.

"Yes. There is this very nosy housekeeper who lives in the next townhouse. She was on her way home from the shops when the argument happened."

For the police to be ready to charge John, they must have made the effort to speak with Mrs. Blanchard, even though Amy and William hadn't shared that information with the detectives. Amy was impressed.

Mrs. Lawrence continued. "Then, when John was arrested for the thievery, which happened when he entered a house through a window, the police decided he was must also have been able to break into your house to poison Mr. Lawrence. That and the threats he'd shouted at his father were enough for them to assume his guilt."

They remained silent for a few minutes. Then William said, "Mrs. Lawrence, because of your situation, I am prepared to secure the services of Mr. Nelson-Graves, a barrister I've used in the past. I will make the payment arrangements with him."

Mrs. Lawrence began to cry. "Thank you so much, my lord. I promise as soon as I secure employment, I will pay you back."

William waved his hand. "We need not worry about that now."

"Will Mr. Nelson-Graves be able to get John out of gaol?" The woman's voice shook, which was not surprising considering that gaol was a terrible place for adults, but much more so for children.

"I will arrange a time for you to visit with Mr. Nelson-Graves. He will be able to answer your questions." William stood and walked to the small desk near the window. He withdrew a paper and pencil from the drawer. He scribbled on it and brought it over to Mrs. Lawrence.

"Here is Mr. Nelson-Graves's address. I suggest you send a missive to his office on Monday and request an appointment. I will send a note also, telling him to expect you."

Just then, the tea tray arrived. "Please stay for a while to partake of the tea, Mrs. Lawrence," Amy said. To make her more comfortable, she and William joined her, since they'd left their own tea at the dining table.

Nothing more of the note was mentioned. After they finished the tea, William arranged for his carriage to take Mrs. Lawrence home, since she'd arrived in a hackney. Amy and William retired to the library to discuss the latest happening in the very confusing murders.

★   ★   ★

The Assembly was well under way when William and Amy arrived the next evening. As promised, after Mrs. Lawrence had left the day before, William had sent a note along to Mr. Nelson-Graves with an introduction to Mrs. Lawrence and the assurance that he would take care of the fees for the barrister's work.

It had taken some persuasion, but he had finally talked Amy out of hiring Mrs. Lawrence. However, he did promise he would help her in attempting to find employment for the woman. He shook his head at the softheartedness of his new wife.

Lady Margaret greeted them as they made their way across the room, dodging dancers in the middle of a lively quadrille.

"I know it's been a while since anyone has asked, but why aren't you two on your honeymoon now that the murders have been solved?"

"Who said they were solved?" Amy asked.

Lady Margaret frowned, looking back and forth between them. "I thought you said the police decided Albert killed Alice and then himself because of guilt?"

"Really, Aunt, you must stay up on these things," Amy said with a smile. "The police visited yesterday and said they had been wrong."

Her eyes widened. "They admitted they were wrong?"

"Actually, it seems their chief investigator thought they were wrong. They came to us to see if we had additional information for them."

"They asked for your help?" Lady Margaret laughed. "My goodness, that is certainly a surprise."

The Misses O'Neill, Mr. Rawlings, and Mr. Davidson joined their group. William's parents strolled up, and the discussion moved to the current book the club was reading, the matter of the dual murders put aside.

"I thought Miss Spencer and you brother, Lord Davenport, were attending tonight?" Miss Gertrude O'Neill said. "At least that is what Miss Spencer said at the book club meeting Thursday night."

Amy shrugged. "I haven't seen Michael all day, actually. He and my papa are trying to put together a business deal that didn't work for them. I believe they were attempting to salvage as much of it as they could."

The musicians began a waltz, and William solicited his wife's hand for the dance. His parents joined them on the dance floor, and Lady Margaret was waltzing with a gentleman he'd seen before but who was not familiar.

Amy looked up at him as they moved into a turn. "I think if Annabelle is at church tomorrow, I will invite her to lunch again. I do worry about her, you know. She is really taking Alice's death very hard. Also, now that a couple of weeks have passed since the murder, she might be able to offer some information to us."

"Twins," William said. "I'm sure it's worse than losing just a sibling."

"Indeed."

Amy glanced over William's shoulder. "My goodness, look who just entered the Assembly."

"Who?" William was not in a position to look unless he swung Amy around, crashing her into another couple.

"Jared."

"Munson?"

"Yes. I've never seen him here before."

William finally got a look at the man. "I believe he's in his cups. At least he seems to be having trouble walking a straight line."

"Oh dear, I believe you're right."

They continued with their dance, William keeping an eye on the young man as he made his way from group to group, not lasting long at any of them.

The music ended and William escorted Amy to the refreshment table to obtain a drink. With glasses in hand, they joined their book club group just as Jared was walking up to them.

He almost stumbled into Amy. "What say you, Cousin, how about a dance?"

"Oh, Jared, I don't believe I can handle another dance. I'm just trying to catch my breath from the last one."

Amy offered him a smile, and William glared at the man. "I think it might be best to take your leave, Jared."

"Why?" He swayed toward William, who put his hand out to keep the man from smashing into him.

"Let me help you to your carriage." William took Jared's arm.

Jared tugged his arm away. "I want to dance with my cousin."

"No." William gripped him again. "My wife does not wish to dance with you."

William signaled one of the footmen who stood along the wall, ready to handle any difficulties. The large man walked over, keeping his eye on Jared. Once he reached them, he took a hold of Jared's shoulder. "I think it's time you left, friend."

"No. I want to dance with my cousin." He looked up at the footman. "My aunt was murdered at my cousin's wedding, you know. Now I have no money." He thumped his chest with his thumb. "I should have gotten everything she had. It should have been mine."

His words were slurred, so William could only guess at what the man said.

The footman placed his hand under Jared's arm and attempted to move him forward. "Please allow me to escort you out, sir."

Jared swung at the man, missed him completely, and ended up on the floor, either knocked out or passed out.

William looked with disgust at the lump of the man curled up on the floor, seeming to settle in for the night. "I will speak with the man at the door and see if they can bring his carriage around."

Amy accompanied him down the stairs to the entrance. Luckily, Jared did have a carriage and driver with him. Two footmen dragged the soused man down the stairs, outside the entrance, and dumped him, not too kindly, into the carriage. One of the footmen tapped on the side of the vehicle, and the driver took off.

Shaking his head, William returned to where Amy awaited him at the door. "He's on his way home."

They returned to the dance and joined the others.

"Is everything well, Wethington?" Mr. Colbert asked.

"Yes. He is on his way home."

Amy looked past him, a huge smile on her face. "Oh, Michael! And Eloise! There you are. I thought you mentioned the two of you were coming tonight."

Hand in hand, the couple strolled up to the group. Miss Spencer stopped in front of Amy, a smug look on her face. She glanced at Michael who grinned.

"What?" Amy said, glancing back and forth between the two of them.

Michael raised Miss Spencer's left hand, where a nice-sized diamond ring caught the radiance from the numerous gaslights. "We're engaged!" she said.

Chapter 36

Amy's newly betrothed brother and her best friend sat along-side her and William in the family pew at St. Swithin's, awaiting Sunday service. Amid shocks and exclamations of good wishes, the unexpected announcement Eloise had made the night before still brought Amy a sense of joy.

Two of her favorite people in the world. After William, of course. She and Eloise, who had been best friends for years, would now be sisters. She'd always adored Michael, her only sibling, and looked up to him, even though they hadn't been raised together. But now they could raise their children together!

Unfortunately, she was certain Papa would not be joining in the sort of felicitations the couple had enjoyed the night before. He had already retired for the evening when they'd arrived home from the Assembly. That morning he had advised them at the breakfast table that he would not be joining them for church.

She had thought it quite wise of Michael not to impart his good news first thing in the morning. Of course, Eloise would be joining them for lunch after church, as was her general practice. Amy admitted to a bit of unease that if the announcement was made to Papa then, it would become very uncomfortable for Eloise. And Michael. And Annabelle, whom she hoped to persuade to join them. She must remember to ask Michael and Eloise not to say anything until luncheon had ended.

'Twas sad they had to hide such wonderful, exciting news.

Amy looked around the church and spotted Annabelle in the Munson pew. She appeared so sad and lonely, sitting there by herself. Amy was about to excuse herself and ask her cousin to join them in their pew when the vicar came out to begin the service.

As always, she found the music, sermon, Bible quotes, and blessings very calming and soothing. It was a wonderful way to end a busy week and reflect on the one to come.

Despite her best intentions to focus on her prayers, thoughts about the week to come naturally gravitated to the murders. Were she writing a book based on what had happened so far, she would have Jared as the responsible killer of Alice. Money is a great motivator. However, that didn't seem to fit either, even though she could not say why. That, of course, would make it obvious he also killed Albert.

As far as Albert's murder, she wasn't sure the son had done it, despite the police's hurry to charge him. Making things easy for themselves seemed to be their method.

The question that always hovered in the back of her mind was whether the same person had killed both Alice and Albert. No matter how she tried to put the puzzle pieces together, Jared was the only suspect so far to fit the scenario of one person killing both husband and wife.

However, if he was not the murderer, that left the uncomfortable fact that two different people had enough anger to kill the Finches. Aside from what they'd discovered about Albert and his strange life, he and Alice had seemed like a normal couple, doing normal things. From what she knew, though it was admittedly not very much, they didn't have a great many friends.

She sighed and concentrated on the final blessing.

The sun shone brightly as they left the church. Before she was able to walk away from them, Amy hurried up to Annabelle.

She linked her arm in her cousin's. "We would love to have you join us for lunch, Annabelle."

The woman looked surprised. But pleased. "That would be very nice," she said.

"Wonderful. Why don't you dismiss your carriage and ride with me and my husband and Aunt Margaret? We will send you home in our carriage."

Annabelle remained quiet as they traveled from the church to their townhouse. She gazed out the window, giving the occasional pensive sigh.

As they all arrived together at the house, laughing and removing outer garments, Amy sidled up to Michael and pulled him aside. "I know you are pleased about your engagement, but I beg you not to speak of it at the table. You know Papa is not going to be happy, and it will only embarrass Eloise and Annabelle to have him bellowing."

Michael hugged her and kissed the top of her head. "Little sister, you are not the only wise one in the family. Neither I nor Eloise will mention our betrothal at lunch. I planned to speak with Father this afternoon once everyone is gone. Including my future wife."

Amy took in a deep sigh. "Thank you." At least she could now enjoy her lunch and focus on Annabelle, who clearly needed some kindness.

Fortunately, it was a quiet, pleasant meal. They did not discuss murder, engagements, or repairs on the Winchester townhouse. There was no talk of missing birds, collapsing business deals, or annoying barking dogs.

Consequently, they spoke of the weather, the poor roads, and the Queen's birthday. Boring, perhaps, but pleasant.

After they enjoyed tea, sweets, and fruit, Annabelle leaned over toward Amy, sitting next to her. "I believe I would like to have William's carriage brought around. I find I fatigue easily and enjoy an afternoon nap."

"Of course." Amy signaled for one of the footmen to approach. "Please have his lordship's carriage brought around and let us know when it is ready."

"Of course, my lady. Right away."

They bantered for a few more minutes with innocuous subjects before a maid appeared to advise Amy that the carriage was ready. She stood and walked with Annabelle to the door. She gave her cousin a hug. "Please plan to visit with us on Sundays. We would love to have you join us for lunch each week."

Annabelle patted her hand. "Thank you so much, dear. You are so very kind."

Amy watched her walk down the steps, holding onto the footman, looking very much like an old woman, and then she returned to the table.

★ ★ ★

The next to leave them was Eloise. William considered that Michael wanted her gone when he confronted his father with his betrothal. His brother-in-law escorted Eloise to her home, which was only a few townhouses away.

By the time he'd returned, they were all settled in the drawing room. Lady Margaret had retrieved her sketch pad and was busy drawing. Amy had picked up her knitting.

William was unsure what she was making and was afraid to ask. Whatever it was, it was lumpy, crooked, and had one or two gaping holes in the center. She was much better off using her spare time to write her books. His fondest wish was that whatever the strange thing was, it would not appear under the Christmas tree in December with his name on it.

"Children, I have received good news," Franklin said as Michael strode into the room. Since he was smiling, he doubted his father-in-law was about to announce his son's betrothal.

"I stopped by the Winchester townhouse late yesterday afternoon. The supervisor informed me that the repairs are almost finished. In fact, we can move back there as early as tomorrow afternoon."

"What about Othello?"

"Who?" Franklin asked.

Lady Margaret huffed. "My bird? He is still missing."

Franklin narrowed his eyes. "And with any luck he will not show up again."

Amy jumped in and patted her aunt's hand. "No worries, I am sure he will once again reappear, and we will see that he is returned to you."

"Father, I would speak with you in the library." Leaning against the fireplace mantel, Michael winked at Amy, which didn't seem to relax the stiffness in her shoulders. His sister did not like confrontations.

"Why?"

Michael straightened and pulled on the cuffs of his jacket. "There is something of importance I must discuss with you."

"Is it business?"

"No."

"Then out with it, boy. I see no reason for us to secret our-selves in the library. It's only family here."

"Very well." Michael clasped his hands behind his back and rocked on his heels. "I became betrothed last night."

For once Franklin was speechless. Then it was obvious to all that the man had understood what his son had said, and what it meant. He narrowed his eyes. "To whom?"

"Miss Eloise Spencer."

Franklin hopped up, his face red and his eyes bulging. "I will not have that hoyden for a daughter-in-law, nor as the mother of my grandchildren!"

William was once again impressed with Michael's calm in the storm. However, his stance and lowered voice were indica-tive of controlled anger. "If you wish to see said grandchildren, you will desist in your insults to my soon-to-be wife."

Franklin slashed his hand in the air. "I won't have it."

"You have no choice," Michael said, his voice even lower.

"I do. I can cut you out of my will."

Michael shrugged. "No matter. I have enough resources of my own. And the title and entailed properties will come to me regardless because of the laws of primogeniture."

Amy stood, her hands fisted at her sides. "Papa, please, stop this. Michael has the right to make his own choice of a wife."

Franklin swung in her direction, the look on his face mak-ing William jump from his seat to stand alongside his wife.

"Stay out of this, girl."

William leaned toward her and spoke into her ear, "I think your father is correct. You need to stay out of this. I suggest we retire to our bedchamber and let them sort it out."

"No!" Amy moved a step away from him, but he followed. "Papa, Aunt Margaret told us how you forbade her to continue her association with the man she loved and banished her to the country. That was not fair, and your attitude toward Michael and Eloise is also not fair."

Franklin sneered. "Indeed. I did interfere with her infatuation with Mr. Harding. And considering how the man ended up drunk and dead in the River Avon, after his shady business deals almost ruined your husband, I think it was a wise decision."

William leaned into her again. "I'm afraid that wasn't a good example to use, my love."

Amy looked up at him. "I'm afraid you're right."

"Then let us leave them to straighten this out." William turned to Lady Margaret. "Amy and I feel the need for a walk in the fresh air. Would you care to join us?"

Lady Margaret hopped up. "Yes. That sounds like just the thing."

The three of them left Michael and Franklin glaring at each other. They retrieved their outer garments and departed.

The bright sun of earlier had been diminished by increasing clouds. Amy shivered and leaned closed to William. "It has become a tad chillier than when we left church."

"We shall walk fast; it will warm us up."

Lady Margaret shook her head. "I do wish Franklin would remember that he is Amy's and Michael's father, and not their guardian, as they are not children. Michael certainly has the right to marry whomever he wishes." She looked over at Amy. "Frankly, I see nothing wrong with Eloise. In fact, I think she would be good for Michael, as he would be good for her."

"I'm glad you see that too, Aunt," Amy said. "As you know, Eloise and I have been friends for ages, and I see her as loving, kind, smart, and loyal. Michael needs a bit of loosening up, and I believe Eloise is just the woman to do it."

They remained on their walk for another half hour or so and then arrived back at the house. "Well, the building is still standing, and I'm hopeful the furniture is not in pieces," William said as they ascended the steps.

Filbert opened the door. "Othello has returned."

"With Persephone again?" Amy asked.

"Yes."

"I am going upstairs and locking that bird into his cage, and he will never again be allowed to leave it." Aunt Margaret handed her coat off to Filbert and hurried up the stairs.

"Things are quiet," Amy said looking around as they entered the drawing room. "And all the furniture is *not* in pieces."

Both Michael and Franklin were nowhere to be seen. William took his most comfortable chair and picked up the newspaper. Amy retrieved her knitted object and began to torture the thing again.

"My lord, my lady." Sally, one of the temporary upstairs maids entered the room.

Amy looked up at her and smiled. "Yes, what is it?"

The young girl cleared her throat and fidgeted with her hands. Finally, after taking a deep breath, she said. "Remember you were asking a while back about the possibility of an extra temporary employee the day Cook greeted us all?"

"Yes?"

"She was here today."

"Who was," William asked.

"The temporary maid. I remembered that Cook had her help in the kitchen while the rest of us were sent to the employee dining room to await Mrs. O'Sullivan. I never saw her again after that until today."

William looked over at Amy. "Where did you see her? Did she come to the kitchen door?"

Sally shook her head, her blonde curls bouncing despite the cap she wore on her head. "No. She was here for lunch today."

Amy took in a deep breath and looked over at William. "Annabelle?"

CHAPTER 37

Amy had barely processed the startling words from Sally when Filbert entered the drawing room. "My lord, the two detectives have arrived and request to speak with you."

Still shaken by what she'd just heard, Amy attempted to compose herself and said, "Thank you, Sally. You may return to your duties."

The maid scurried away just as the detectives entered the room. Again, not waiting for permission.

"Good morning, my lord, my lady," Carson bowed, very unlike him with his distaste for the nobility. Perhaps his actions had something to do with the smirk on his face.

"Sunday, Detective?" Amy said as she waved to a chair near them. She was unable to stand herself, Sally's news having weakened her knees. And, truth be known, her breathing wasn't too steady either.

Although he appeared much hardier than her, William also looked a bit shaken.

Annabelle? According to Sally, Annabelle was the extra employee whom Cook thought she counted, and this was troublesome. That was the day Albert had been poisoned, as the only meal he'd eaten that day was breakfast. As much as her heart attempted to shout "No!," her brain said Annabelle had most likely taken her anger out on the person she was certain had killed her beloved sister, not wanting to wait to see if he would be convicted and sentenced.

But her cousin had always seemed so kind and sweet. For goodness sake, she attended church most every Sunday! However, poisoning was a very passive way to kill someone, and based on Amy's research, a more common method for women to use.

All these thoughts were running through her mind as the detectives spoke while she had paid them no heed. William, however, seemed to be engaged with the conversation.

"What you are telling us, then, is that, in your opinion, Mr. Jared Munson did away with Mrs. Alice Finch at the wedding breakfast because he wanted her money, and you believe she had threatened to cut him off? And Albert met his end thanks to his son, John Lawrence, who despised the man?"

"Yes. And threatened him before a witness." Carson's smug look was almost comical, based on the information they'd just received from Sally. Which Amy had no intention of sharing with them. Especially since she was still processing the stunning news herself and certainly didn't want poor Annabelle tossed into gaol before Amy had the chance to clear the matter up.

"The reason for our visit is to thank you for the little assistance you provided, and to tell you the murders have been solved, so you may stop whatever investigation you thought would help us."

Despite her current mood, Amy almost laughed out loud.

"And the chief investigator agrees with this?" William asked.

"He will." Carson nodded. "We have a solid case against them both. They are currently in custody, and we will be seeking formal murder charges against them from the magistrate tomorrow."

William looked over at Amy and shrugged. "Well, if those are your conclusions, then I wish you luck in getting the chief inspector and the magistrate to move ahead with your plan."

Carson narrowed his eyes. "What is that supposed to mean? I guess you think you have it solved another way? You and your wife, the murder mystery author?"

William raised his hands as if in surrender. "I can honestly say we do not yet know what we believe to be true."

Amy nodded. That was a good way to put it since they'd yet to dissect or discuss the recent information.

Carson waved his hand. "That is why it is always best to leave these things to the professionals."

Amy was polite enough not to remind them that she and William had already solved prior murders that they had fumbled. What she wanted more than anything was for them to leave so she and William could consider this latest startling news.

Apparently, William thought the same. He slapped his hands on his thighs and rose. "Well, thank you, Detectives, for coming on a Sunday to ease our minds that the murderers have been identified. We don't want to detain you, assuming you have other and better things to do on a Sunday afternoon."

The detectives scrambled to rise, Detective Marsh quickly closing his notepad. Amy stayed in the drawing room as William escorted them to the door. Most likely to make sure they left.

After a few minutes, William reentered the room and collapsed into the chair across from Amy. "Well, then."

"Indeed. I don't know where to begin," Amy said. "If Sally is correct—and I see no reason why she would lie—Annabelle was the woman who came into the house the morning the temporary maids arrived and then left, never to be seen again."

"I think in all fairness to your cousin, we should visit her and see what she has to say for herself."

Amy breathed a sigh of relief. "Yes. I believe you are correct."

They were soon ensconced in their carriage on the way to Annabelle's house. "I wonder how the discussion between your brother and father went?" William asked. Her husband was apparently trying to distract her, but aside from the carriage collapsing around their ears, nothing was going to take away the magnitude of sadness and concern she felt.

She shrugged. "As neither one of them was home when we returned, I can't imagine. I do know when Michael makes up his mind about something, he doesn't change it. And from what I've seen when he and Eloise are together, there is a great deal of affection there."

"What I suggest is that you find someone for your father."

Amy burst into laughter. "Surely, you jest. Papa never showed much interest in my mother. I mean, they got on all right—when they were together. She lived in Bath, he lived in London. They both seemed quite satisfied with the arrangement."

"Quite odd, actually," William added.

"Yes. I never thought so myself until I got older and saw what other situations married couples had. What of your parents? Were they happy in love?"

William leaned back in the chair and rested his foot on his knee. "Happy, I believe. I'm not sure if theirs was a great love match. They were certainly fond of each other."

"What do you think of her marriage to Mr. Colbert?"

She almost giggled when he frowned. "Lust, that's all that is. And they are both much too old for such nonsense."

"Oh please, William. Both your mother and stepfather are very fond of each other. Why, he makes her sit at the front of the book club meeting each week so he can gaze upon her."

William snorted. "Ridiculous."

Inevitably, they turned to what was occupying their minds. "Despite what we just learned, I find it difficult to believe Annabelle was involved in Albert's death," William said.

"Not when you consider how much she loved her twin sister. Whether we, or anyone else, did not believe Albert killed Alice, it appears as though Annabelle was convinced that he had. And decided to administer her own punishment to the man."

"I wonder how she knew to sneak in with the other temporary maids?" William asked.

"I imagine when we confront her, we will find that out." Amy climbed from the carriage and shook out her skirts. "We might as well get this over with. Just to give Annabelle the benefit of the doubt, I do not want to alert the police until we talk to her."

The dead weight in Amy's stomach and the ache in her heart grew heavier as they made their way up the steps. How did one accuse a family member, someone one has known all their life, of murder?

★   ★   ★

"Are you ready?" William asked before he dropped the knocker.

"No. But we have no choice. We cannot allow John to pay for a crime he did not commit."

They continued to stare at the door for a few minutes. "We must go in, Amy," he said softly, reaching over to take her hand.

She sighed. "I know." Her eyes filled with tears as she regarded him. "This is probably one of the most difficult things I've ever done in my life."

"Yes, I know." William dropped the heavy door knocker. A staid-looking, older butler answered the door. His pale blue eyes had faded with age, and the little bit of hair he had retained was smoothed back, barely covering his scalp. "Yes?"

"Lord and Lady Wethington to see Miss Annabelle Munson," William said.

He nodded and backed up, waving to a small room off the entrance hall. "If you would be good enough to wait there, I will see if Miss Munson is accepting visitors."

After about ten long minutes the butler returned. "Miss Munson awaits you in the drawing room. If you will follow me," he said.

William felt the reluctance in Amy's demeanor as they climbed the stairs and followed the butler to the large, airy drawing room. Annabelle sat on a blue and green striped settee, a pink and white china teacup sitting on a small table next to her. She smiled as they entered and waved toward a matching settee.

"Please, come in and have a seat." She looked at them with tears rimming her eyes. "I've been expecting you."

CHAPTER 38

Amy took a deep breath and settled on the settee, William at her side, still holding her hand.

"Why do you say you were expecting us?"

Annabelle blinked to remove the tears from her eyes. "When that maid saw me during lunch today, I knew it was all over. I probably should not have gone to lunch at your home, but I am tired. So very tired. I want it to end."

Amy lowered her voice. "End what, Annabelle?" She was still unable to confront her cousin with the awful suspicion.

"That I killed Albert. Or whatever his name is. Wicked, wicked man that he was." She raised her chin. "I am not sorry. I know I will end up in hell because of that, but I could not help myself."

"I assume you were convinced he killed Alice?" William asked.

Tears popped into her eyes, and she jumped up as if shoved from behind. "No! He made *me* kill Alice!"

"What!" Amy and William said at the same time.

Annabelle began to pace. "Yes. I killed them both." She turned to them, sitting like stone statues. "It. Was. A. Mistake!!" She raised her hands and looked up at the ceiling, a wrenching cry of agony coming from her lips.

Amy licked her dry lips. "I don't understand."

Annabelle swiped at the tears streaming down her face. "Albert was a horrid, horrid man. He was so mean to my sister." She turned and faced them, her hands fisted at her sides. "Do you know how many times I held my beloved sister in my arms as she wept over his dalliances? How many times she blamed herself—herself!—for his behavior? As if she were somehow lacking?"

She snorted. "Alice felt she wasn't a good enough wife." The rage in Annabelle's face, the tension in her body was enormous. She had carried this burden for weeks. Amy was amazed she had not suffered an apoplexy.

At that very moment, Annabelle took a deep breath and seemed to compose herself. "I had finally convinced her to file for a divorce. I hated—*hated*—seeing her suffer. Then, after a visit with her solicitor, she changed her mind. She said the solicitor had advised against it. Told her a divorce was difficult for a woman to obtain.

"Albert, on the other hand, could get one—the cad—by claiming adultery on her part. Can you imagine? The disgrace and scandal that would cause? Plus, he would never do that and cut off his source of income."

Amy exhaled, not realizing she'd been holding her breath this entire time.

Annabelle walked to the window of the drawing room and looked out. "I hated him. So much. So very, very much."

William cleared his throat. "Can you tell us how this all came about? Your sister's death?"

She turned back, her eyes snapping again with anger. "Yes. I had it all planned out. If she couldn't be free of the man, I would free her. Give her her life back."

Stumbling to the chair closest to her, she collapsed. "At your wedding breakfast, I put a large dose of *Atropa belladonna* in my champagne glass. Then I walked over to where Albert and Alice were sitting. I engaged them in conversation, and when he was distracted, I switched glasses. My poisoned one for his."

She gazed off into space, leaving Amy wondering if she was going to continue. After about a minute, she looked directly at them. "For the first time probably ever, Albert decided to be nice to his wife. She loved champagne."

Annabelle covered her face with her hands. It took her a couple of minutes to compose herself. "When I saw Alice collapse and noticed the two glasses in front of her, and none in front of her bloody husband, I knew what had happened."

She stood again and threw out her hands in supplication. "I killed my own sister. My twin. The other half of my soul. Do you have any idea how much that hurt? How much I hated Albert Finch at that moment?"

Once again, she returned to the chair she'd been sitting in when they had arrived.

"How did you know to arrive at our house with the group of temporary employees?" Amy asked.

Annabelle tilted her head and frowned. "You told me."

Amy was taken aback. "I told you?"

"Yes. We had tea together at Sally Lunn's. We were talking about your family staying with you, and you mentioned you had hired temporary help and they were to arrive the next morning."

It took Amy a minute or so to go over their conversation that day and remember.

"Lord Wethington and I are hosting my family for a couple of weeks."

Annabelle perked up. "Indeed? Why is that?"

"They had some issues with flooding during the last two storms. Apparently, there was an unknown leak in the roof, causing damage that required repairs to the bedchamber floor."

"It is quite nice of you to allow them to stay while they have repairs done on their townhouse. But I imagine it makes for quite a disruption in the household."

"To some extent that is true, but we have contracted with an agency to send additional temporary help for a couple of weeks. I believe they are expected first thing tomorrow morning."

"Ah, yes. I remember now."

Annabelle smoothed out her skirt. "I assume you will contact the police now?"

Amy wished she could say no, but that was not possible. Perhaps Annabelle would get off easier when she explained her situation.

Murder is murder, Amy, she told herself.

She nodded her head. "I'm afraid so."

"Ah yes. I assumed that." Annabelle picked up the teacup next to her. "However, I can relieve you of that duty."

Amy frowned. "What?"

Annabelle rested the teacup next to her chin. "If you will excuse me, I will be joining my beloved sister now." She nodded toward the desk across the room. "You will find all the information you need in that envelope."

With those confusing words, Annabelle downed the tea.

Suddenly realizing what her cousin meant, Amy jumped up and ran toward her. "Annabelle, no!" She shook her shoulders. "You can't do this!"

Annabelle smiled up at her. "'Tis done."

Within seconds, she slumped forward. Amy continued to shake her, the tears streaming down her face. "Annabelle, no! We can work this out. Please."

She felt warm hands grip her shoulders and pull her back against a strong, hard chest. "No, sweetheart, Annabelle was correct. It is done."

Amy turned in William's arms. "This is terrible. I never wanted her to do that."

He led her back to the settee and wrapped her in his arms. "Of course you didn't." He placed his knuckle under her chin and raised her head so he could look into her eyes. "Don't you understand? She planned to do this. She had the poison at hand. She left a note. I'm sure it is a confession. There was no way you could have been prepared for this."

★ ★ ★

It took William close to a half hour to calm his wife enough to leave the house. He took the letter Annabelle had left and stuffed it into his pocket. Then he advised her housekeeper that their mistress was deceased. After that, it was almost another hour to soothe the staff and give orders for the detectives to be notified by sending a note to the police station with instructions for them to visit with him and Amy at their townhouse.

He was quite concerned about Amy. She had suffered a couple of shocks, and it would be best to get her home and possibly even summon a physician. Truth be known, he was quite saddened himself.

Given the story they had just heard, he almost felt as though Annabelle had been justified in doing away with her brother-in-law. But the law was the law, and no one had the right to take another person's life. Regardless of the motivation.

It was a quiet ride back to their townhouse, and Amy was so limp in his arms, his worry for her grew. Once they stopped in front of their house, he squeezed her gently. "Sweetheart, we've arrived home."

She sighed and sat up. He climbed out and helped her from the carriage. Slowly, they made their way up the steps. Once Filbert opened the door, William said, "Please send for her ladyship's maid."

Amy looked up at him. "Why?"

"You've had quite a shock. I think resting for the remainder of the day is in order."

She rallied herself. "No. We have things to do. I am well."

He studied her pale face and her eyes, swollen from crying. "I don't think so. It is better if you allow me to finish this up."

"I am fine. We started this together, and we shall end it together."

'Twas probably best not to argue with her, lest she become even more agitated. "Very well. I shall send for tea while we await the police."

She nodded.

They entered the drawing room, and Amy sat while he gave instructions for tea to be sent in. The house was quiet, which led him to believe Lady Margaret, Franklin, and Michael were all away from the house. A good time to get this all sorted out.

Amy wandered the room restlessly. He kept an eye on her, still concerned for her state of mind. Once they were settled with their tea, he withdrew Annabelle's letter from his jacket. "I believe reading this before our detective friends arrive is a good idea."

Amy nodded.

He opened the envelope and read:

"I killed them both. Alice, by mistake; and her dastardly husband, Albert, on purpose." He looked up at Amy and shrugged. "That's it. Just her name written below it."

The front door opened, and expecting to see Filbert announcing the detectives, William watched as Lady Margaret glided through the doorway to the drawing room. She took one look at Amy and came to an abrupt halt. She looked over at William. "What's wrong?"

William no sooner finished the sad tale than Franklin and Michael entered the room. Tension radiated off them both. Apparently their discussion about Michael's engagement had not gone well.

Amy's brother studied them for a minute. "Are we about to receive bad news?"

William waved to the chairs. "You might as well take a seat."

Once again, he related the story. Lady Margaret still seemed to be recovering from the shock, a cup of tea in her hand. Michael and Franklin soon held snifters of brandy.

"That is a terrible story," Michael said.

Lady Margaret shook her head. "That poor woman. What she must have gone through."

There was to be no relief for them that afternoon. The detectives arrived just as Franklin and Michael rose to excuse themselves.

"I believe I will depart also," Lady Margaret said as she eyed the two men.

"Why did you send for us?" Detective Carson asked as he and Detective Marsh settled into the chairs just vacated by Amy's family.

William picked up Alice's note and handed it to Detective Carson.

He scanned it quickly—not that there was much to read—and glared at them. "Where did you get this?"

"We had reason to believe my cousin, Miss Anabelle Munson, had something to do with Mr. Finch's death. When we arrived at her house, she confessed to killing them both."

Carson continued to stare at them, various thoughts passing over his face. "She says here it was a mistake." He shook his head. "She was never on our list of suspects."

Not very impressed with their suspects, it was hard for William to condemn them since Annabelle had not been on his and Amy's list either—only the woman who had arrived with the maids and disappeared. Which, of course, ended up being Annabelle.

"Yes. She killed her sister by mistake," Amy mumbled.

Picking up the explanation, William told the entire story once again. Ever the dutiful recorder, Detective Marsh scribbled ruthlessly in his notepad.

Once William ended the tale, Detective Carson held up the note. "I will keep this."

William nodded, only too happy to have the blasted missive removed from his wife's sight.

"We may need you to answer more questions, so please don't leave yet for that honeymoon of yours until you hear from us," Carson said.

"Honeymoon?" William said. "What's that?"

★ ★ ★

The next morning, William sat in his study, reading over contracts that his man of business had sent over. Amy rested on the settee near the window, once again attempting to add to her knitting project, the identity of which grew more dubious each day.

She'd tossed and turned all night, soft moans coming from her when she did manage to sleep. He'd offered, last night and then again this morning, to summon a physician, but she'd refused.

A soft knock on the door preceded Lady Margaret entering the room. "How are you feeling, Amy?"

"I'm fine," she said.

Lady Margaret sat alongside her and took her hand. "Well, I have good news for you."

"Excellent," William said. "We could use some good news right about now."

She smiled. "The repairs are complete. Franklin, Michael, and I are moving back home today. You might be interested to know that I just came from there. I went around the back of the house to enter through the garden, because the workers were carrying out their leftover bits and pieces of wood and paint supplies. You will never guess what I found on the back step of the house."

"What?" Amy said.

"Feathers. Othello's feathers."

William laughed. "Then he *was* trying to return to his house. Are you sure he is not a pigeon carrier?"

"And Persephone found him." Amy grinned at William. "I told you my dog was smart."

"Oh, one more thing. Michael left early this morning and gave me this note for you."

Amy frowned. "He left me a note? You only live two streets over."

Lady Margaret shrugged. She pointed to the envelope. "What does he say?"

Amy withdrew a folded paper from the envelope and scanned the words, her face breaking out into a bright smile. "Michael and Eloise have eloped!"

ACKNOWLEDGMENTS

Thank you to my agent, Nicole Resciniti, who works so hard on behalf of her clients.

Gratefulness to Faith Black Ross, editor extraordinaire.

A tribute to Agatha Christie, whose wonderful stories motivated me to write a cozy mystery.

Admiration for Charles Dickens, whose work, *The Mystery of Edwin Drood* inspired the title for my story.

Kudos to my family, who put up with me always sitting behind my computer and mumbling about death, murder, and mayhem.